LOVE CAROUSEL

LOVE CAROUSEL

A Korean pop fiction novel by
KPOPALYPSE

Book three of the Shin Hana series

LOVE CAROUSEL

A Korean pop fiction novel by KPOPALYPSE

Book three of the Shin Hana series

This book is a work of fiction. Any references to historical events, real people or real places are used fictitiously. Other names, characters, places and events are the products of the author's imagination, and any resemblance to actual events, or places and persons, living or dead, is entirely coincidental, even if such resemblances might take certain well-informed individuals down memory lane...

Text copyright © 2024 Kpopalypse
Cover art illustration by Caius Augustus
www.artstation.com/caiusaugustus

The immoral rights of the author have been asserted.

Print ISBN: 978-0-6457192-6-0
E-book ISBN: 978-0-6457192-7-7

For all the caonimas.

101. PHONE CALL

"So, now that you're on television I suppose I should try to care a little about your rubbish group. What's the name of it again?"

"Halcyon."

"That's such a shit name. I can tell Mr Park thought that one up. That name has an old man smell about it. Only someone rich and out of touch with reality could conjure something like that up."

I'm sitting on the bench in our agency building's small outdoor yard, talking to Sooae on the phone. Sooae is the girl who I met at Club Soap, our CEO Mr Park's brothel, and she's a laugh riot. I can't stop myself from giggling as I listen to her continue to roast our idiotic CEO.

"He's loaded and he treats us employees like shit. I'm at least ninety percent sure he's a paedophile, too. He's got that vibe."

"I can fill in the extra ten percent."

"What do you mean?"

"You haven't seen his partner?"

"Since when has he had a partner?"

"As long as I've been training."

"Don't tell me she's a kid? No way!"

"I don't know how old exactly, but she's younger than me, and I joined this group straight from school. She even told me once that they were going to get married but they couldn't because it wasn't legal yet."

"How do you have dirt on him like this that I don't even have? I thought I knew everything about that son of a bitch!"

"Him and his partner don't seem to have much in common except that they're both great oversharers of shit that I really don't want to know."

"I bet you hear a lot of stuff while you're in there. Why don't you tell me all about the members? Give me the dirt! I need some entertainment, it's a slow night."

"Well, there's Iseul..."

"I already know Iseul's a fucking moron. Skip that bitch, please."

I start giggling again; she clearly knows Iseul well. Good that she doesn't want to talk about her because I don't really want to think about that bitch any more than I have to either. Sometimes I feel like if Nari wasn't the leader of our group, Iseul would turn to bullying me relentlessly. But then sometimes she's really nice and helpful to me between the bitchiness and snobbishness. I don't really know what to make of her. Sooae continues.

"What about the girl you came here with?"

"That's Caitlin."

"Is she nice? She seemed okay."

I hesitate for a moment.

"Yeah."

"I saw that news article. Is she really a pothead?"

"Yes!"

"She's your girlfriend, right?"

I hesitate again – I don't know how to respond to this. I guess she is, but how do I put it exactly? A simple "yes" doesn't seem like it would really explain it. Sooae then starts laughing.

"Oh wow! You're so obvious, Hana!"

How can she tell this over the phone, I have no idea. I feel awkward, I can't think of anything to say. Sooae continues.

"Does she treat you right?"

"Yes..."

"You sound unsure."

"She's really nice, but we're very different."

"You know, she was popular that night we met. I still get some of our regulars asking when she's coming back, and she was only doing the reception desk! She could make serious money here."

I don't want to think about this.

"Can we move on?"

Sooae starts laughing loudly again through the phone.

"No, no we can't! This is interesting! How long have you two been together?"

"We met while training. So not that long I guess."

"Is it weird having a girlfriend and having to constantly live with them all the time along with four other people all close together? You live on site, right?"

"Yeah, we do. It's annoying. We don't ever get to do anything much together, there's no privacy unless we sneak around."

"You should try living somewhere else."

"We're not allowed to. I'm not sure how we would do that anyway even if we were allowed. We have no money."

"Get Caitlin to work here! That'll bring in the money!"

"No! Shut up!"

Sooae starts laughing.

"I'm just kidding! Anyway I'm sure the money will start coming in soon now that you're known. Assuming your CEO isn't just funnelling it back into his shady business ventures. Anyway, tell me about the others. Who's the short girl?"

"That's Shu."

"She's cute, I like her."

"Everyone does. I can't stand that Chinese bitch."

"You hate her because she's Chinese?"

"No, I hate her because she's annoying. I hate all of that stupid *aegyo* bullshit she does. She never quits with that garbage. She has such an irritating personality. I don't get what people see in her, in that fake-cute routine."

"She's definitely the popular one in your group by the look of it. All the TV shows and articles kind of focus on her."

"I can't explain it. I guess she's not a bad person or anything but she drives me up the wall."

"Wow, you have issues. Just promise me you won't be nasty to her."

"I would have been way nasty to her already but Caitlin won't let me. Neither will our leader."

"Who's the leader?"

"Nari."

"She's the one with the muscles?"

"That's her."

"I think that's cool that she's buff. Too many people in idol groups have exactly the same look, she's attractive but she's a bit tough, I like that. What's she like?"

"Super driven. She's a real workaholic. She's all about success and fame, and all that."

"Okay, that's kind of boring. I like her less now. Does it burn her that Shu is more popular?"

"I have no idea. I couldn't be bothered to ask her, I don't care about things like that."

"Is she a good leader though?"

"She's pretty intense but she's okay. She's a bit uptight. She doesn't really get on my case because we're both good dancers. She's always roasting Youngsook, the tall one, because she can't dance that well."

"Youngsook looks a bit out of place in your group."

"She can sing though. Someone has to."

"Oh right, so she's an actual musician? Not like the rest of you frauds, then?"

I start giggling again. It's funny because it's true, none of us have anything like Youngsook's singing talent.

"Hey Hana, I've got to go, a regular just showed up. Talk later, okay?"

"Sure."

Sooae hangs up her phone in my ear. I lie back on the bench and stare up at the night sky. I'm glad that she rung, it's great that I've found another person I can connect with outside the group, even if she is a bit strange. It's also good that our group has become successful to some degree, although who knows how long that will last and if we can maintain it. It's good just because I don't want to have to quit being here and go back to living with my mother and going to school. I don't really feel like I fit in with the idol life either, but it's better than the alternative. However I also know that nobody is an idol forever, so at some point I'm going to have to work out what it is I actually want to do with my life. I have no ideas about this. What skills do I even have beyond being able to dance a bit? How would I even make my way in the world? What do I even want? I know that I want Caitlin, I know that whatever I end up doing, I want to be with her. Beyond this, everything is uncertain.

102. BRIEFING

"*Annyeong haseyo,* Mr Park CEO!"

We all bow in unison before Mr Park, our CEO. We're standing before him in the gym, in our usual lineup, from left to right: Iseul, Shu, Nari, me, Caitlin, Youngsook. Standing next to Mr Park is Ijun, his "partner" or whatever. For some reason she's wearing a *hanbok* with a small handbag around her shoulder instead of her usual school uniform, although both the *hanbok* and the handbag have exactly the same type of design motif that her usual school uniform has, with the same black and red trim. As usual, she's playing with her phone and ignoring us completely. Mr Park smiles at us, he seems happier than normal.

"Today I want to discuss with you all some of the upcoming schedules and plans that have been put in place for Halcyon. With our recent achievements comes the responsibility to capitalise on and make the best of our positive outcomes. Dedicated effort will be required from..."

Mr Park suddenly stops talking. He turns to look at Ijun, and says nothing. After about ten seconds, Ijun recognises that there's an awkward silence in the air, and looks up from her phone back at Mr Park. They continue to stare at each other for another ten seconds. Mr Park then raises his eyebrow with an expression that indicates he's very unimpressed with her. Ijun slowly puts her phone away in her handbag and then glares angrily at Mr Park, who seems satisfied with this action and returns his gaze to us.

"Dedicated effort will be required from each member of the team, so we are giving you as much notice as possible of upcoming events so you can all prepare yourselves appropriately. Firstly, we are pushing the release of 'Love Carousel' forward. As 'Show Me Love' has become popular with the public, we need a similar song to make the most of this popularity, as this is what the public will be expecting from us next. 'Love Carousel' is much closer to the uplifting feel of 'Show Me Love' and will resonate better with our existing fanbase, whereas 'Love Light' has a more reflective feel, so we will halt promotions for 'Love Light' for now and pick them up at a later stage."

I hear Iseul breathe a sigh of relief, which she doesn't try to hide. Mr Park completely ignores her and continues.

"We are also booking more extensive live performance activity as well as extra variety show appearances. We have already booked the comeback debut on Music Train, as well as appearances on Platinum Hour, Idol Enquiry and

Summer Soak Festival. There will also be promotional activities leading up to these events, such as more fan meetings, live streaming and more."

I feel my heart sinking. I don't know the other names, but I know Music Train. That was the show with the producer/director Mr Jeong, who insists on meeting every performer after they've been on stage, and who has already assaulted me twice now. I was hoping to never see him ever again in my lifetime, but it looks like we'll be forced to cross paths at least once more.

"There is also news on some individual activities. Caitlin and Shu, please take a step forward."

Caitlin and Shu both take a step forward. What could possibly have been offered to *both* of them at once? They couldn't be more different.

"We have secured for you both photoshoots for DGT Magazine. This is a high fashion publication that is sure to raise your profiles. Congratulations, be sure to make the most of this chance for your own benefit and the benefit of the group."

"Thank you, Mr Park CEO!" says Shu. Caitlin just smiles, as her and Shu both bow and return to the lineup.

"Youngsook, please step forward."

Youngsook steps forward nervously.

"An outside producer has expressed some interest in harnessing your talents. We are in negotiations currently with their agency. If this comes to fruition, you will have some new collaborative musical opportunities. Be sure that you lose some weight between now and then, there is no need to bring embarrassment to yourself and the organisation."

"Thank you, Mr Park CEO," replies Youngsook, as she steps back into the lineup. She's clearly not happy about being told to lose weight by the CEO, but this is hardly the first time that's happened.

"Nari, please step forward."

Nari takes a step forward.

"You have been asked to be interviewed for... I forget the name..." Mr Park then turns and looks to Ijun, saying nothing. Ijun shrugs at Mr Park.

"I don't remember it either. What?"

They stare at each other for about ten seconds in silence, until Ijun finally realises what Mr Park wants her to do. She rolls her eyes, pulls her phone out of her handbag, and spends a few seconds looking something up.

"It's called... Women's Definition."

"Oh. What is that? Jog my memory, please. As I recall, it's not a music publication?"

"It's a women's fitness website, Mr Park CEO."

Ijun shows her mobile phone screen to Mr Park. I can't see what's on her screen, but Mr Park looks unimpressed and grimaces.

"A very strange place to promote. However they seem to have an audience, so perhaps something will come of it. Nari, we are organising an interview soon. Please use the opportunity effectively to further promote the group activities."

Ijun pulls her phone away from Mr Park's vision and starts playing with it, while Nari bows to Mr Park.

"Thank you Mr Park CEO, I won't let you down!"

Nari rejoins her place in the queue.

"Hana and Iseul, please step forward."

I step forward, and Iseul does the same. What on earth could involve the two of us?

"I am disappointed to report that neither of you have managed to attract any attention for individual activities."

Oh. *Nothing.* I guess that does actually make sense. Mr Park continues.

"I must say that I am..."

"That's not true, Mr Park CEO!" interrupts Ijun, while continuing to play with her phone. Mr Park turns to Ijun, looking annoyed.

"Ijun, look at me."

"You're lying! I won't look at you."

Ijun refuses to make eye contact and keeps playing with her phone defiantly.

"Ijun, put your phone down!"

"You're the one who told me to get it out again!"

"Ijun..."

Mr Park makes a grab for Ijun's phone, but Ijun is ready for it, she holds her phone out of his reach.

"I won't look at you if you lie!"

Ijun suddenly runs out of the gym, through the door to the admin area and disappears. Mr Park doesn't bother to go after her, he instead turns his attention back to myself and Iseul.

"We did have an opportunity?" asks Iseul.

"Hana did, you did not. I didn't mention it, because it's not something worth following up."

"Can I at least know what it is?" I ask.

"No you cannot. It won't help your career. One more thing, Hana."

"Yes, Mr Park CEO?"

"Getting Halcyon back onto Music Train took some considerable effort by our team. Be sure that you don't do anything to endanger this second opportunity. Do you understand what I am telling you, Hana?"

"I understand, Mr Park CEO."

"You can both step back into the queue."

Myself and Iseul both step back.

"Any other questions? Raise your hand if so."

Everyone in the group looks at each other. I'm too shocked by what just happened with Ijun to even be able to think of anything, I already asked my only question which didn't get an answer. I notice Iseul has her hand up.

"Yes, Iseul?"

"Given that some of us are now getting photo shoots from *real* photographers, do we still have to work with Gisang?"

"Yes."

"Why him? Can't it be literally anybody else?"

"Gisang has a reputation for excellent work. In fact, it is his work with Caitlin and Shu that has allowed us to put the group in the sights of the photographers from

DGT. There is a reason for our method, and it is not your place to choose who you have to work with."

"A good photographer is not the only reputation he has."

"A good photographer is the only *proven* reputation that he has."

Iseul sighs deeply, but doesn't say anything more, she knows it's useless to argue with Mr Park. Nari shoots her hand up.

"Yes, Nari?"

"Given Mr Jeong has assaulted Hana on more than one occasion, can we get some assurance of protection when we have to meet on Music Train?"

"Is this all you girls can think about? Will every question be this? You are on the cusp of fame and fortune, and you are only worried about this?"

"I'm trying to look out for the team, as the leader. This is my duty and responsibility."

"Am I to believe that Hana did absolutely nothing to provoke Mr Jeong? As the leader, you do not seem to know your team very well at all. Yet another failure of your leadership."

Nari glares at Mr Park and says nothing. I can tell that she's angry. I wish she would scream at him or something, but I know Nari is too disciplined to let herself loose like that in front of the CEO and potentially lose everything she's worked for. Mr Park looks us over.

"If there are no other questions, that is all."

We all bow. Mr Park leaves the room quickly without a goodbye, I guess he's now going to catch up to Ijun. We all step out of our lineup and form a loose circle, as we look at each other.

"I can't believe we're going to be doing Summer Soak," groans Iseul.

"What's Summer Soak?" I ask.

"It's an outdoor stadium show that they have right in the middle of summer where the performers just wear swimsuits and hardly any clothes and they get squirted with water while they sing."

"That's allowed?"

"It's not only allowed, it's the whole *purpose* of the event."

"So it's like a big beach party! Being squirted when it's hot would be nice!" says Shu.

I roll my eyes internally at Shu, trust her to be annoyingly positive about it. Meanwhile Caitlin runs off in the direction of the dorms, without a word.

"Shu, it's totally just for perverts," says Iseul.

Shu's face turns slightly sour. Youngsook suddenly starts laughing at Iseul.

"It's not just men who go to that event. Don't blame other people just because you got tattoos that you don't want anyone else to see!"

"You sound like my dad."

"You sound like *my* dad!"

Nari interjects. "Iseul has a point. It will be a good event if we perform well, but we have to be careful."

"I thought you *wanted* to be famous?" Youngsook replies. "People who perform well at Summer Soak go hugely viral!"

"Yeah, so our dancing has to be perfect, we need to..."

Youngsook starts laughing even harder and cuts Nari off.

"Fuck 'dancing', I'm talking about getting wet!"

Nari groans and goes to say something but stops when she sees Caitlin run back into the room, phone in hand.

"Here, check it out! I found the video from last year's event. Let's take a look and see what we're in for!"

We all gather around Caitlin's phone screen. It shows a big stage, some boy band is singing. I recognise Lixin, from my meeting with him, I guess this must be his group Star-D. The boys are taking turns singing and squirting the audience with water cannons by the side of the stage. The audience are getting revenge by shooting the band members with water guns as they sing.

"It's a big water party! This looks like fun!" says Shu, while jumping up and down. Ugh.

Caitlin puts her fingers up to the screen and zooms in.

"Look at Jaesung, he looks fucking hot. Those white T-shirts don't leave a lot to the imaginat... oh shit! Look at those abs, goddamn!"

The boys in Star-D all remove their T-shirts at the same time and throw them on the stage floor. The screams from the crowd increase wildly. Youngsook cranes her neck to get a better look at the action.

"Wow, I didn't know Troy was that jacked," says Iseul.

"I'd ride him like a mechanical bull!" adds Youngsook.

"Those girls in the audience better not look at Lixin too hard, he's my baby!" says Shu.

Nari clears her throat loudly.

"All of you, wipe the drool from your mouth and find a girl group. Looking at the boys isn't relevant, we need to know what *we're* in for."

"Looking at boys is always relevant at least to me," replies Youngsook.

Nari shakes her head disapprovingly at Youngsook. Caitlin scrolls to another video that has a group of about a dozen female performers. I don't recognise any of them.

"Who are these people?" I ask.

"You don't know White Iris?" asks Caitlin.

"Why would I?"

"You live under a rock," Iseul snorts.

"Shut up, Iseul!" Nari claps back.

Iseul doesn't say anything in response, which is great. We crowd around the screen and watch the girls of White Iris. They're all wearing combinations of bikini tops and short shirts and dancing what is obviously a routine as tightly choreographed as our own. Every now and then, jets of water spray up at them from the crowd. The girls look uncomfortable, like they're struggling to maintain focus on the routine.

"I am so *not* doing this," says Iseul.

"Yes you are. We all have to put in our best effort," Nari replies.

"You know I can't do this."

"It's not everyone else's fault you got a stupid gang tattoo. Have you ever thought about maybe getting it removed?"

"Are you kidding? I would literally be murdered."

"Maybe you should have thought of that before you joined an idol group."

"I didn't know I was going to be in a dumb idol group, did I? Anyway our CEO knows that we can't let people see that tattoo, so I'm definitely not going to have to do this, which is great. The rest of you can do it without me."

"Nonsense. You have to do it. We'll get you a swimsuit that covers your back if we have to."

"No way. Still not doing it."

I sigh and continue to watch the girls of White Iris as they struggle through their routine. For once, I agree with Iseul. I really don't like the idea of being ogled in swimwear either and I don't want to do this bullshit any more than she does. If she finds a way to evade this nonsense, I hope that she finds a way to take me with her.

103. PUBLIC IMAGE

"Start it up, I'm ready."

"Sure, remember don't rush the opening."

"I stopped rushing the opening months ago."

"Just making sure."

I'm holding myself in the starting position of the "Love Carousel" dance, waiting for Nari to start the recording. Nari's assessing my dance routine individually in order to help me correct any weak spots, the other girls are practicing by themselves on the other side of the gym, waiting for their turn to be called by Nari. After a few seconds the speakers crackle into life and I begin the opening movements. I work through the slow, controlled opening section, which is actually the hardest part, and wait for the cringe lyrics to appear, which is my cue to speed up.

It's time to go for a new ride / I don't know who I'll be meeting today / Maybe it's you, could you be the one / I'll let destiny determine my fate

The rest of the dance routine is easier from here, I'm not worried about it, I've done it so many times already.

As I know I won't make mistakes, I stop thinking about the dance routine. It's all muscle memory by now. I start thinking instead about the bullshit words to this song. I'd really like it if our group could get some better lyrics one day, but I guess it's probably never going to happen.

Can you feel the heat rising / The tension of uncertainty / Anything could happen under the starlit sky

I don't know what this song is about, I guess it's just Mr Nam the producer's juvenile sex fantasy or something, it's probably what he sings to himself while he tries to scheme up ways to drug us and record us in secret. I hope we get a new producer one day.

It's a love-love carousel / Can you feel-feel my heart / This night, this time made for

Suddenly the recording stops. I freeze in position and look at Nari.

"What was wrong with that?" I ask.

"Nothing, you did great. Marie's here."

Marie, our annoying Greek makeup artist and stylist, walks into the centre of the gym, wheeling her usual suitcase behind her that converts into a makeup stand. I hate her because she's always so harsh with applying makeup, but I guess she's not here to do our makeup as we don't have a performance for a while, which means she's probably just here to talk to us about something. The other girls notice that Marie is here and everyone walks forward to within earshot so she can tell us whatever it is she needs to tell us.

"Hello girls. I'm here today to do some preparation work on your public image. By now you have all seen the style sheets for 'Love Carousel', yes?"

We all nod.

"So there are some changes to styling that we need to do in advance of the debut stage. I will consult the sheet, as I can't quite remember who had what..."

Marie pulls out a plastic sheet folder, it's the same one that the rest of us were given a while ago with the "Love Carousel" concept drawings in it.

"...here we go, there's quite a few changes. Youngsook, you are going blonde for this comeback. Caitlin, we are going to also add some blonde streaks to your hair. Iseul, no change, Shu we just need to change your fringe a little, Nari the drawing here is actually wrong, we're going to add some silver streaks for you, and Hana, we need to cut a lot of length off to get you this pixie cut. Okay, who wants to go first?"

Oh no.

"I'm not getting a pixie cut! No way!"

Marie stares at me coldly.

"What's the problem this time, Hana?"

"I don't want my hair cut!"

"Why do you have to always give me problems? Why can you not just do as you are told?"

"Why do I have to get my hair cut?"

"It's the concept. You have known about this for a while now."

"I'm not doing it!"

"Hana likes her hair. Can't we just get her a wig and put her hair under it or something?" Caitlin asks.

"No, it won't work. She's got too much hair and it's too thick, it would look bulky. We're after a light, breezy look."

Why is it only me who has to cut my hair? I like my hair how it is, shorter hair is weird and far too exposing, I like the protection of longer hair. I feel safer, like people can't look at me, they can't perceive my whole features unless I let them. It's not much of a barrier I guess, but it's something close to me, something I control, and I don't get to control much. I've never had short hair since I was a child and I'm not comfortable with going back to short hair at all, especially not here, in this world run by weirdos and creeps. I stare at Marie and say nothing.

"We're trying to make you popular, yet you make it so difficult. If you won't have surgery the least you can do is..."

I've heard enough.

"Get lost! I'm not getting my hair cut!"

I run off out of the gym quickly in the direction of the dorms. I'm just going to curl up in bed and tell everyone to go fuck themselves. I manage to get a few metres into the hallway when I hear footsteps increasing in loudness right behind me. I try to increase my pace but a heavy weight pushes hard on my back and forces me down to the floor. I go sliding along the hallway tiles to a stop, and then twist my body so I'm facing up and can see who's responsible, even though I already know who it is. Nari hovers above me, she has pinned me down by straddling my torso with her legs. I wriggle around to try and break free but there's no point, Nari is way stronger than I am and keeps me in place easily just by increasing the pressure of her hips, she doesn't even need to use her arms. I'm simultaneously jealous, irritated and slightly aroused by her strength.

"Are you going to cooperate?"

"No! Why would I?"

"There's no getting out of this, Hana."

"I'm not letting her do it!"

"Yes you are."

Nari smiles at me for a brief second. I'm not sure what that smile is about, but I don't like it, because I know what it means; Nari knows she has the upper hand. I know it as well, but I don't see why I should make this any easier for her, or Marie. Why can't I have my own hair? Why do I have to do this? Nari gradually releases the pressure from her hips, but grabs my left wrist with her right hand at the same time.

"Get up."

Nari starts applying some kind of upward force to my wrist and forearm so my arm is bending backwards unnaturally. The pain locks my forearm in place and is intense, I have no choice but to stand up and move in exact synchronisation with Nari so I don't cause myself even more agony. She slowly marches me back through the hallway and out to the gym, past the other girls who are all looking on curiously, to the far end of the gym where Marie has one of the wooden classroom chairs waiting for me.

"Sit," Nari orders, like I even have a choice. She's still forcibly directing me with her wrist lock, so I have to move where she moves. I sit down in the chair. Nari lets go of my wrist finally and I wince in pain as I flex my hand back and forth, trying to work the soreness out. Meanwhile, Marie grabs a comb and starts flicking it around my hair, inspecting it.

"You have split ends everywhere. A haircut is going to do your hair some good, definitely. You should have cut it a long time ago. You know, I don't have to make it dead short, I can get a pixie cut effect by just removing to shoulder length and clipping back the ends, then twisting them inward."

I start thinking of what insult to hurl at Marie and whether I can run off somewhere else this time, like into the yard or out the front door. Nari seems to read my thoughts, she kneels down behind me and wraps her arms around my torso forcefully, so I'm stuck in the chair like a straitjacket and can't move.

"There's two ways this can go. Either you cooperate with Marie and she works her magic so you can retain as much length as possible, or you be an uncooperative bitch and run away and I will catch you and bring you back here and she will give you the shortest, most severe pixie cut you've ever seen. Which is it?"

Having Nari's arms around me like this is making it hard to think straight. She has so much force in her grip.

I start thinking about what it would feel like to have her push me down into my bunk and kiss me. That would be nice. I mean, it'll never happen, she doesn't seem to have a lesbian bone in her body, but I can dream. Maybe Caitlin is right and I'm not so monogamous by nature because I keep having thoughts like this. But thoughts aren't a crime, are they? It's not the same as doing the action, right? I look over at Caitlin, who is watching me, as are all the others. I can't quite read her expression. I wonder what she's thinking.

Nari interrupts my train of thought.

"Which is it, Hana?"

"Which is what?"

"Are you going to be good?"

I sigh. "I guess so. Please just do the shoulder length."

"Good, I'm going to let go, and you're going to stay right there, completely still, for Marie, got it?"

I nod and Nari gradually releases her grip. I sigh with both yearning and relief that the pressure of her arms is off. I watch Marie as she whips around some more with the comb, inspecting my hair, and then grabs a large pair of silver scissors. As Marie makes the first cut, I see a length of my hair fall to the gym floor. I instantly burst out crying, but I try to remain as still as I can manage.

"Come on, you big baby, it's just hair. It grows back."

With each new cut that Marie makes, my sobbing intensifies. I look over at Caitlin again, she looks back at me with a worried expression. I wonder if she understands.

104. DISTRACTION

"Look at this. This is bullshit. Ijun, can we please get something done about this. No human can survive on this amount of food per day."

Youngsook points her hand-held video camera at her own dinner bowl, which contains our new regulation meal; half a boiled chicken breast, half a hard-boiled egg, and a single piece of lettuce. She's filming for the next episode of our reality television show. Ijun isn't in the room with us, but since she has to edit all the footage we take into the final reality show, we all know that she will have to watch this, so we use the opportunity to air our grievances. Ijun doesn't seem to mind.

Shu looks at her own bowl and then at the camera. "It was a whole chicken breast yesterday! What happened?"

"They're probably making us cut back in preparation for the comeback," says Nari.

Youngsook swivels the camera around so it's pointing back at her own face.

"Seriously Ijun, please try and get something done. I know it's all up to Mr Park CEO and he probably doesn't let you decide much, but the new dance routine is really hard and I don't want to be fainting in the middle of it from lack of nutrition. Please help us if you can!"

"I've been to the hospital seven times since I joined this group. I don't like the hospital," says Shu.

I don't have anything to add, so I just start eating my food quickly before anybody has thoughts of taking any of it off me. In less than ten seconds, I'm done and push the bowl away.

"Fast eater?" Youngsook asks.

"Yeah I'm done, I'm going outside for some air."

"Anything to say for the documentary before we lose sight of you?"

"Yes, I hate our new concept, it stinks. Bye now."

I get up and walk quickly out of the dining room, through the hallway and gym, through the glass sliding doors, into the enclosed yard area. I take a few deep breaths and sit on the metal bench. A few minutes later, I feel my phone vibrate in my tracksuit pocket. I take it out and check the message.

Caitlin: want some company?

Me: yes – tell the others to fuck off and leave us alone out here though

Caitlin: hahahaha see you soon

I'm glad Caitlin's coming out here. It will be good to get some time alone with her, even if it's only for a few minutes before evening dance practice starts. Even though we live together we don't actually get to spend that much time with each other, simply because we're also living with four other people at the same time. We can't just behave like a couple whenever we want. After a minute I see Caitlin walk up to the glass door and slide it open.

"Hey there. Can I sit?"

I smile at Caitlin and nod. Caitlin sits down, straddling the metal bench, and faces me.

"You're still bothered by your hair? It's a shame, I think it's cute!"

Caitlin runs a finger over the side of my neck, where my new shoulder-length hairline ends. I involuntarily tighten my breath.

"Don't!"

Caitlin pulls her hand away immediately.

"Wow. Okay."

I try to calm my breathing down. I like Caitlin's touch, but I'm not used to it on my neck without the hair there. I know I'm probably making way too much of a big deal about this, but I also can't help it. I feel like I'm not in control of the reaction. Caitlin looks me up and down, observing my movements.

"Something's really wrong. This is much more than a fashion thing for you, isn't it?"

I look at her. I don't know what to say, so I just stare.

"I won't make you talk about it if you don't want to. Come here."

Caitlin stretches out her arms to me, inviting me to draw closer. I slide over so I'm next to her, and she embraces me, holding me close to her torso while stroking the back of my head. I start sobbing silently into her shoulder.

"Hey, it's okay. I'll protect you. Hey, I've got an idea. I'll be your long hair."

Caitlin starts giggling as she waves her head over mine in an exaggerated way so her own long hair dangles right into my face, smothering me and making it hard to breathe. It's a completely stupid gesture and it makes me laugh a little. I actually do feel slightly better. I blow Caitlin's hair away from my mouth a little so I can talk.

"Stop being dumb!"

"You like it though. Made you feel better, didn't it?"

"Okay, I'll admit that cheered me up a little. But I can't talk with... hey!"

Caitlin grabs me and pushes me so I'm lying down on the bench, then climbs on top of me, straddles my waist with her legs and dangles her hair in my face some more. It's successfully stopping me from talking but it's also distracting me from being upset. I spit strands of Caitlin's hair away from my mouth, while she laughs. After a few more seconds of trying to make me choke on her hair ends, Caitlin leans down towards me and gently kisses me.

"I'll look after you, Hana. I promise."

I draw Caitlin down towards me and squeeze her tightly.

"Hey lesbians, no sex in the yard!"

The unexpected yelling makes my heart jump. Caitlin turns around and looks up. It's Youngsook, standing in the sliding door entrance.

"I told you not to come out here!" Caitlin replies.

"We're starting gym now. It's distracting!"

"Nobody's making you look, pervert!"

Youngsook rolls her eyes.

"I don't know if you two lovebirds noticed, but the sliding door is glass? It's a bit hard not to look when you're doing that shit right in full view! I'm really happy for you and all that, but can't you fuck somewhere else?"

"We're not fucking, you moron!"

"Well, whatever lesbian shit you're doing, then!"

"Where exactly do you suggest, then?" Caitlin says to Youngsook while humping me with an exaggerated pelvis motion. She's being deliberately stupid, I lose it and start giggling. Caitlin and Youngsook also both start laughing.

"I don't know! Just get in here, you idiots!"

Behind Youngsook I notice Nari standing and glaring at us with folded arms. She has less of a sense of humour about this than Youngsook.

"Nari looks like she's shitty at us, we'd better stop," I whisper to Caitlin.

"Fuck that, all the more reason to keep going!"

Caitlin starts humping me again even harder and we both burst out laughing until we fall off the bench together. I'm grateful to Caitlin for cheering me up. She always seems to know what to do to make me feel better. I hope that we never have to part for long.

105. UP TO SOMETHING

"This is so fucked. What are we going to do?"

"I don't know either."

Myself and Iseul are in the agency bathroom, helping each other into our sparkly light blue summer dresses, the costumes for the upcoming "Love Carousel" performance. Today is the day we have to do the photoshoot for the promotional pictures. This would be fine, but there's one problem; the photographer is Gisang, Iseul's dad, Mr Park's brother and an incredibly gross pervert. I link up the hooks at the back of Iseul's dress while she sighs. We're both disturbed by the prospect of this shoot, but her probably even more so than me, given that this lecherous creep is her own father.

"I can't believe Gisang isn't in jail yet," Iseul groans.

"Wasn't he getting sued for something?"

"He was, there was a big sexual harassment case, but Han Chinhwa dropped the charges just the other week."

"Why?"

"Gisang threatened to counter-sue for defamation if she won."

"He can do that?"

"Yeah."

"But how is it defamation, if he did it?"

"If he suffers reputation loss, it still can be."

"That's such bullshit. What a shit system. Hey, you're done, do mine now please."

I turn around and Iseul starts linking up the buttons and loops at the back of my dress. After a minute she's still not done with it.

"Everything okay back there?" I ask.

"It's fine, my hands are just shaking. This is really upsetting me, having to work with him."

"Why don't we kill him then? Since we can't rely on the law to do anything about it?"

"You're not serious."

"Who says I'm not?"

"No, Hana. Not possible."

"Why not?"

"Are you for real? He might be a complete piece of human garbage and he probably *does* deserve death, but he's still my dad."

"He's not *my* dad, I don't give a shit. I'd waste him in an instant if there was a way I could get away with it."

"No Hana, just no, you idiot. I can't order a hit on my own flesh and blood, that's ridiculous."

"So what *are* we going to do then? Just put up with this shit?"

"I don't fucking know *what* to do."

"I do."

"Look, if he was just some random guy for me like he is for you, I admit this would be an easier situation. Anyway you're done."

"Let's go out there and face the music, I guess."

We both take a few deep breaths and stare at each other.

"Hana, I feel like an idiot saying this, but do you want a hug or something?"

Being hugged by Iseul, on top of whatever horrors Gisang is going to inflict on us? I cringe internally at the thought.

"No, it won't help. Nothing's going to help. Let's just get this over with."

We walk out of the bathroom together and into the gym. Gisang already has his camera gear set up, a bright rectangular light on a stand, plus some strange fabric cones on stands and his camera tripod. The other girls are all here, but Gisang isn't. Nari looks at us and anticipates our question.

"He just went to the toilet, he'll be back in a moment. He just finished with me and Youngsook, it's your turn next."

"He did some kind of weird couples thing with us, it was totally dumb," adds Youngsook.

Nari laughs. "Yeah, I guarantee you'll both hate it. And after the couples shoots with all of us he's going to do solo ones where we take off the dresses. Not looking forward to that."

"Yeah he wants us in some lingerie or something."

I feel a shiver run across my body. I definitely don't want Gisang taking underwear shots, of any of us.

"Fuck, can't we get out of this bullshit somehow?"

Nari looks deep in thought.

"Normally your non-compliance is a pain in my ass, Hana, but I'm with you on this one. Trust me, none of us want to do this. I'll try to talk him down when the time comes."

Before I can think of any options, the door to the admin area opens and Gisang walks in. He strolls to the centre of the gym and looks at myself and Iseul.

"Ah, just the two girls I wanted to see! Over by the wall lit by the floodlight, please."

We both walk unenthusiastically over to the bright spot on the wall, while Gisang takes position behind his camera.

"Okay, now can you two put your arms around each other and can we have a few playful, seductive poses, sort of a flirty lesbian vibe please."

I sigh and look at Iseul. This is going to be fucked. I can see Iseul is fed up and about to say something. I know there's nothing I can do about this photo shoot existing, so I'm just going to let Iseul and Gisang argue it out, and plan my revenge later.

"You're not fucking serious, Dad?"

"Yes I'm serious. Do it. Don't worry, you don't have to get too explicit with it. Just hold each other close and lift up each other's dresses a little."

"DAD, NO!"

"You told me in our last shoot that Hana's a lesbian, I'm sure she'll show you the way if you're struggling."

"Oh screw off, Dad!"

Iseul looks and me and I look back at her. It's obvious that she's not at all comfortable with this, and neither am I. Cautiously, I put my arm around Iseul's lower back and lean forward into her in a way that I hope Gisang thinks is just me trying to look seductive or something but is really so I can talk quietly into her ear without him hearing.

"This is fucking bullshit. I'm so sorry, Iseul."

"Maybe I'll take back what I said earlier. I'll give it some thought."

"Hey at least he's not touching us yet... oh shit, he's coming up to us..."

I feel pressure on my back as Gisang walks up beside us and pushes us closer together with his arms, so our bodies are touching. He then grabs my hand, and forces me to pull the bottom of Iseul's dress up to her thigh.

"Don't be afraid of each other, girls. Nobody's going to be convinced if you two seem afraid to get close to each other."

"You disgust me!" Iseul hisses.

"Love you too, babe. Now get to work."

Gisang wanders back behind the camera. I feel like an idiot pressed up against Iseul and clinging onto her dress. As awkward as it makes me feel, I can't let go of it because Gisang will just get annoyed at me and who knows what will happen after that.

"I guess you're getting that hug after all," Iseul says.

"Yeah, I guess I am. Let's just try and get this done quickly so it's over."

Iseul's face is red with embarrassment, or maybe it's rage, I'm not sure which. We reluctantly cooperate and make some "seductive" poses while leaning into each other, pressing against each other, and hiking each other's skirts up. I guess it's not very racy really, but the fake intimacy with Iseul of all people is not something that I'm comfortable with, and I dread seeing how this is going to turn out in the final pictures. I wonder how obvious my true feelings about this will be. After a couple minutes, Gisang stops taking photos and peers out from behind the camera, smiling at us.

"Okay, we're done! Good job, girls. Not so bad, was it?"

"You're sickening!" Iseul grumbles.

Gisang ignores Iseul's insult. "Caitlin, Shu, you two are up next. Get over here against the wall, and face the light."

Caitlin and Shu walk up and assume the position, while I walk back with Iseul to join Nari and Youngsook as they look on from the side.

"Told you you'd hate it," says Nari.

"You're not kidding," I reply.

"Don't worry, I wasn't going to let Gisang do anything too extreme."

"You'd stop him?"

"You bet I would. In fact I already did. He wanted way more skin in this shoot and he also wanted you two to kiss each other but I talked him down, I said that there was no way you'd agree to that."

"Thanks, I appreciate it."

"Hey Hana..."

"What?"

"It's nice to see you learning some manners."

"Oh fuck off, Nari!"

Nari chuckles a little. "Hey, check out at Caitlin and Shu. I think they're up to something."

I look over and see that Shu's whispering something in Caitlin's ear, while Caitlin nods. Gisang then clears his throat.

"Sorry to interrupt the conversation, girls, but we've got a shoot to do. Shu, can you please lift up Caitlin's dress for me and do some flirting."

"Yeah, sure! I can do that!"

Shu smiles and then lifts Caitlin's dress all the way up past her waist, so her ass is completely exposed. Caitlin starts laughing and immediately starts trying to swat Shu's arms away from her dress while backing off.

"Hey! That's too much for our family friendly group!"

"I don't care! I'm going to free the Caitlin ass!"

"You're not going to do shit!"

"You can't run! I'm going to show your asscheeks to the world!"

"You've got to catch me first!"

Caitlin backs off across the wall and completely out of the photo equipment zone. Shu doesn't care and keeps trying to grab Caitlin's dress, and Caitlin runs away. Shu starts chasing Caitlin around the entire gym while they both scream and laugh.

"I'm going to slap your ass until it jiggles!"

"You're too jiggly as it is to catch me!"

Gisang suddenly whistles loudly.

"You two quit mucking around and get back into the camera field now! We've got a shoot to do!"

Caitlin runs back into the lit zone, with Shu still chasing her and trying to slap her ass for some reason. Caitlin pulls up next to the light and Shu runs straight into the back of her, sending them both tumbling to the gym floor, and taking the light down with them. The light makes a loud crashing sound as it shatters, sending shards of glass scattering across the gym floor.

"STOP! Get up and get away from there!"

Shu looks up at Gisang with an apologetic expression.

"Oops! I think I broke it! I'm sorry!"

Gisang looks furious.

"You stupid bitch! That light costs a fortune! Are you going to pay for that?"

"Don't worry! We could fix it!"

"With what?"

"Could we use sticky tape?"

"Don't be stupid!"

"What about glue? Does anyone have glue?"

Gisang glares at Shu and Caitlin, red-faced. He looks like he's going to explode.

"That light was worth more than your parents' yearly salary and it's completely wrecked! You can't just fix it easily, you idiot! You'll be punished for this! Get up!"

"But my parents earn a lot?" says Shu.

I look over at Caitlin, who is lying on the floor, picking bits of glass out of her clothes and laughing to herself. She looks at me and smiles. There's no way that her and Shu didn't plan this.

106. THE GIRLS

It's late, and we're all in our bunks in our tiny dormitory room that's smaller than the size of my entire bedroom at home. Shu and Iseul are both asleep. Youngsook is sitting up in bed playing with her phone. I'm not sure what Caitlin's doing as she's in the bunk above mine, but she hasn't said anything for a while so she's probably also sleeping. Nari is still in the gym, doing something, I don't know what and I really don't care, exercising maybe. I'm lying down in bed, reading through fan mail, silently to myself, trying to wear out my brain enough to the point where I feel tired enough to sleep. Way more people write to us now, we all get a lot of mail, it's great for insomnia.

Hana, when I first saw you, I knew you were the one for me. You are like the adorable little sister I never had. I wish that I could meet you properly. I beg that you look my way when I see you next. I am wealthy and have the means to take care of your every need. All you need to do is pledge your love for me, and that you want to be with me, always. I will describe for you my appearance and clothing so you can recognise me when we meet next. I am 49 years old, male, and I weigh 102 kilos...

Fuck, what a loser. I don't want to read any more of what this person has to say. I throw the letter on the small pile at the end of the bed which I'll put in the rubbish in the morning. I open up the next letter and read.

I saw how you looked at Caitlin on that TV show at the farm. You're a dirty bitch and you need to be taught a lesson. I know you're performing soon. I'll get up there and rape you right there on the stage, right in front of everyone, expect it...

I'm not reading any more of this either. I guess I would normally be scared by such a threat, but it's so extreme that it's impossible to even take seriously. It seems like normal people aren't interested in writing to us, so we only end up with mail from idiots. Not that I'd consider myself very normal either, but I wouldn't waste my time writing to some minor celebrity who I don't even know. I can't even wrap my head around what kind of stupid person would do that. I feel my phone vibrate under my pillow. I pull it out to take a look at whatever it is I've been sent, it can't be any worse than the garbage I've been reading tonight from fans.

Ijun: promotional pictures have been posted on the company social media profile for "Love Carousel". Please take a look.

I navigate to the True Miracle Entertainment profile page to see what's been posted. It's a bunch of pictures that we took of ourselves months ago, from our own individual social media profiles. The company have just recycled them by adding some filters to them, and some text with "Love Carousel", the company logo and the comeback stage date. They didn't use any of the recent pictures that Gisang took.

"Did you just get the message about the promo pictures?" Youngsook asks.

"Yeah, I had a look. Why are they all old stuff?"

"I guess Gisang didn't have enough pictures done before we broke his light, and they didn't want to delay the comeback any further."

"That's good. That shoot sucked and the pictures would have been some sleazy creep stuff."

"Yeah his pictures do kind of have a porn vibe to them, even the ones that don't show skin."

"I swear it's his creep energy."

"Are you sure you didn't enjoy getting close to Iseul?"

I look over at Iseul's bunk. She looks fast asleep. It should be safe to talk about her behind her back.

"Of course not, don't be gross."

"I thought I might have detected a bit of chemistry there."

"You're deluded."

"Are you sure?"

"She's not my type. Why would you assume that I like her?"

"Well, you *are* lesbian..."

"I'm not a... look, you like boys, right?"

"Yeah, and?"

"Well, do you like every single boy that you meet, just because they're a boy?"

Youngsook starts laughing.

"Well normally I'd say no, but I'll admit that the enforced isolation from boys in this place is lowering my standards a little!"

"Whatever you say."

Youngsook sits up in her bed and looks at me.

"Hey, Hana... that reminds me..."

"What?"

"I can't believe you're not one of the girls yet?"

I just stare at Youngsook. What the fuck is she talking about? Is this some weird exclusionary bullshit? How am I supposed to take this? Youngsook sees my confused expression and starts playing with her phone.

"Don't worry, I'll invite you. Check your phone, I'll send you a link."

I look at my phone which flashes up a new message.

You have been invited to the group "girls". Click the link to accept.

I accept the link and suddenly I'm part of a chat room.

Youngsook: hey everyone I thought I'd invite Hana in

Instantly the screen starts flooding with messages.

Ora: Hi Hana!

Gyeongja: HANA!

Amna: hi Hana!

Gyeongja: HANAHANAHANAHANAHANA

Sumire: greetings Hana!

Astrid: hi Hana! Where are you from?

Gyeongja: HANA! HANA! HANA! HANA!
Ora: Astrid, Hana is in Youngsook's group
Amna: is Hana as clumsy as Youngsook
Gyeongja: IT'S HANA!
Youngsook: Amna, that's not possible
Astrid: a great warrior has arisen
Ora: Hana is the real deal. She takes care of business.
Amna: does she ever
Gyeongja: HANAAAAAAAAAAAAAAAA!
Sumire: Hana are you okay? Say something!
Ora: Hana is shy. Give her a moment.
Sumire: No way? Shy? How?
Gyeongja: HANAAAAAAAAAAAAAAAA!
Astrid: Hana, the destroyer of worlds, an introvert?

I look up at Youngsook, and I can almost feel my jaw hit the floor. She *knows*. They *all* know. Youngsook walks over to my bunk and sits next to me. She smiles down at me and starts typing into her phone. I look back at my screen to see what she's writing.

Youngsook: give Hana some time, she's a bit emotional
Gyeongja: WE LOVE YOU HANA
Youngsook: maybe a lot of time
Youngsook: she didn't know that you all know
Youngsook: about some of her hobbies
Amna: it's okay we can wait for quality

I can feel myself getting upset. I try to hold it back, because I have a question, and I need an answer right now, before I start crying so hard that I can't speak.

"Who, from our group, is in this group?"

"Caitlin and Nari don't know about it. The rest are in."

That means Shu. *Shu also knows.*

"How long have..."

Youngsook smiles at me and gently reaches down, holding my hand.

"A while."

107. COMEBACK

"You still have vomit on your chin."

"Oh my god are you serious..."

"Yep! Big orange chunks of puke!"

"Oh sweet lord..."

Shu giggles while Youngsook runs off to the bathroom to clean up. We're all in our "Love Carousel" costumes, waiting to go onstage and Youngsook has been doing one of her usual pre-show purges. I don't know why Youngsook gets so nervous about being onstage, she has more ability than any of us. I'm feeling nauseous about our comeback stage too, for a different reason; at some time tonight I'm no doubt going to run into the Music Train PD, Mr Jeong. The last time we met, he was thrown out of a restaurant for assaulting me in public, right at the table. Of course I may have annoyed him just a little bit by being rude but it's not like he didn't deserve it. Who knows what he's got in store for me this time but I'm sure it won't be anything good.

"Look, it's Yohan!" says Iseul.

"Where?" asks Nari.

Iseul points down the corridor, where several groups are all lined up, waiting for their turn to perform. We all turn out heads to look. We *all* know who Yohan is, even with Shu and Caitlin's foreign backgrounds, and my own exceptionally sheltered upbringing, we all still know of him. Yohan is one of the members of EB-K, one of the biggest, most successful Korean idol groups to ever exist. Unlike us, and probably unlike every other person in this corridor with us, he's a real celebrity, a household name in many countries. Neither of my parents cared about music at all, but even *they* know who EB-K are. We watch as Yohan, dressed in a bright green suit and with black slicked-back hair, talks to someone at the far end of the corridor, an older man who looks like one of the staff. It's hard to get a good look at either of them as they converse with each other at the far end of the long corridor filled with members of other groups and trolleys full of stage equipment.

"Why is Yohan here?" asks Caitlin, craning her neck to try and get a better view of him.

"He's going to be doing some announcing for part of the show tonight," replies Nari.

"Our part?"

"I wish, but I doubt it."

"Wow, he looks so different to on television," says Shu.

"How?" asks Nari.

"He seems greasier. His skin is weird."

"You can tell from that far away?"

"I have excellent vision! I can determine greasy skin from a long distance!"

Mr Park suddenly appears in front of us.

"Look sharp, girls! You're on in a minute! Remember same drill as last time, the mics are off but the monitors in your ears are on. The crew will instruct you through these. Where's Youngsook?"

"Cleaning up!" says Shu.

"What happened?"

"Well, she was in the hall here with us, and she did a big vomit, so she went into the bathroom and got rid of the vomit and then she came out but there was still more vomit so she went back. She's very nervous. Look, there she is!"

Youngsook rushes up to rejoin us, while fidgeting with her in-ear monitors.

"Sorry everyone! Sorry Mr Park CEO! How do I look?"

"Like someone who is too fat and lazy to be an idol! Now get ready, the stage call will be any second! Don't mess it up this time!"

I start adjusting my own in-ear monitors so they're more comfortable. This time all our microphone and monitor sets are big and black with white highlights, they don't match the summer dresses that we're wearing at all. At least they're more comfortable than the stupid ones we've had in the past that were fashioned like flower petals and coloured to match our outfits.

"Be ready to head to the stage in five seconds."

That's the live sound engineer, talking to us through the monitors. We all line up in our usual order and wait. I take a deep breath to relax myself, although I barely feel nervous at all. I just have to get through the opening moves of the dance routine, and I know I'll be fine after that.

"Go. Now."

We file out through the door and onto the stage, quickly taking up our starting positions for the "Love Carousel" dance. This is a preparation that we've practiced hundreds of times in the gym, we all find our positions easily on the dimly lit stage area.

"Music starting after four clicks, in four... three... two... one..."

I hear four clicks and then the opening bars of "Love Carousel". The stage lights gradually come on and I work my way through the slow dance movements in the opening section. I notice that we actually have some cheering from the audience this time; the last time we performed on Music Train, the stage was dead quiet during the opening of the song. I guess we really are getting a bit popular.

It's time to go for a new ride / I don't know who I'll be meeting today / Maybe it's you, could you be the one / I'll let destiny determine my fate

I feel like I got through that first section okay, at least I didn't fall and bust my ankle, so that's an achievement. Everything gets easier from here for me, I just have to watch out for the others and hope nobody messes up. The next part I have to "sing" but I'm not really singing it, just moving my mouth in time to the words.

Can you feel the heat rising / The tension of uncertainty / Anything could happen under the starlit sky

That's it, I'm done with the miming part now as well. I can't really see the audience as the lights are too bright, so I focus on being aware of my surroundings as we move into the big chorus section.

It's a love-love carousel / Can you feel-feel my heart / This night, this time made for us to be together / To do whatever our hearts please

Everyone seems to be getting it so far, which is a huge relief. Although Youngsook's stage fumbling was what made us go viral, we can't just mess up all the time. I know that we have to prove that we're a competent group for people to like us. While I'm not that invested in our popularity myself, I know that I don't want to be sent back home so it's important that our group at least stays in the game so that doesn't happen. I'm determined to never live with my mother or go to school ever again. I watch for the upcoming rap section, which fortunately I don't have to do much with.

I know that you don't understand the reasons / My heart only goes where it pleases / Do you think we could be together / In this small space, in this short time / Would it be enough to make you mine

While I have to keep facing forward to the audience, I notice out of the corner of my eye that Iseul is struggling. She looks like she's fading fast. Iseul's been pretty quiet today in general, she didn't even use the opportunity to be in the corridor with a bunch of people from other groups to chat up boys and exchange phone numbers like she did last time we were here. As we move through into the next pre-chorus and chorus, I try to keep an eye on her.

In the cold light of morning / There will be no regrets / We know that we followed our hearts / I will board the carousel again / And let destiny determine my fate

As the bridge section plays, there's a bit of a break in the dance routine where we're still for a while. I notice Nari is propping up Iseul's arms so she stays in position. Suddenly I'm distracted by a harsh crackle in my in-ear monitors, and a new voice.

"Hana, you bitch. You worthless slut. I'm going to get you after the show, so you'd better be ready. Don't think you can get out of it. You'd better play nice when I see you if you want a career."

That's Mr Jeong's voice. He must have entered the control room to say that to me just now. What a piece of shit, trust him to use this chance to get revenge. My heart starts racing. How am I going to get out of this? We're all going to have to hang around and wait for him after the performances are over. I need to work out a way I can avoid meeting him.

The song finally kicks back into the last chorus and then it's over. We all hold our ending pose. I can't quite bring myself to smile so I just do some heart shapes with my hands and stare vacantly at the nearest camera. The crowd cheers loudly, they love us somehow.

"When the lights go out, exit stage right."

That's not Mr Jeong, that's the live engineer, he's handed the microphone back over. Thank fuck for that, I sure don't want to hear that piece of shit Mr Jeong's voice again, now or ever. The lights dim and we re-emerge in the hallway. Mr Park is waiting for us, he holds out a small bag in front of us.

"Everyone put your monitor equipment in the bag. No breakages this time?"

"I think Iseul's a little broken!" says Shu.

I look over at Iseul, she's barely even conscious.

"Are you okay?" I ask her.

Iseul's eyes roll back in her head and she suddenly falls forward, nearly hitting my head with hers. Nari quickly reaches out and grabs Iseul's arm, stopping her from landing on me or falling further. Nari then tucks Iseul into her side to keep her stable and upright.

"We need to get Iseul to the hospital," says Nari.

"No, you girls need to wait here for the PD," Mr Park replies.

Nari looks at Mr Park angrily.

"We can't just wait here with Iseul passed out!"

"We can get medical help for Iseul, but we can't afford the risk of being seen as unprofessional. You must all stay here and wait for the PD."

Nari sighs and turns to the rest of us.

"An ambulance will take forever. Iseul's cars are useful, but who do we call for a quick ride when it's Iseul who needs the hospital?"

"What's going on?"

An unfamiliar voice. We all turn around. It's Yohan, in his green suit, staring at Nari and Iseul. We all stare at him, speechless. He looks at Nari.

"Let me see if I can remember who is who in this group, I'm sorry but I'm terrible with new groups... you're Nari, right?"

Nari nods. She seemingly doesn't know what to say. I think she's a bit star-struck.

"And who is the girl that's collapsing? That's... Hana?"

"No, this is Iseul."

"Okay. Give me Iseul."

Nari walks Iseul over to Yohan, who grabs Iseul and lifts her up with his arms. Yohan looks at me.

"Okay, so that means *you* must be Hana."

I smile a bit. The idea of someone like Yohan knowing who I am is pretty amazing.

"It's me, Hana."

"Come with me. Follow me out to my car."

I look at Mr Park, and he just motions for me to go with Yohan. I guess Yohan outranks him. I trail behind Yohan as we walk through the corridor.

"I'll just need you to open doors for me, Hana. Can you get the big double-doors up ahead?"

I race up to the end of the corridor and swing open the double-doors so Yohan can get Iseul through them. We walk through the doorway, out to the underground car park.

"Okay, and now the doors to my car. Reach into my front pocket and grab my keyring. There's a black rectangle there with a blue button."

I hesitate. Yohan might be a celebrity and a big deal, but I'm not reaching into any man's pants for anything. Yohan looks at me and sighs.

"Hana, I know what you're thinking. Look, I can't do anything to you, I have my hands full carrying Iseul, right? Don't worry, nothing's going to happen."

I really don't want to do this. I'm not convinced. I stare at Yohan's front pocket silently. This is so awkward.

"I have a partner anyway, if anything happened he wouldn't approve. In fact I should be the one being cautious of you!"

Yohan smiles at me. Knowing that he has a male partner makes me feel a bit better about it, with any luck he's not into girls at all. I reluctantly reach into his pants and find the keyring. Fortunately I don't feel anything else while I'm in there. I pull it out and press the blue button on the black rectangular piece of plastic. A black car in the parking lot flashes its lights and makes a clicking noise.

"Open the back door and I'll put Iseul in."

I open the rear door of the car and Yohan slides Iseul into the back seat so she's laying across it.

"Now get in the front."

"Where am I going?"

"To the hospital. Someone has to stay there and mind her. Come on, let's go."

Yohan doesn't know it, but he's saving me from having to deal with Mr Jeong. How do I explain that to him and thank him? Should I even talk about it? What if him and Mr Jeong are friends? I decide not to risk it, instead I quickly walk over to the passenger side and get in Yohan's car. Inside it's the most luxurious car I've ever seen, even more so than the limo I rode in with Iseul. As Yohan starts the engine up and pulls away, out of the carpark and into the night, I run my hands over the black leather interior.

"This is a nice car. Thank you for taking care of Iseul."

"Take a card from the dash."

Yohan points to a small pile of black business cards in a little card holder next to the dashboard, I reach over and grab one. It has Yohan's name and phone number.

"Why do you want me to have this?"

"Hana, do you know why I came to see you?"

"I thought you were coming to get Iseul because she was passing out?"

"No, I actually came to see *you*. I just happened to notice Iseul when I arrived. I mean, I can't just ignore something like that, can I?"

"I guess not...?"

I'm starting to feel nervous. I'm in the guy's car, and I've only just met him, and he wants to see me for... some reason? I really hope this is nothing weird.

"So I wanted to talk to you privately, because I want to get you on board with something that I'm planning, which isn't something for everyone to know."

"Oh?"

"You're lesbian, right?"

"I'm n... wait, is it that obvious?"

"It's pretty obvious to me. I was ninety-nine percent sure! Thanks for confirming!"

I sit back in my seat and sigh.

"Hana, I'm trying to start up a network for people like you, and me, and others in this industry, who are LGBT. There's a lot of us, but we have to stay silent, and there's no support, no resources for us, nowhere to go if we need help. Having our whole lives in the closet is devastating for our mental health, but what can we do? If I was ever outed, my career would be done for, and I imagine it's the same for others. You seem like a pretty straightforward sort, who would want to get on board with this."

"What do you want me to do?"

"Just take my details. This is still in the planning stages, I don't know yet what this support network is going to look like, or how we can operate it away from the *sasaengs*, without them finding out about it. I'm just laying the groundwork for now. I'll be in touch in the future."

"Okay."

"I just want to use my position to try and help. Oh, and if you know anyone else who would be interested..."

"Caitlin might."

"Who's Caitlin?"

"My... partner, I guess? She's in the group with me."

"Which one is she? Sorry, I'm bad with names."

"She's... the one with..."

"Oh wait, I think I know."

"You do?"

"Yeah. She got arrested for drugs, didn't she?"

"That's her."

"What happened there, she got off?"

"Yeah, they just let her go."

"She's lucky."

"She's definitely got the gift of being able to talk her way out of situations."

"I know some guys who will be a bit sad to find out she's taken!"

"Too bad for them. Mind you, Caitlin's a bit of a tart so they might still be in luck, you never know with her."

Yohan laughs as we continue to drive on, into the night.

108. HOSPITAL

I'm sitting on a chair in the hospital ward, next to Iseul's bed. It's busy here, with doctors walking noisily up and down the white tiled corridors attending to patients, and constant annoying announcements echoing between staff members over the public address system. Iseul is fast asleep, with an intravenous drip connected to her arm, feeding fluid into her veins; this is the standard treatment for whenever we pass out onstage or during training. Myself and Shu have been admitted multiple times each, but this is the first time Iseul has needed to go to hospital for this reason. Sitting here is boring, so I get out my phone, I want to see what our performance of "Love Carousel" looks like. I do a quick search but I can't find any videos of it yet. I guess I'll check again later, there's bound to be some soon. I've been here for a while now, I wonder how Caitlin is doing. I start texting her.

Me: hey

Caitlin starts writing back immediately. I guess she's back in the dorms by now.

Caitlin: hey Hana, how's the celebrity life? What just happened to you and Iseul?

Me: Yohan dropped us at the hospital, I'm still here now waiting for Iseul's IV drip to run out so we can come back to the dorm. You're back at the agency?

Caitlin: The PD lost interest in us as soon as he found out that you had split, he was super pissed and we just left

Me: good, I hate him. He said he was going to come looking for me after the show, making threats, through my in-ears.

Caitlin: yeah, I know THAT feeling

Me: I'm so lucky to have gotten out. What if I have to meet him again.

Caitlin: don't stress. We'll think of something.

Caitlin: that's insane that we met Yohan though

Caitlin: do you realise how mad Iseul is going to be once you tell her that Yohan touched her and she wasn't conscious enough to experience it?

Me: she might remember some of it maybe, she was still standing, kind of

Caitlin: I don't know, she looked pretty out of it

Me: I'm going to have some fun with her when she wakes up, it can't be long now, it's already been hours

Caitlin: enjoy, see you soon

I'm bored so I check the "girls" chat group, it's just constant chatter in there between the Pearlfive members and some other people I don't know, the text is going by too fast for me to even follow what they're talking about but it's nothing that makes any sense to me. It's too much effort to engage with right now, I don't have the mental energy for it. My phone vibrates in my hand, I have a new message notification. I open the message.

Sooae: I just saw that comeback. Your new song sucks just as much as your others.

Me: I know, right? The same guy who wrote the other songs we do wrote it, can you tell?

No response yet. I look over at Iseul, she's still asleep. Her drip only has about a fifth of the fluid left in the bag, that's good because once it runs out the nurse will detach it from her arm and then we can leave here. I want to go back to the dorms so I can see Caitlin again. I feel my phone vibrate in my hand. Sooae has replied.

Sooae: Yeah, sure can. Hey is Iseul alright? I could tell on the TV that she was struggling hard

Me: she passed out just after. We're at the hospital. She's alright, she's just getting fluids.

Sooae: that's ridiculous. Why was she like that?

Me: we get fed nearly nothing. Even less just before an important show, so we don't weigh over.

Sooae: fucking idol system. Anyway enough about you and your shit music that sucks, let's talk about me and my completely excellent music. Did you listen to the song I sent you?

Me: fuck, I totally forgot about that. Sorry. I'll get around to it.

Sooae: no, listen to it NOW, bitch! I've been waiting long enough!

Me: fine

I scroll back through Sooae's messages, looking for the song that she sent. Eventually I find it.

Me: how do I play a song on here?

Sooae: just tap it, you dumbass

I tap on the music icon that says "Kimchi Slappers". Immediately loud music starts blaring from my phone, feeling self-conscious I quickly turn the volume down. The song starts with just a guitar noise, but it's so amped up that it sounds like a broken electric saw. Then some drums come in, with a mindless rhythm that's slightly irregular in a way I can't describe, certainly impossible to dance to, and then finally some girl screaming over the top. The voice sounds like angry yelling, and then sometimes like the girl is gargling blood, it's just crazy, nothing like normal singing. I turn it down even further as I notice Iseul moving, I think I've just woken her up. I start texting Sooae while I watch Iseul stir.

Me: what is this. this isn't even music

Sooae: better than your garbage, what do you know about music

Me: I don't need to know about music to know this stuff isn't music

Sooae: go fuck yourself hahaha

Me: hey Iseul is waking up, I gotta go look after her

Sooae: okay, tell her she's a bitch for me

Me: will do, talk later

Sooae is funny, I love her personality and how she just insults everything but in a good-natured way. I need more people like that in my life and less uptight people like Nari and Iseul. I look at Iseul who is definitely awake now. She's just realised that the drip needle is in her arm, she sits up carefully and rubs her eyes.

"What happened to me?"

"You passed out after the show."

"Oh right. Why is it *you* here and not Ijun? Isn't it Ijun who always stays at the ward?"

"Not this time. What's the last thing you remember?"

"We got off the stage... and Nari helped me down, and then there was a guy... I'm a bit foggy from there."

"That was Yohan."

"What?"

"Yohan took us to the hospital. He literally picked you up and carried you out to his car, while I held doors open for him."

"You're full of shit, Hana."

"No I'm not. Ask the others."

"You're such a liar."

"And you know what else?"

"What?"

"I put my hand down his pants."

"WHAT?"

"He needed someone to open his car doors up while he was carrying you so I had to reach for his keyring in his pocket to unlock them."

"You are so full of shit! You're such a liar!"

"It's true!"

Iseul stares at me for about ten seconds.

"Actually, now that I think about it, you're not a *good* liar. You're completely transparent when you try to lie, because you're so stupid. So it probably *is* true. Oh wow, fuck you. Fuck you so much, *wangtta* girl."

"Fuck you too!"

"I'm going to bully you so hard when I get out of this hospital bed, you skank. You can be my dance-shuttle, you can do all my dance routines for me."

"No you won't. Because I have this."

I take out the card Yohan gave me and wave it at Iseul.

"What the fuck is that shit?"

"Yohan's card with his contact details. Be nice to me and you can have it."

"Dumb bitch, I've already got his number... oh wait, no I don't, he's the only one who I'm missing! Fuck! Oh wow, really, fuck you so much. No, seriously. Screw off, I hate you so much now, I hope you die soon. Imagine the experience of meeting Yohan being wasted on an ugly dyke like you. There's no justice."

I put Yohan's card away and smile at Iseul. She looks like she wants to get out of bed and fight me, but she can't move from where she is due to the drip still being in her arm. Serves her right for being such a bitch.

109. THE BIG MEET

"Oh wow, look at them all!"

Shu points to the glass double-doors at the end of the large meeting hall. From our sitting positions, behind long white tables on the stage, we can see the queues of people, lined up for this event; the fan meeting to promote our new "Love Carousel" comeback. We're all dressed in the same summer dresses that we performed the song in. A pathway is marked out and cordoned off with metal barricades to contain the fans who will soon be here, lining up to meet us. Security staff are positioned around the floor, preparing themselves for the crowd to be let in. I scan over the blue-suited staff and look for Petal, my favourite security guard but she doesn't seem to be here.

"How many of them are there?" Shu asks nobody in particular.

"At least a couple hundred," replies Nari.

"It's going to be so loud when they all come in here, with the wooden floors and glass walls and everything," says Youngsook.

Mr Park walks to the front of the stage and faces us.

"Okay girls, we're just about to open the doors. Remember to remain seated, be polite and be charming. Fans can talk to you and ask you to sign items, they can also give you gifts, but they cannot reach over to you or touch you in any way without permission. Call security if you have an issue."

"Yes Mr Park CEO!" we bow and reply in unison.

Mr Park walks off to the far edge of the stage, this means it's time for the fans to be let inside. The double doors open and the fans come flooding in. Instantly the security team springs into action, directing the crowd to designated seats and navigating them in an orderly manner to the stage, one by one. Fans gradually come up to the tables as directed. So far my table is empty, which is good, the less people I have to talk to today, the better. Youngsook was right, it's instantly noisier in here due to the chatter of the fans. I look at the crowd and wonder what would even motivate someone to attend an event like this.

"Hey, Hana!"

The voice startles me. A fan has sat opposite me and I didn't even notice. It's a young, skinny guy with a bowl cut.

"Oh, *annyeong!*" I bow sheepishly.

"Wow, you look just like your pictures!"

"I do? What pictures?"

"These pictures!"

He produces a photobook, it's a photobook for the "Love Carousel" comeback. I didn't know this existed.

"Can I take a look? I haven't seen this yet."

"You haven't seen your own photobook?"

"We don't get to see much."

He slides the photobook over the table, I open it up and take a look. As I flip through the pages I can't help but start laughing. It's exactly the same images that Ijun sent to us, the ones that we took ourselves.

"What's funny?" he asks.

"They just used our social networking pictures! Our agency is so cheap!"

"You shouldn't say that! Aren't they supporting your fame? You should be grateful!"

I don't even know what to say to that.

"Look, do you want me to sign this or what?"

"Sure, can you please sign the picture of you, on the bed? That's my favourite picture!"

"Okay."

I flip through the photobook until I find the picture that I took of myself in the dorm bunk. In this photo I have my head on the pillow, and I'm looking up at the camera. I grab a marker on the table and sign my name next to the picture. I notice this picture looks a bit different to when I took it, but it takes a few seconds to realise why.

"Hey I had long hair when I took this. They've edited the photo around the edges!"

"Wow, that's so clever!"

"It's so annoying. I miss my long hair. Hey, what does that text say, under the picture?"

"You can't read it?"

I squint at the text, there's something printed below my picture but I can't read any of it, it's too small. I try to move the book around in the light so I can focus on it better but it doesn't help.

"It's so tiny. Who can even read this?"

"That's easy to read. You need glasses, Hana."

"I do not. Anyway, what does it say?"

"It says: *Thank you to all our fans for your unwavering support, your passion gives us energy and joy, which we hope to return to you through our brighter dedication to our performance, we love you all so much – Hana.* That's beautiful, Hana!"

"I didn't write it."

"You didn't?"

"Does it sound like something I would write?"

"Yes?"

I stare at him blankly.

"Look, is there anything else?"

"You're a little different to how I expected, Hana."

"Okay then, bye now."

I close the photobook and slide it back over to him. I couldn't be bothered talking to this person, he obviously has a strange impression of me. He gets up and leaves nervously. I immediately sigh with relief.

Nobody else has gotten into my chair yet, so I look next to me to see how the others are doing. Caitlin is on one side of me and Nari on the other, both have their hands full with greeting fans and signing books. I watch

Caitlin smile to fans as she bows and talks to them, I notice that every one of Caitlin's fans is a guy.

"Hi, Hana!"

Another person has sat down in my chair without me noticing.

"Oh, *annyeong!*" I bow sheepishly again, trying to compensate for my lack of attention.

"Remember me?"

I look at the person, a young woman. I don't remember her.

"It's okay, you were looking at Caitlin! I'm sorry to interrupt! I'm Lim!"

"I'm sorry, I meet a lot of people. Who are you?"

"You remember our chat last time? Feminism...?"

That's right, Lim is the person who told me what feminism was, at the fan meet for our debut.

"Yes, I remember you now. Hi, Lim!"

"So did you read about feminism?"

"Actually I did!"

"What do you think?"

"I liked it, but sometimes women are bitches too, you know? Like, men not being allowed to have rights is a no-brainer, but sometimes women don't deserve any rights either. I certainly know a few who deserve no rights at all."

"Hey, can I whisper something to you?"

I'm allowed to veto this type of request, but because it's from a female fan, I'll allow it.

"Yeah okay, go ahead," I nod.

Lim bends over the table at me to whisper in my ear. I stand up and bend forward towards her. I notice a security guard looking in my direction; he's checking if I'm okay with this, as this activity isn't allowed unless I permit it. I give him a quick thumbs up and he gives me a nod back. Lim puts her lips directly up to my ear.

"Hana... are you lesbian for Caitlin?"

I sit back down and look at her. I don't know what to say or where to look. Lim starts grinning at me. Am I this obvious?

"Wow, you're totally red-faced!"

I put my head in my hands to try and hide how much I'm blushing. I can't believe a fan has brought this up.

"Don't worry Hana, I won't tell!"

"How..."

"You look at her, like, *all the time*. I'll show you!"

Lim gets out her phone, and shows me a fan-made video: "Hana staring at Caitlin compilation". She presses play and I watch. The video starts with a clip from when we did the farming TV show. When Youngsook is chopping rice I'm barely paying attention and talking to the others, but when Caitlin starts doing the same activity, I can be seen staring intently from the corner of the screen. The video edits to zoom in on my face and emphasises my stare with a stupid duck-quacking sound effect. The next clip is of us getting ready to do our school stage, it shows me staring at Caitlin while in the ready position before the music starts. Then there's a clip of our debut stage, and once again I'm staring at Caitlin the same way just before the song comes on. Then the screen cuts to when we were on Joong & Kwan, that stupid idol show. The video plays the same duck sound effect each time I take a look at Caitlin, and they've edited together just these parts plus superimposed a number on the screen which increases each time I'm caught. At one point when everyone is facing away from me I look at Caitlin up and down for a few seconds very obviously, this is represented by about ten quacks in a row and the number going up very quickly. At the end of the video I've checked out Caitlin fifty-seven times according to the counter.

"I can explain! For the dances, I use her movements to cue the start. For the farm thing..."

"You don't have to explain anything! It's already very obvious. Don't worry I'm not going to make a big deal of it. I just hope that one day you can express yourself more freely."

I sigh.

"A lot of people are really looking forward to that day. Anyway, it's good to see you!"

Lim leaves and I feel a sense of relief again. Just because she's right doesn't make it any less awkward. I barely have time to catch my breath when someone else sits down in the chair opposite from me, I'm ready for it this time and bow.

"Hello, Hana. It's good to see you."

It's another guy, slightly older than the one before, he seems like he's in his late twenties. He sits down placidly, he seems harmless enough.

"Hi there."

"I saw you when you performed at the Air Force base. Is it true that you like guns?"

"Yes! You're in the Air Force?"

"I'm a guard there."

"Do you get to shoot people a lot? Have you shot a lot of people?"

"What?"

He seems a bit offended. I guess I'd better explain.

"Sorry, I'm not criticising. I'm interested in a job where I can shoot people. Do you think I could be a guard?"

"Oh. Actually it's mainly a lot of waiting around."

"Do you sometimes wish people would try to invade your base so you could just shoot them?"

"That thought hasn't crossed my mind. If you wanted to be a guard you could sign up for training. There's a lot of discipline though, more than being an idol."

"You haven't been an idol, how would you know?"

"You haven't been in the military."

"I don't think I want to if there's lots of people telling me what to do."

"Maybe that's for the best Hana. It's good to meet you though. I'd hate it if you weren't in Halcyon and got another job. You're my favourite in the group."

"Oh. Why?"

"You don't seem to have so much of a filter like the other girls. They all know what to say and do. You just seem to be a bit more true to yourself."

"It's hard being true to myself. This place is so full of weirdness that sometimes I feel like I don't know what my true self even is."

"You see, any other idol wouldn't say something like that. Anyway take care of yourself Hana."

I bow and he gets up and leaves. A few seconds later another man sits down, a young guy.

"Hi, Hana! You're so pretty!"

Oh no, he finds me attractive. I'd better be rude to him so he goes away.

"Can you do a smile for me?"

"No. Agency says it's not allowed. They tell me I've reached my smile quota. Got anything for me to sign?"

"Can you please sign my book?"

He slides his photobook over. I sign the front cover without even opening it up and slide it back.

"I was hoping you could sign the page with your picture on it."

"I could, but I won't."

"Why not?"

"I've reached my picture-signing quota too."

"You know I always thought you were my ideal type in the group but now I'm starting to reconsider."

"Well now that's a shame. Anything else you want from me today? Do a little dance perhaps?"

"No thanks. I'll be going now."

"Bye then."

He gets up and leaves quickly. The next fan is a lady. She's clearly pregnant, and she has a baby with her. She's not even sitting down, she just stands there holding her kid in her arms. Oh my god, what is she even doing here, doesn't she have better things to do?

"Hello Hana!"

"Hi."

"Can you hold my baby? I want to take a photo of you with my baby!"

"It's dangerous for kids here, what are you doing? No!"

"Come on, just quickly! Hold my baby!"

She holds her gross kid out in front of her, expecting me to take it. Not a chance. I instinctively back away.

"If you drop that fucking kid, it hits the table."

I wave for a security guy, but they're all distracted. How typical, never paying attention when they're needed. I keep scanning the room for a free guard while she talks.

"No need to be so rude."

"Yes there is. Don't bring your kids here."

"Some idol you are."

I finally catch eyes on a guard and wave him over.

"This lady is pregnant and she has a baby with her."

"That's allowed in here," the security guard replies.

"That's allowed? Really?"

The lady looks at me with total smugness. I just want to smack her. I can't deal with her, I have to completely offend her so she'll leave.

"Hey what's the sex of the one on the way?"

"I don't know yet. We find out next week."

"You should abort it, just in case."

"What?"

"There's a fifty percent chance it might be male. Do you really want to risk it?"

The lady looks at me, speechless. I give her the fakest smile possible and she storms off. What a fucking idiot. The next person comes up, a young man, but before he can say anything or sit down we're interrupted by a loud scream, followed by the sound of scuffling and tables moving. Something's happening on the other end of the row of tables where we're seated, on the other side of Nari. I stand up to take a closer look. The security guards have grabbed hold of a guy by Shu's table, they start escorting him to the side of the stage and out of the building. Another guard is comforting Shu, who is curled up and lying on the ground. Whatever altercation just happened, I missed it.

"Are you okay, Shu?" asks Nari.

"That was scary! He grabbed me!"

More security guards come up to the stage and motion for everyone to back away.

"I'll be okay, everyone! Just give me a moment!" says Shu, as the guard with her helps her onto her feet and back into the chair. Less than a minute later she's diligently back to greeting people and everything proceeds as it was before. I turn back to the young man and we both sit down.

"Hello, Hana! I'm a huge fan!"

"Oh. What do you like about me?"

"You're... um, you sing well!"

"Sing well, since when?"

"On your songs!"

"You know that's not even me singing on those songs, right?"

"Really? You sing live though, right?"

"No, we just mime it."

"Are you serious? I thought you were musicians?"

"We're not musicians, we're idols."

He doesn't seem to know what to say.

"Look, do you want me to sign anything?"

"I don't know... I'd like the actual singer to sign it."

"I can arrange that. Give me your photobook."

He hands me the photobook. I get up, walk around behind Caitlin, and tap Youngsook on her shoulder with it. Youngsook, who's busy talking to a fan and signing something, turns around and stares at me.

"What's this for?" she asks me.

"My fan wants the 'actual singer' of my lines to sign the book, that's you. Want to sign it for me?"

"Sure, I'd love to."

Youngsook opens the photobook up to the page with the picture of me on it, and signs it quickly: *I totally sung all my parts on this record, for realsies – love, Youngsook sorry I mean Hana.* I burst out laughing.

"That's fantastic, thank you!"

"Anytime!"

I go back to my chair, resume my seat, and slide the photobook back to the guy.

"Here you go. Signed by the actual singer. Enjoy."

"But... I don't like Youngsook, she's not as pretty."

"She's still out of your league."

"Yeah that's true, but my job isn't to be an idol."

"Hey you said you wanted the singer. She's the singer. Make up your fucking mind what you want."

He starts talking but I've stopped listening. I'm busy looking at the crowd behind him. There are still hundreds of people here, this event is going to take hours. I'm sure that being a more popular group has its benefits, but this certainly isn't one of them. I can't wait to be anywhere else.

110. TERMINATION

"It's eight o'clock! Thank god!"

All of us collapse on the gym floor at once. We've been practicing the "Love Carousel" dance over and over all day to iron out the last few kinks in the dance routine before we take it on the road, as we have a large amount of shows to do in a few days.

"I could fall asleep right here," says Shu, while lying face down on the wooden floor.

"Me too," says Iseul, putting her head on Shu's thighs.

"Hey I'm not a pillow!"

"Technically, you are a pillow at this moment."

Nari gets up and skips over to the hallway door.

"Since you're all lazy, I'm first for the shower, you can all decide who's next, see you in three minutes."

Nari runs off quickly to start the showers up as we all have to shower within the fifteen-minute time limit or the water gets cut off. We all start looking at each other to organise some sort of order for showering for the rest of us when the administration door opens and Mr Park walks in.

"Hana, get up!" he yells.

I'm exhausted. I just want to lie here for a few seconds.

"Hana, get up now!"

"Can it wait one minute please? I just need to catch my breath."

Mr Park walks up to me, bends over, and grabs my head by the earlobe.

"Ah, that hurts! That's attached, you know!"

"We're going to my office, right now, Hana!"

I have no choice but to follow Mr Park seeing as he has my ear in a super-tight grip. There's no chance of me getting out of this, he's definitely the strongest sixty-year-old man I've ever met. He's obviously really angry about something too, which is obvious by the way he's grabbing me, I've been dragged by the ear by mad teachers before and this feels just like that. I awkwardly walk with him through the admin area and into his office. He deposits me into the chair opposite his own, and lets my ear go. He then takes a seat behind his desk.

"Am I in trouble?" I ask.

Mr Park doesn't say anything, but starts looking in a cupboard behind his desk for something.

"Look, Mr Park CEO, if I've done something wrong, I'm like really sorry and..."

"SHUT UP, Hana!"

I stop talking. There's no use continuing when he gets like this. After a couple minutes Mr Park pulls out some sort of document and places it on the desk.

"Sign this."

"What's this for?"

"Frankly Hana, I've had enough of you. You don't listen to anything I tell you, you have a constant attitude, and you reflect that attitude not just to your team here, but also to the staff, the clients we engage in order to boost your career, and even the group's fans. You have the lowest popularity rating, the lowest amount of utility in the group, and it's clear that you're never going to improve, nor do you want to. The attitude that you exhibited at your fan meeting was the last straw. Do you know how many complaints I've received?"

"How would I even know that?"

"That was a rhetorical question. Do you know what a rhetorical question is?"

"Is that a rhetorical question too?"

"It's clear that you don't want to be part of the team. Sign this. It will get you out of your contract without a termination fee. You will then be sent back home, and we can both forget that this all happened."

No way. I'm not going back home, to live with my mother, and go to school again. I'd rather die.

"This isn't fair! It's not my fault I'm not protected! The fans are all creeps and your industry friends have assaulted me! Why do I have to always act like everything's fine?"

"I am not discussing anything. I am over talking to you about it. This is not up to you. Just read and sign."

Mr Park places a black pen on the desk beside the document. I'm expecting myself to burst out crying, but instead I feel oddly numb. I start reading through the document. It's pretty hard to understand quickly as it's written in that funny legal way just like my initial contract was, but it does seem to say that I'll be released with no penalty. The document also says that I'm forbidden from saying anything about my activities at the company to anyone, and also that the company is cleared of any wrongdoing for anything that happened while I was here. No wonder he wants me to sign it, he's covering his ass should I try and seek some legal advice for anything bad that happened. Not that I could even be bothered with taking legal action or would even know the first thing about how to do that, but it's nice to know that Mr Park is a manipulative criminal right to the end.

"What if I don't sign? What are you going to do?"

Mr Park just looks at me, threateningly.

"I don't have a choice, do I?"

"You do have a choice, but you have only one correct choice."

The door to Mr Park's office opens, and Ijun walks in, dressed in her usual black and red school uniform and carrying a pink laptop.

"I told you not to interrupt!" Mr Park yells.

Ijun doesn't say anything back or even acknowledge his annoyance. She walks up to Mr Park's desk, opens her laptop up on it, and shows him the screen. He sits there and reads the screen in silence, taking his time, while she looks at him with a blank expression. As he keeps reading, he seems less upset.

"You're showing me this now? Not half an hour ago?"

"I only just got it now."

"Nice timing."

Mr Park turns to me. He looks at me for a full minute while saying nothing. Meanwhile Ijun starts looking at the paper on Mr Park's desk that I'm supposed to sign.

"Mr Park CEO, you were about to fire her? Really?"

"Like I said, nice timing."

"Like *I said*, I only just got this! It's not my fault!"

Mr Park sighs and looks at me.

"Hana, get out and close the door behind you. This doesn't concern you any longer."

Ijun looks at Mr Park defiantly.

"Hana has a right to know what is going on!"

I'm confused as hell.

"Am I being let go, or not?"

Ijun looks at me.

"I will tell you what's going on privately, since Mr Park CEO for some reason would rather not."

Mr Park goes to say something but Ijun cuts him off.

"I don't care, Mr Park CEO! She has a right to know! Hana, come with me. Nothing bad will happen. Come."

I look at Mr Park. He doesn't look at me, only Ijun.

"Come back here when you're done."

Ijun nods. Mr Park then waves silently at me, signalling for me to leave with Ijun. I follow Ijun out of Mr Park's office, back into the gym which is now empty, and outside through the sliding doors into the park area. Before I can get a single word in or even sit down, Ijun starts addressing me.

"You need to lift your behaviour immediately. We had dozens of complaints about your idiotic conduct at the fan meet and social media is now on fire, thanks to you. I've been busy putting out that fire, but you were minutes away from being kicked out."

"I don't want to be kicked. The fans are assholes, I can't help it sometimes."

"Yes you can help it, and you will help it. I know the fans suck, because I'm the one who has to handle the fallout every time you show an attitude. I'm as sick of your nonsense as Mr Park CEO is. You're making my life very difficult right now."

"My life is difficult too. It's not right, what happens here."

"You're here, so you have to play the game, and put up the required public image. We all do. I know it's hard but you can't just tell everyone how you feel all the time. If you need to express yourself, talk to the girls in private. Got it?"

"What good will that do?"

"You'll get to be in the group tomorrow, that's what it'll do."

"Okay. So am I kicked out or not?"

"You got lucky."

"What happened?"

"You got a sponsor. Not sure how, but..."

"A sponsor? Who?"

Ijun holds up her phone and points to the logo on it. I notice that it's a new phone, she's upgraded it from when I last saw her with her phone.

"Hancel want you, and Shu, as brand ambassadors. They were very specific about only wanting you both, as a package deal, and not the others. Mr Park tried to talk them into just Shu, but they weren't having it."

"Why us?"

"I don't know, but the money is big so we're not going to be asking too many questions. This is a big contract, Hancel are huge. The amount they're paying for this will recoup the entire group's debt in one hit. It's a big enough amount for Mr Park CEO to forgive everything you've done wrong so far, and you've done a lot wrong so far. So try not to mess this up with any of your usual behaviour."

"I'm sorry. I don't mean to let the team down. I just find it so hard to control myself. I don't know what's wrong with me."

"That is your problem to figure out, Hana. We all have problems."

"Ijun... can I talk to you honestly?"

"What is it?"

"This place... it's kind of fucked up, isn't it? You see the stuff we send on video, right? You understand, right?"

"Things will be hard for a while yet. But they will get better soon, at least for you girls."

"Just us?"

Ijun just stares at me.

"Go to your dorms."

"I'm sorry?"

Ijun points in the direction of the glass door.

"Go! Do it now. Don't say anything more."

I know better than to go against an instruction from Ijun. I quickly walk through the gym. As I reach the hallway I sneak a quick look back at her. She's sitting on the bench, facing away from me, staring at nothing. I walk into the dorms. The others are all sitting up in their bunks, except Youngsook, I guess she's showering.

"You look shaken. What happened?" Nari asks.

"I nearly got kicked out."

"What? Why?"

I climb into my bunk. I'm not very keen to talk about this, but I guess I have to.

"Mr Park said he's had enough of me. I only got to stay because I got a job offer or something at the last minute, some advertising thing I think."

"That's nonsense, he can't kick you out. You're a good dancer. I won't allow it. If he tries to kick you out again, come straight to me."

"Yeah, whatever. What will *you* do?"

"I'll tell him that if you go, so will I."

Nari seems adamant. I'm surprised that she's in my corner this much. I know that I've annoyed her a lot in the past.

"I thought you'd be glad to be rid of me?"

"Well, actually..." starts Iseul. *That fucking bitch.*

Nari throws her pillow at Iseul, hitting her in the face.

"Shut the fuck up, Iseul! We support each other in this place! We're a team!" Nari says.

"Excellent shot!" laughs Caitlin, jumping down from her bunk to retrieve Nari's pillow. Caitlin pokes Iseul playfully a couple times in the face with the pillow.

"Stop that, you whore," Iseul grumbles, swatting the pillow away.

Caitlin smiles and throws the pillow gently back to Nari, who catches it and then looks at me.

"You might be an annoying bitch, Hana... but you're *our* annoying bitch. We have to stick together in this place. Also you're the only one who keeps up completely with me on stage with the routines, I need that. You're not going anywhere."

"I don't keep up?" asks Shu.

"You're good, Hana is better. And you know I'm not biased!"

"Oh." Shu looks a bit dejected. *Good.*

"She's just a bit snappier, that's all. Maybe Hana giving you some dance lessons would be helpful for you."

Oh no, Nari. What the fuck.

Don't you dare volunteer me for this shit.

Anything but teaching the aegyo Chinese dwarf.

Nari sees the look in my eyes, there's no doubt that she knows exactly what I'm thinking.

"Not only would it be a good exercise for you to get better at dancing, but it would be a good exercise for Hana to get better at being a decent human being. That way, you can help each other. What do you think, Hana?"

Nari gives me a big grin. I stare back at her flatly.

"Sounds fantastic," I reply, trying to make the sarcasm in my voice as obvious as possible.

"Well, I'm the leader, so you don't have a choice. You might as well learn to love it."

The dorm door opens and Youngsook comes in, she's just finished her shower. She puts her finger up to her lips.

"Hey, everyone – quiet! Listen!"

We all stop talking. Youngsook opens the dorm door a little wider. The sound is dull at first, but as we listen closer, it becomes easier to hear. It's Mr Park, yelling.

"Who is it?" asks Shu.

"It's Mr Park!" replies Youngsook.

We keep listening. I can't hear what exactly is being said, but it's pretty clear that he's having an argument with someone. I can't hear the voice of the other person, only Mr Park's voice, getting louder and louder.

"I'm going to find out what he's saying," Youngsook says.

I'm pretty sure that this is an argument between Mr Park and Ijun, and it's probably about our conversation, so I'm curious about this too.

"I'm coming too!" I whisper to Youngsook.

I follow Youngsook out of the hall and into the gym. The arguing sounds like it's in the admin area next door, it sounds a lot louder in here than in the dorm. I still can't really catch more than the odd word of what's being said. I tap Youngsook on the shoulder.

"We look suspicious as fuck. Let's pretend that we're exercising or something so it doesn't look like we're listening in, but more like we just happen to be here. Just in case someone bursts through the doorway. I'm in enough trouble for one day, I don't want to risk pissing him off even more."

"Yeah good idea, we can do some warm-ups I guess."

I start practising my leg stretches and splits on the gym floor. Youngsook is still a bit too transfixed by the argument to do anything other than listen. Suddenly we hear the sound of smashing glass, the loud sound makes me involuntarily shiver. The argument then continues. Youngsook isn't scared but seems confused.

"What broke?"

"Sounds like a glass panel."

"Damn, he's angry. Who's he talking to?"

"It has to be Ijun. I know it for sure."

"Think she's okay?"

"Who knows, I didn't hear screaming or anything?"

The arguing suddenly stops. I look at Youngsook, and she looks back at me. We both listen carefully. A new noise then starts up, a deep thumping noise that repeats at regular intervals. It sounds like furniture being moved around.

"What the fuck is that?" I ask Youngsook.

Youngsook thinks about it for a few seconds, she looks as confused as me. Suddenly she bends over and puts her hand over her mouth.

"What? What is it? Are you okay?" I ask.

Is Youngsook in pain? I walk up to her closer and realise that her face has gone bright red. She has her fingers between her teeth; she's not in pain, she's trying to stop herself from laughing out loud. She tries to say something to me but can't do it because she's laughing silently too hard.

"You're laughing? Why? What is it?" I whisper.

Youngsook tries to say something again but she can't get the words out. The thumping noise gets louder, and suddenly I hear moaning. Okay, now I realise what it is I'm hearing.

"Oh no! This is gross! I don't want to listen to this!"

"I'm sorry, Hana... I don't know why I'm laughing! This isn't funny at all, it's horrible! But I can't help it!"

"Never mind, let's get the fuck out of here!" I whisper.

Youngsook nods, her eyes are now watering. We run quickly out of the gym and back to the dorms, Youngsook covering her mouth and doing her best not to scream out in laughter on the way.

111. TRAVEL

"Why do you have your seatbelt on?"

"Just because."

I'm staring out the window of the van as our group drives down the highway to Busan, where we've been asked to do an event of some sort. Mr Park is driving, the rest of us are in the back, along with Marie, our stylist and makeup artist. Marie is right at the back of the van doing Shu's makeup. Caitlin is sitting next to me, the others are all asleep; we use any downtime opportunity to sleep where possible. I watch as we overtake other vehicles on the highway. I don't know how fast we're going but it's definitely faster than the speed limit. Caitlin grabs my hand and holds it gently.

"You're worried about safety after what happened to Pearlfive, right?"

"Of course. Do you blame me?"

"No. But it's pointless to worry so much."

"Yeah I guess Mr Park is going to drive as fast as he wants. Not much we can do about it. I still feel anxious though."

"You need a distraction."

Caitlin is right, maybe I can think of something else to get my mind off the danger of travel. I remember the "girls" chat group that Youngsook invited me to. I pull out my phone and take a look at the chat history. It's just a bunch of nonsense that doesn't make any sense to me.

"What's that?" asks Caitlin.

"It's a chat group. Youngsook invited me to it."

"Can I join?"

"I'd invite you, but I don't know how."

Caitlin looks over at Youngsook, who is fast asleep.

"I don't want to wake her. Ask the others in the chat, maybe?"

That's a good idea. I start typing into the chat.

Me: hi, it's me, Hana

The chat responds instantly.

Gyeongja: HANAAAAAAAAAAAAAAAAAA

Sumire: Hi, Hana!

Ora: Hi!

Astrid: the warrior speaks

Do these girls have nothing else to do other than be on chat all day?

Me: hey can I invite someone here?

Ora: I bet I know who!

Ora: I already have her number so I've sent an invite.

Ora: I should have done it earlier, but didn't think of it. Haven't been feeling the best. Recovery, you know.

I show Caitlin my screen. She pulls out her phone and joins the chat.

Caitlin: hey
Gyeongja: HEY HEY HEY
Ora: hi babe, sorry I took so long to drag you in here
Sumire: Hi Caitlin!
Astrid: Hello!
Caitlin: so where's the party?
Gyeongja: PARTY?
Gyeongja: WHERE IS THE PARTY?
Gyeongja: CAN WE HAVE A PARTY?
Gyeongja: PARTY PARTY PARTY PARTY

Caitlin starts laughing.

"Is this Gyeongja girl insane or what?"

"She's different!"

"You went to that funeral with her. Is she like that in person too?"

"Pretty much!"

"You know, she has a point. We could use a party. Something to look forward to. There's so much work and so little downtime. We could invite these girls for a get-together, and some boys too."

"Does it have to be with boys?"

"It's a party, we should cater to all types. Just have to work out how to get away with it. I might ask Iseul about it when she wakes up, she seems to be able to arrange anything. Is she in this group?"

"Our whole group is now, except Nari."

"That's cool, Nari won't go to it anyway."

I turn my attention back to the chat.

Me: we are seriously going to organise a party

Gyeongja: PAAAAAAAAAARTYYYYY

Gyeongja: WE'RE HAVING A PARTY

Ora: Are you serious?

Gyeongja: PARTY PARTY

Gyeongja: PARTY PARTY PARTY

Ora: I'm still a bit injured, so is Sumire. Give us a few more weeks.

Caitlin: It can wait. When you get better we'll do it!

Gyeongja: PARTY PARTY PARTY PARTY

Gyeongja: YOU'RE THE BEST HANA

I have to stop using this chat. Reading Gyeongja's spam is wearing out my brain.

Me: My group will update you

I put the phone down and look out the window. I notice Caitlin also puts her phone away and starts shifting in her seat, closer to me, so our sides are touching.

"Hey, Hana... the others are asleep... and Shu's in the back with Marie, the highway noise is pretty loud, so I don't think they can hear us..."

Caitlin starts touching my hairline around my neck with her fingers. It makes me flinch a little.

"It's weird when you do that."

"I know. That's why I'm doing it. I think if I do it slowly, you might get more comfortable with it over time."

Caitlin continues to gently stroke my hair around my neck. I begin to relax a little.

"I guess that could work. I'm sorry I'm so jumpy."

"It's fine. A little at a time. Don't worry, I'll still touch you in other places, when I get a chance."

"Not a lot of chances, are there."

"I know. It sucks, hey."

Caitlin leans in further and starts kissing me along my neckline, then moves to my lips. Her kisses are passionate and firm, their force pushing me deeper into my seat.

"I'm done! Who's next? Everyone's asleep? Oh my..."

Fuck. It's Shu, being as loud and annoying as possible, of course. Caitlin giggles and keeps kissing me. I'm finding it hard to reciprocate because Shu is so annoying, the mood is now well and truly broken.

"I'm not asleep anymore," groans Youngsook. "Guess I'll go next, seeing as the two lovebirds are busy."

"Just try and be quiet, don't wake Nari up on your way through," Caitlin says while nuzzling my neck.

I suddenly hear Nari clearing her throat.

"Too late. Hey, stop that, you two!"

Caitlin sighs.

"We'll pick this up later," Caitlin whispers to me.

"When?" I reply.

"I don't know. But we will."

112. HIGH-TOUCH

"Team, it's nearly time. Remember when I give the signal, follow the two white lines on the ground. Iseul will be first, go in order, single file. The lines will take you out to the audience area, but they'll be behind a barricade. Don't walk outside of the white lines, don't stop to interact with fans or take any objects from them, you can wave and smile but that's all. Move quickly to the stage. Once you're there, bow and greet the audience as we rehearsed. Then you'll be asked the questions by the MC, and you'll be given a microphone to answer. Do you remember the three questions, and your answers?"

We all look at Mr Park and nod. I adjust my "Love Carousel" summer dress which is feeling a little lopsided for some reason.

"Yes, Mr Park CEO!" we say in unison.

"Once you've said your answers to the three questions, then remain in line, and the audience will line up for the high-touch. After the high-touch is over, you will be given the signal to leave, then follow the white lines back to here, backstage, in opposite order, Youngsook will be first. All understood?"

What the hell is a high-touch? I have no idea. I look at the others, looking for any reaction. None of them seem too concerned about whatever this is. We all nod again.

"Yes, Mr Park CEO!"

A man with a headset microphone interrupts Mr Park and says something to him that I can't hear. I assume he's the one giving the signal. They start talking to each other for a while. The conversation seems a little tense, like something unplanned might be holding things up. I might as well use this opportunity to find out what I'm in for here, seeing as how nobody has bothered to tell me exactly. We're standing in the carpeted backstage room in our usual lineup order, which means that Caitlin's standing on my right side and Nari on my left. I figure Caitlin might know what I want to ask, but Nari, being Nari, will *definitely* know. I tap her on the shoulder to get her attention.

"Hey, no-one has told me, what's a high-touch?"

"It's no big deal. We just line up on a stage, and the audience walks by and touches our hands."

"What, they just touch our hands... and that's it, then they leave?"

"Yes. One by one."

"Just our hands?"

"Just our hands. Like a high-five."

"Oh... what's the purpose of that?"

"It's so they can say that they touched their idol."

"What? That's so dumb!"

"Don't worry, it's nothing. I know it's weird but you should be flattered that people want to high-touch you. To some of these people, you're their dream girl. The one they fantasise about. It's a big deal to them that they managed to touch you, even just one time, for half a second. They'll remember that moment forever."

"That's actually completely messed up. I feel sick."

"It's just another part of the job."

"I'd like to 'touch' a few of these fans if you get my meaning."

"Okay girls, let's go!" Mr Park yells.

Iseul quickly walks between the two white lines, and we follow her in single file, through a door, into a room labelled "green room" which is actually completely red for some weird reason, then through another door into a hallway. We can hear the audience getting louder as we approach a set of open double doors.

"Wow, they're loud! They love us!" says Shu, who starts skipping along the white line path. I try to ignore this typically Shu-like display of *aegyo* cringe as we keep walking through the double doors and find ourselves in the audience section of a small concert hall. The screams and whistles from the crowd become deafeningly loud as we enter. The white path marked out for us follows a line around the edge of the seating and up some stairs to the front of the stage. We're protected from the crowd by a row of grey metal barricades that contain the audience at chest height with about three metres of clearance between them and the designated path for us to walk. There's also a row of security guards who all look attentive. I feel somewhat comforted, this venue seems to know what they're doing as far as security goes. We all smile and wave to the crowd, except Shu who also starts jumping up and down and shouting. The crowd wave back, some of them hold signs and objects but I can't really focus on any of them, there's so many. We ascend the stairs and reach our designated standing places on the stage. The MC is here, a man who looks to be in his thirties, holding a silver microphone.

"Everyone please give a warm welcome to Halcyon! Please make them feel at home!"

The crowd roars. We all bow and wave.

"We are Halcyon! *Annyeong-haseyo-Halcyon-imnida!*"

We don't have microphones so we shout as loud as possible. I'm certain that we can't be heard over the fans cheering. The MC walks over to Iseul's side and smiles.

"Thank you Halcyon for that introduction! I'll point the microphone at each of you in turn, so you can say your names for the audience, one by one!"

The MC points the microphone at Iseul.

"Hi, I'm Iseul! Nice to meet you!"

Iseul bows and waves to the audience, they cheer politely. The MC moves on to Shu's position.

"Hi I'm Shu! It's great to be here! Yay for Busan!"

Shu starts jumping up and down on the spot and waving both hands around high in the air, like she's trying to wave to every single audience member at the same time.

The crowd love this, she gets lots of cheers. The MC looks a bit taken aback by Shu's extreme reaction. He tries to point the microphone at her face to encourage her to stop jumping around so much and say something more but it doesn't work, Shu's bouncing around so much that it's impossible for him to even focus it on her mouth. He gives up and moves onto Nari.

"Hi, I'm Nari, the leader! We are honoured to be here today in Busan to perform for you!"

Nari bows and the crowd cheers politely. The MC points the microphone at my mouth. What do I say? I'll just keep it simple I guess.

"Hi, it's me, Hana! It's great to be here!"

That's all I can think up. I bow a little and the crowd cheers politely. I hear a stray "I love you, Hana!" in the crowd somewhere, it's a female voice. I smile a little. It's good to know that I have female fans. The MC moves onto Caitlin.

"Hi everyone, I'm Caitlin! I've never been to Busan, nice place you have here! Can I move in?"

Lots of cheers and a little laughter, the crowd like her. I notice the MC quickly looking Caitlin up and down, as he then moves onto Youngsook.

"Hi, I'm Youngsook! It's great to be in Busaaaaaaan!"

Youngsook sings the last syllable of the word "Busan" right at the top of her vocal range. The crowd love this gesture. The MC walks over to Youngsook's side so he's not obstructing the view of any of us.

"I'm Jake Cho, your MC for the concert this evening! Thank you Halcyon!"

Jake pauses to let the crowd cheer some more. Next is the completely scripted part of the interview.

"Halcyon ladies, can you tell us a little bit about what you have in store for us tonight?"

Jake hands the microphone straight to Nari.

"We're really excited to be here, so we're going to perform our very best for you! It's our first time as a group performing in Busan! We promise to bring you our very best performance of all our songs! You'll cheer for us, won't you?"

Nari puts her left hand up to her ear, while pointing the microphone to the audience with her right hand. They cheer wildly. Nari smiles and gives the microphone back to Jake so he can ask the next question.

"Halcyon ladies, do you have any special messages for the fans who have come to see you tonight?"

Jake hands the microphone to Shu, who reaches for it expectantly.

"We are so happy to see you! We have been getting all your letters and messages and receiving all your love! We are very excited, and we plan to return that love tonight, to all of you! Please expect us fondly and keep us in your hearts!"

Shu smiles and passes the microphone back to Jake.

"So ladies, I've heard a rumour, that you've been working hard to please the male fans, and to make this performance extra sensual tonight, is this true?"

Jake passes the microphone to Caitlin.

"No comment!" says Caitlin, giving Jake a smile and a not-very-subtle wink. A bunch of men in the crowd start hollering. Caitlin passes the microphone back.

"I've heard Halcyon girls are renowned for their sexiness, can you verify this?"

This isn't in the script, it was supposed to end here. Where is this going? The crowd starts hollering again. Caitlin doesn't seem bothered, she takes the microphone off Jake before he can even hand it over.

"We've heard these rumours too. We don't know who is spreading these *scandalous rumours* about us, but our lovely fans will all find out the truth tonight, we promise you this!"

Caitlin smiles and holds out the microphone for Jake. The crowd goes nuts with cheering and whistling.

"Since this is the case, can you girls do some sexy poses for us? As a preview of tonight, perhaps?"

We all look at each other in somewhat of a panic. I have no idea what to do. Caitlin senses it immediately, she grabs me and starts rubbing her leg up against mine like she's doing a sexy dance of some sort. It's pretty awkward but Caitlin is doing the move in a deliberately exaggerated manner which also makes it kind of funny, I can't help but laugh and go with the flow. The other girls pair off and start doing the same, taking their cue from Caitlin, with Nari rubbing up against Youngsook and Shu rubbing up against Iseul in the same way. It's ridiculous and embarrassing but it works, it gets lots of hollers and also laughter from the crowd, they seem to sense how stupid this is and that we're not entirely comfortable with it.

"That's great ladies, everyone please give them a round of applause for being such good sports!"

The crowd claps politely.

"Now we're going to start the high-touch portion of the afternoon. Everyone please form up at thc side of the stage, security will usher you up the stairs. Halcyon girls, please step back behind the line here, and the audience will greet you, one at a time!"

Jake points to a yellow painted line on the stage and we all stand behind it. The security start organising the front rows of fans into a funnel so they can be sent up to the stage in an orderly manner. After a couple minutes the fans walk up beside us in single file. I watch Iseul receive the first fan so I know what to do. Iseul holds out her hand at shoulder height and touches the palm of the first fan, a young guy. She makes eye contact, smiles, says *"annyeong!"* and bows to him. Then the fan walks to Shu who does exactly the same thing. Okay, I guess that's all I have to do, I guess it's not so bad. I hold my hand out and wait for the fan to come to me. When he arrives he bows and says his greeting, and I do my best impersonation of what Iseul did. As soon as the fan leaves, another one appears behind him and I repeat the process a few seconds later. Then the next one, and the next one.

"Hana, wish me luck in Virtuous Assault playoffs!"

I'm interrupted by a voice that is a bit more abrupt than the rest. It's Jihu, the gamer, who I invited to our dorm to play with Ijun a couple months back. What the hell is he doing in Busan?

"Annyeong... sorry, what playoffs?" I ask.

"My e-sport team is competing in the national pro league later this year!"

"Okay! Good luck, Jihu! Kick some ass!" I say as I wave.

Jihu waves back as he disappears from view before I can ask him why he's here. I quickly turn my attention to the next fan in the line. How many people are crammed into this theatre, at least a couple hundred, maybe more. A few more fans go by. By seeing them individually like this, I can get a feel for the age and gender of our fans. I think our fans here are about three quarters male, to one quarter female, that's not a very good ratio. I wonder what we can do to increase our female fans. The fans are mainly late teens and early twenties, there's a few older fans too but not many. I notice some fans are happier to see me than others, for the majority of these fans I'm probably just in their way of seeing one of the more popular girls. More fans go by, we're getting through the crowd quickly, quicker than I expected. I only have to spend a couple seconds with each fan, we'll be done in a few minutes. I notice that as each fan completes the high-touch, they are escorted out along a pathway, to somewhere outside the hall, another room in the building perhaps. I try to determine a pattern in the fans that specifically like me, hoping maybe I have more females who like me, but I can't really tell if the ratio is any different. Suddenly I feel something on my back.

"Hey, careful!"

It's Caitlin's voice, it's her hands on my back. I guess I lost my balance and fell backwards, she just caught me before I fell completely over. I notice that I'm feeling a little dizzy and my vision is a bit spotty. Caitlin keeps a hand around my waist as we continue to high-touch fans. Eventually they're all gone.

"Hana's starting to check out here," Caitlin says.

Someone else says something I don't quite hear. I walk off the stage, with Caitlin's arms still around my waist. I realise that I feel not just dizzy but weak. Something's up to my lips, it's a bottle with a drink in it of some sort. I grab it and drink it while I'm walking, it's cold and tastes sugary, like berries. I'm not conscious of where I'm going. I feel like I'm drifting, so I'm just going to go with whatever happens. I feel something soft by my head. I look around and realise that I've been taken to the "green room" where Caitlin has laid me down sideways onto one of the couches. That's nice of her. It's comfortable here, and very red.

"How are you feeling?" Caitlin asks.

"Hi, Caitlin... I'm good now, I think. You feel good."

"I'm not Caitlin. You sure you're okay?"

I realise I'm actually talking to Nari.

"Oh. Where's Caitlin?"

"She's with the others."

"The drink was nice."

"Electrolytes. I'll get you another soon. You should still be okay for the show in a few hours if you have more to drink and get some rest now."

"Hey, thanks."

"We look after each other. It's okay."

Now that I'm lying on the couch, I feel a little bit better already.

"Hey, Nari..."

"What?"

"Can I get a towel or a wet wipe or something?"

"What for?"

"I just had to touch all those gross people's hands."

"Just get some rest, Hana."

113. BASEMENT

"Hanahanahanahanahana...."

Oh no. It's Shu, waking me up. Someone kill me.

"Screw off! Can't I sleep?"

"We're nearly home, Hana! We have to get out soon!"

I groan, open my eyes, rub the sleep out of them and look around. I'm sitting in the rear of our van, the girls are all here. Caitlin is sitting in the seat next to mine, also waking up, and Shu is leaning forward over both of us, the others are all organising their bags and getting ready to exit the vehicle. I notice Marie our stylist isn't with us, she must have been dropped off earlier. I look out of the window, it's night. I recognise the street we're on, as we go by the bus stop a couple blocks down from the agency building. As we drive up to the front entrance, Shu points at some people in front of the main doors, just standing around.

"Who are they?" Shu asks.

We all look but nobody responds. I expect the van to slow down to a stop at the front entrance, but instead we keep going.

"Why aren't we getting out?" Shu asks while looking around at all of us. She's so irritating, I just want to slap this fucking midget but I know I can't because everyone will get upset and punish me.

"Because the van's still moving you stupimmfhfhh..."

Suddenly Nari reaches over and shoves her wrist sideways into my mouth so I can't speak.

"Don't say something you'll regret!"

I sigh and stop trying to talk. Nari takes her arm out of my mouth and smiles.

"That was close, Hana! Wouldn't want to have to reprimand you for being mean, now, would we?"

I decide to not push my luck any further, and look again out of the window. Our van is circling around the building, it comes to a stop by a garage entrance at the rear. A grey metal door slides open and the van rolls forward, coming to a stop inside a large parking bay. The van door slides open and we all slowly get out, stretching our limbs to get rid of the stiffness from the road.

"Oh wow, look at these fancy cars! Look at the cute red one!" Shu squeals.

Shu wanders around the parking bay, inspecting the cars from different angles while we wait for Mr Park to emerge from the driver's seat of our van. He seems to be taking his time so I wander around looking at the vehicles to kill time, and so do the other girls. The parking bay has a black sedan with tinted windows that looks very luxurious, a white sedan that looks identical to the black one in every detail, a large silver motorbike and a tiny red sports car. All these vehicles are completely shiny and spotless, they all look like they've barely been driven. I've never seen any of these cars before, but I guess they must belong to Mr Park. There's also another black passenger van here just like the one we've been riding in, except it's damaged. There are some scratch marks on the side, and a bunch of tools on the ground next to it, I guess this vehicle is being worked on. I stand next to the van and look at my reflection in the side door, which is distorted from where it's been dented on the side by something.

"Pay attention girls, let's go!"

Mr Park yells and beckons for us to follow him. I didn't notice he had exited the vehicle we were in. I let the other girls go first, and follow after everyone else, directly behind Caitlin. We walk through a door and down a concrete corridor, that I recognise from when Mr Park was sick and Ijun gave us temporary access to this area under the ground floor. I start thinking about what me and Caitlin did together the last time we were down here. I wish we could meet again down here but we can't do anything about that right now.

"Oh my god..." I hear Caitlin giggle. She falls back in the queue so I catch up to her, and points to the bottom of a doorway as we pass it. I notice there's a light coming through a crack in the bottom of the door.

"What is it?" I ask.

"He's totally growing weed in that room!"

"How do you know?"

"That's a grow light! Also, can't you smell it?"

Now that Caitlin mentions it, the marijuana smell is definitely pretty heavy down here, much more than I'm used to. I didn't notice it much before, as Caitlin smokes quite often so I've gotten used to a light marijuana scent lingering near her.

"Yeah, I can... wow, that reeks!"

"There must be heaps in there!"

Caitlin reaches out and twists the door handle, it turns a little. She smiles at me and I give her an impatient stare. I really don't want to go in that room.

"Hey, can we keep moving?" I ask Caitlin.

"It's not locked! We could take a look!"

"I don't want to get in trouble. I nearly got kicked out of the group the other day, I'm probably on really thin ice right now. Please."

"I guess you're right. I'll check it later."

I'm not as fascinated by this as Caitlin obviously is. Fortunately she's given up on the idea of going in there. We quicken our walking pace to catch up to the others, following them out of the corridor and up the stairs to the office area. Mr Park retreats into his office without a word and we file through the hallway into our dorms, I guess he's exhausted too. As soon as we get into the dorm room we all sigh with relief and collapse onto our bunk beds.

"I'm exhausted! I will sleep now!" says Shu.

"I can't believe we have to go for another drive tomorrow," says Iseul.

"Hey at least we don't have to train when we're on the road," replies Youngsook.

We all lie in silence for about a minute. I think about looking at my phone but I decide not to worry about it, I'm too tired to be staring at screens, I just want to sleep. I kick off my shoes and get under the covers, without bothering to take any of my clothes off. As I try to drift off to sleep, I hear Nari and Iseul talking.

"Those are some nice cars out there."

"He's rich, of course he has nice cars."

"Where does he get the money from?"

"Us, I guess, maybe. Plus his other businesses. You know, those totally legit ones he has."

"I wonder if we'll ever actually earn some money for ourselves."

"How should I know. I'm too tired to think about that right now."

"Doesn't it bother you though? That we might not ever get paid? I'm going to ask to see our financials."

"Good luck with that."

"There'd better be some payment at some point soon. I don't want to be doing all this leading of you people for no damn reason."

"Hey Nari, can I ask a question?" says Caitlin.

"Sure, what is it?"

"Since you're the leader, do you want to lead us all into the Land of Nod by shutting the fuck up so we can get some sleep?"

I start laughing and so does both Youngsook and Caitlin. I then hear a soft pillow noise which is no doubt Nari throwing a pillow at Caitlin's head.

"I'm looking out for all of you idiots, you know!"

"Yeah and we appreciate it... but now isn't the time? Let's talk again about this later."

"Fine."

Nari doesn't say anything else. I start thinking about money. I guess money has never mattered to me as I've always had none, plus no freedom to spend any even if I did have some. Even though I've never owned anything much, I've always had my basic needs looked after, that's been equally the case at home and here. I guess that might change one day, so I should think about how to prepare for that if it does happen. If I do end up getting kicked out of here, I don't want to have to live with my mother again, that would be intolerable, I'd rather be a financially independent person. However I have no idea how to even go about that, or what I would need to do. I barely even have any skills as an entertainer let alone in the real world outside of this place. Would I just live on the street? How would I even do that? I'm so unskilled that I wouldn't even know how to be homeless properly, I'd have to ask another homeless person. How do other people handle these questions? Why is my life so weird and pathetic? These thoughts turn over in my mind as I gradually drift off to sleep.

114. HANCEL

"Here we go, five... six... seven... eight..."

"Why do you start the count at five?"

"Starting at five is how dancers do it. You know this. Come on, Shu, pick it up and stick with me. On the count of eight, please."

I get ready to start the pre-chorus part of the "Love Carousel" dance again, this is the part that Nari wants me to get Shu up to speed with. I watch Shu steady herself on the gym floor. Behind me, Nari watches us both silently, to make sure I'm teaching Shu correctly and not giving her a hard time. The other three girls are working on routines at the other end of the gym.

"Five... six... seven... eight..."

Shu suddenly starts the dance a beat early. Why?

"Stop, Shu!"

"What was wrong with that?"

"You were too early. You were supposed to start on the count of eight."

"That was on the eight?"

I sigh.

"Yes you were on the eight, but when I say 'on the count of eight' the routine actually starts after the eight. You have to let the eight run its course before you start."

"Then you should say 'after the count of eight' so it's less confusing."

"Everyone knows what 'on the eight' means."

"But I did it on the eight!"

"Okay, whatever, just do it after the eight, please. Let's go again. Five... six... seven... eight..."

I pick up the dance but then stop. Shu is just standing there.

"Why didn't you start, Shu?"

"I was waiting for the eight to run its course."

"You only need to wait for one beat."

"How do I know the course isn't bigger than that?"

"Every beat is just one beat long. They are all equal."

"Then how come they have different numbers?"

"Because they have to go in order."

"But why does the order matter if they are all equal?"

"Oh my god Shu I swear that I'm going to break your stupid face open in a fucking second!"

"Hana, shut up!" Nari yells.

"Shu is pissing me off! She's doing it on purpose!"

The door to the admin area opens and Mr Park walks into the gym. Following him is another man, who I've never seen before. Both Mr Park and the other person are dressed in sharp-looking black suits. It's unusual for Mr Park to be dressed formally, so I guess he must be trying to impress the visitor.

"Shu and Hana, just the two girls I wanted to see. Please allow me to introduce you to Mr Wu Yichen, External Talent Liaison Manager for Hancel."

Yichen is tall and skinny, with black hair in a short bowl cut and a gaunt, ugly looking face. He seems quite young, for an important person, he couldn't be older than twenty-five. I guess this person is the one saving my career, I'd be back at my mother's place if it wasn't for him. I'd better be respectful. I bow at ninety degrees.

"Annyeong hasimnikka!"

Yichen bows back and smiles at me, looking me up and down silently. I know that look. I'm glad I'm wearing my gym tracksuit today and not anything that shows skin. I feel any slight respect or gratitude I had for him quickly evaporating. Shu also bows to Yichen at ninety degrees, and says something long and complicated in Mandarin. What the fuck was that Chinese word salad? It must have worked, Yichen is smiling and nodding, they're now talking to each other in Mandarin, having a full conversation. Yichen is now completely ignoring me, that's great. I'm not sure if this is a good thing or a bad thing as far as my employment goes, but it's good from the point of view of me not having to deal with this Chinese asshole. Shu definitely has the upper hand here as far as forming a good relationship with Yichen, and that's fine, I don't mind, it's not like I want to deal with him and if she can take the heat off me I won't complain. He hasn't even said anything in Korean yet, perhaps he doesn't even speak it, which makes me wonder what he's even doing here or why I have to meet him. Wow, they sure seem to be getting along, Shu seems really in her element talking to this guy. I look over at Mr Park, he's beckoning to Shu to come forward over to the admin area. Mr Park says something more basic in Mandarin to Yichen. Shu, Yichen and Mr Park then all walk over to the admin area door. Am I supposed to come with them? I try to make eye contact with one of them but nobody is looking in my direction. I look over at Nari instead, who fortunately is paying attention and seems to sense my confusion.

"Wait there, Hana!" Nari says to me quietly while putting her hand up, motioning for me to stay put.

Nari then runs up to Mr Park to get his attention before he vanishes through the admin door. Mr Park looks at Nari, who then points to me. Mr Park makes a "no thank you" type of face and then disappears through the doorway, with Yichen and Shu following right behind him. I breathe a sigh of relief as they vanish. The rest of the group have all stopped practising and look at me.

"Well, that was strange, who was that?" asks Caitlin.

"That guy is Yichen, he's from Hancel. They want me and Shu for... something. I don't know what yet. I guess we're advertising their phones or something."

"Why just you two?"

"Who knows. But he's apparently the reason I'm not kicked out of the group."

"Not yet," says Iseul.

I glare at her.

"You might get kicked as soon as the advert is over. As soon as Mr Park has his money."

I don't like Iseul being so blunt about it, but I know she's right, there's no guarantee that Mr Park will want me after this deal is done. Hopefully I do this thing for Hancel and get popular enough to be worth keeping around for more work, but who knows if that will happen. I can't even guess at how good or bad I'll be because I don't even know what I'm supposed to do for them yet. Hopefully the fact they chose me means they've chosen me for something that I'm good at. What would be the point otherwise? I guess I'll find out what I'm supposed to be doing for them soon enough.

115. STREAMING

"Hana, come here. Sit down in the chair and face the computer, it's ready for you now."

It's late at night and I'm sitting in the dining room, with Ijun. She's on the opposite side of the table and has just finished setting up her laptop, which is what I'm going to be using for a livestream. I've never done anything like this before, but she's going to help me with it I guess. I focus on the screen, most of the space is taken up with a display of the laptop camera, which is pointed at me. Beside the camera feed is a small chat area, where people are typing stuff. It's hard to read as it's moving by so quickly, but it's mainly just a stream of random emojis.

"Hana, pull the screen towards you a little, so the camera captures all of your face and upper body better. Nobody wants to see the space above your head."

I move the top of the laptop screen as Ijun instructs. My face is now more central on the screen, but the different angle also makes the text harder to read.

"Can I make the words bigger?"

"Hold down the control key and press the plus key a bunch of times."

I do what Ijun says and the font becomes bigger, taking up more of the screen, while my image becomes a little smaller. Fine with me.

"Okay, that's better, thanks. What do I do?"

"Just say hello, talk to them."

"But I don't have anything to say to these clowns?"

"Just follow the rules, and remember that I'll be watching the chat too, on my phone, and moderating it. I'll sit behind the screen so they can't see me. Anything that you shouldn't be answering, I'll just wave to you or look at you. So watch for my signals, but try not to make it too obvious that you're looking at me, okay?"

"Okay, sure."

"Try to keep the vibe light and fun. Go for the easy questions, avoid anything weird or controversial because you probably won't be allowed to answer it anyway so don't try. When you're ready, unmute yourself."

I look at myself in the camera feed and straighten my pyjama collar up. I'm in my pyjamas because it's late and it means I can slip straight into bed once this is over with. Also my pyjamas are thick flannelette and not revealing at all so I figure they're not likely to excite any weirdos who may be watching. I press the unmute button and take a deep breath, then smile at the camera.

"Annyeong haseyo yeoreobun, je ireumeun Hana-imnida!"

Instantly the chat speeds up, rocketing along with emojis and greetings that I have no time to read before they scroll off the top of the page. How am I supposed to read anything at this speed? I look at Ijun. She looks back at me with an annoyed expression. I shrug at her; I can't talk to her obviously, but I just try to convey with my facial expression *what the fuck am I supposed to even do if I can't even read this?* She seems to sense what I want and reaches her hand around to the touchpad. She moves the pointer over the chat, which freezes the chat window in place, so I can read it. I ignore the emojis and just focus on the text.

Hana!!!!!!!!!!!!!!!

My bias

About time, why is this stream so late

Does she know what she's doing

Hi Hana, please notice me!

Hot pyjamas, this will be a satisfying stream

Hi Hana!

I read her lips earlier, I think she called us clowns

How are you, Hana?

There's only one question so far, so I'll go with that.

"I'm good! Hey I'm new to all this I haven't done this before, it's my first livestream! So I might be a bit confused. Wow, you guys type a lot, so sorry if I miss anything. I'll do my best, okay?"

I move the pointer away from the chat window so it can load more messages. The chat window is instantly flooded with more text and emojis.

Hana!

We love you Hana!

What did you eat today?

What are you wearing under your pyjamas? Describe it, as much detail as possible please

When is the next Halcyon song, Hana?

I look over at Ijun, she's using her phone, doing something. I look back at the chat and notice that the "pyjamas" question isn't in the chat anymore, I think Ijun just deleted it. I think about what question to answer. I don't know when the next Halcyon song is so I'll go with food I guess.

"What did I eat today? Well, I had..."

Ijun suddenly glares at me. I don't think she wants me to answer this honestly.

"...I had food! It was nice. Yes. Yummy food."

Ijun seems to calm down a bit, she resumes watching the chat.

Notice me, Hana!

Wow, she's nervous

Blink twice if your CEO is pointing a gun at your head

We're worried about you, you girls faint on stage a lot

#freeHana

When's the next song, Hana

I look at Ijun for a reaction but there isn't one, so I guess I'm okay to answer this song question.

"I don't know when we have another song. I'm sure that we will have one at some point. They don't tell us stuff too far in advance."

I hear the door to the dining room from the admin area open, and look over to my side, it's Mr Park. He ignores me and looks at Ijun.

"Come here."

Ijun glares at Mr Park and waves her arms silently. I think she's trying to convey to Mr Park that she's busy and he needs to keep his voice down. I don't really care about these two having another fight so I look back at the chat.

Hi Hana!
The shorter hair looks cute, keep it that way
Where are the other girls
Are you lesbian
We love you Hana!
I think the staff are talking, Hana tell them to shut up
What's your favourite colour

"The other girls are sleeping. My favourite colour, I don't know, I haven't really thought about it."

I look over at Mr Park again, he's gesturing to Ijun to come over to him. Ijun rolls her eyes, sighs and gets up out of her chair.

"Be good," Ijun whispers, pointing to me, before walking briskly out of the room with Mr Park. Now that she's gone I guess I can relax a little.

"Maybe it's red. Red like the blood of people who annoy me. I'd like to see more of that colour soon."

Hey Hana sing us something
Hi Hana!
Hana has no media training I swear
Hana who is your favourite in the group

Hana lesbian queen
Where can I get pyjamas like that
Hana what do you think about the death penalty
Look at Hana's cute short hair

Ijun isn't around so I might as well have a little fun with the chat.

"I like Caitlin."

The chat instantly responds.

Caitlin I knew it
Caitlin <3
Hanalin ship is leaving port
Can we have Caitlin on the stream too please I don't care if she's asleep wake her up
I think death penalty is okay for murderers don't you
We all like Caitlin too
What do you think about the Middle East
Hana lesbian confirmed
Imagine what sort of nightclothes Caitlin would wear

"Murderers, I think it depends. For killing men, you should just get a warning. For killing women there needs to be a more serious punishment than death. Maybe they should keep you alive and just torture you every day. Where's the Middle East, is that like Daegu? I haven't been to Daegu yet, but Nari is from Daegu. Do you like Nari?"

Hahahahaha
Hana you're the best I love you
Have you noticed how shredded Nari is
Daegu LOLOLOL

Not the middle east of Korea you idiot omg

Hi Hana!

You said you like guns, what do you think about gun control?

Who cares about Nari, where's Caitlin at

Killing men is a minor crime, truth

These questions are disrupting my rhythm

Hana didn't pay attention in geography class

"Nari is very fit, she works out a lot. I mean we're in the gym all the time anyway, but she really loves it for some reason. Yes I think gun control is important, but I'm really bad at it. My shots just go everywhere. I hope to improve but I don't really get a chance to practise."

I hear the door open, Ijun comes back into the room quickly and resumes her place in the chair opposite mine. She looks unhappy about something. She takes her phone out and stares at it. I guess I'd better tone it down a bit now that she's back in the room. I look back at the chat.

Hana your hair is so pretty

No shit this girl is cute but she's such a dumbass

Hana please notice me

Just keep talking, Hana, I'm nearly there

Some guy at my school is being an asshole what should I do Hana help me

"Hey don't call me dumb. It's not my fault I don't know random facts and stuff. I'll deal with you. You know, I don't like my hair. I want to grow it out again but I have to keep it shorter for now, CEO says so. The guy at school, send me his details. I will talk to him. I promise he will be nicer to you after."

I look at Ijun, she looks back at me with a withered expression. I'm not sure if she's reacting to what I just said, or if she's just read through the chat history, or something else is annoying her.

"...because I'm so charming, you know? Hey chat, I have to be good, don't ask me anything too weird, okay? I can't answer weird stuff, I'll get in trouble! Just ask nice things!"

Hana is legit crazy

Hana you ARE weird stuff

She has no filter, that's why we like her

Hana will shares in global freight companies rise or fall this quarter?

Hi Hana!

Fuck, I just messed up my screen, was worth

When are you going to come out

Pick my lottery winning numbers pls

This is the best livestream ever

I look back over at Ijun, she has one hand on her phone and the other hand scratching her head. She looks a bit stressed out, I guess that might be my fault, but hey this nonsense wasn't my stupid idea. I'm really not enjoying being put under pressure like this. Hopefully I won't get asked to do this crap ever again.

116. RIDER

"Oh my god, I was dying up there!"

Youngsook dives face first onto one of the many couches which are arranged in a loose circle around the otherwise bare concrete room. We've just gotten off the stage from another performance, this time at an army base.

"What a show. The audience went crazy!" says Nari.

"I can't wait to get these fake eyelashes off!" says Iseul.

Nari and Iseul both sit down on a couch together. I'm exhausted, I find an empty couch and collapse into it. Lying on my side across its length, I watch as Mr Park enters the room after us, followed by some soldiers.

"Girls, don't get too comfortable. We'll be leaving soon, make sure you have everything together to get back on the van, don't leave anything behind."

"Yes, Mr Park CEO," says Caitlin as she joins me on the couch, sitting next to my head. I lift my head up and she slides her legs under it so I can use her thighs as a pillow.

"Miss, where would you like me to put these?"

A soldier appears in front of us. He's tall, muscular, and carrying a couple of thin cardboard boxes. Caitlin reaches up and opens the lid of the top box, and then quickly closes it again.

"Are these for us? Wow, thank you!"

"Courtesy of the staff, our pleasure, miss. To say thank you for your performance tonight!"

The soldier smiles at Caitlin. Caitlin points to a table in the middle of the room that I've only just noticed.

"Just on the table over there, please."

"Yes, miss!"

The soldier puts the boxes on the table.

"What are those?" I ask Caitlin.

"Pizzas."

"For real? They're giving us pizzas?"

"Pizzas?" says Youngsook.

I become conscious of a strong food smell. It brings back memories, I haven't had pizza since I was a child and my father bought some for the family, a very rare occasion that stopped when he disappeared from my life at age eight. I'm suddenly sad and desperately hungry.

"Take those away please, the girls are on a strict diet, there was nothing about this on the rider. They can't have so much carbohydrates," orders Mr Park.

"Yes, sir!" says the soldier, picking up the boxes again and leaving the room.

"Oh for fuck's sake," says Caitlin under her breath.

I internally sigh. I lower my excitement levels again and stare into space. I notice that a lady in military uniform has appeared and is talking to Mr Park about something, I can't quite hear what's being said.

"Nari, come here," says Mr Park.

I watch Nari get up and walk to Mr Park. They start talking, Mr Park looks like he's introducing Nari to the military lady, they bow to each other. Then all three of them leave the room, back in the direction of the stage.

"What's happening?" I ask.

"I think Nari and Mr Park are going on a tour of the base!" says Shu.

"Hey, where did that soldier with our pizzas go?" asks Youngsook.

"Move your head, Hana," says Caitlin.

I lift my head up so Caitlin can stand up. She walks over to the door where the soldier with the pizza went into, and opens it. The door is ajar enough for me to see what's beyond it, it's an underground car parking space.

"Hey, he's right there, at the vehicle barricade. Wait here everyone, I'm going to get our pizzas back."

Caitlin vanishes into the exit and closes the door behind her. We all look at each other.

"Think she can do it?" asks Iseul.

"It's Caitlin," replies Youngsook. "She'll find a way."

A few minutes go by, or maybe more than a few minutes. I lie still and try to doze off to sleep but I can't, I'm too conscious of my stomach rumbling.

"She's taking her time," says Iseul.

"Maybe *he's* taking *his* time!" replies Youngsook.

Iseul and Youngsook both start laughing, when the door slowly opens. It's Caitlin, carrying the pizza boxes.

"Oh my god!" says Shu.

"Good work!" says Iseul.

"Thank you!" replies Cailtin, putting the boxes on the table and opening them up. "Oh my god, it's *bulgogi* and cheese. What a topping! This is going to be amazing!"

All of us instantly get up from the couches, run over to the table and start grabbing pizza slices. I find a slice and devour it as quickly as possible, the fatty meat and cheese tastes heavenly and instantly makes me feel better. Ten seconds later it's gone already and I grab another slice. I can't stop eating. Mr Park could return at any moment, I have to make sure I eat as quickly as possible. Looking around the room I can tell that the others are thinking the same; we could get this food taken away from us again at any time. We have to make the most of this.

"Damn, this is some good pizza," says Caitlin.

"Why is it so cheesy?" asks Shu, as she awkwardly tries to swallow a mouthful of melted cheese.

"That's what pizza is. Don't they have pizza in China?"

"They do, but it's not so cheesy like this. This is like a lake of cheese!"

"Be honest, Caitlin. Did you suck his dick for this?" asks Youngsook.

Iseul spits pizza out of her mouth in laughter.

"No! You're filthy! I would never!" replies Caitlin.

"Bullshit you wouldn't! You were taking your sweet time out there, you totally sucked his dick for sure!" says Youngsook, giggling.

"I did not!"

"I don't believe you! Hey don't get me wrong, I'm grateful that you're such a dirty slut."

"I didn't do shit! Screw off, you're just jealous."

"Maybe I am, but that doesn't mean you didn't do it."

"I didn't do anything like that. I was just nice to him, that's all."

"And that's it?"

Caitlin pauses slightly and smiles.

"More or less!"

Youngsook bursts out laughing.

"I can tell you're lying! You're so full of shit, Caitlin! You at least gave him a handjob. Or something, I don't know what, but it definitely wasn't just a case of 'Oh hi there mister, can I please have those pizzas?' 'Why yes Caitlin, here they are, please enjoy!' 'Oh my gosh, why thank you kind sir!' 'You're welcome young lady, fare well on your travels!' You definitely did something out there."

Iseul and Youngsook both start laughing. Caitlin is trying not to laugh as well but she can't keep a straight face.

"Fuck off, idiots! You two are clowns!"

"I'm amazed you've got room for any pizza left after all the cum you've just been swallowing."

"Oh my god, just be happy I got the pizzas for us! Do you want me to give them back?"

"No! I want you to become his sex slave so I can eat pizza every day."

I pick up two more pizza slices and take them back to the couch. I'm enjoying eating far too much to even give a shit about this dumb conversation. As soon as I sit down one of the doors to the room opens and Nari walks in. I become tense for a moment but relax again quickly as I realise she's alone, Mr Park isn't with her. Nari stares at us all with her mouth open.

"What the hell? We got pizza after all?"

"Not officially, but we do. Have some!" says Iseul.

"It's extra cheesy!" says Shu, holding up a pizza slice and catching the strands of cheese on her tongue.

"You can thank Caitlin," adds Youngsook.

Caitlin smiles at Nari, who looks back at Caitlin with a suspicious expression. Neither of them say anything to each other.

"What happened to Mr Park?" I ask Nari in between mouthfuls.

"Oh he and that woman he was with told me to leave and come back here, I'm not sure why."

"Are you going to have pizza?"

Nari looks at the pizza in silence for a while. She's obviously hungry and exhausted just like we are, we've all been completely overworked ever since the start of promotions for our new song. However I also know how intense Nari is about her own dieting and exercise. She never misses gym, often does extra workouts late at night when we're all in the dorms, and as far as I know she sticks to the agency diet. She stands there, looking at the pizza and thinking about it, probably weighing up how many slices it would take to ruin her career and her physique.

"Go on, have some!" says Shu.

"If you knew how much cock Caitlin had to suck to get us these pizzas, you would have some right now just to honour her sacrifice," says Iseul.

Youngsook starts laughing.

"I don't know about sacrifice, he was hot!"

"Oh my god, *shut up* you two!" says Caitlin.

Youngsook and Iseul both continue laughing their heads off, they think this is hilarious for some reason.

"Okay, fuck it..."

Nari walks over to the table, picks up a slice of pizza and starts eating it. We all immediately cheer and applaud.

"About time!" says Youngsook.

"Just one slice. I'll burn it off back at the dorms."

"Don't be afraid to live a little, Nari!"

Nari then turns to all of us.

"Hey, grab the slices you want and Caitlin give the empty pizza boxes back to that guy quickly. Also make sure your hands aren't greasy and your mouths are clean, no stray food. I don't think Mr Park is coming back soon, but if he does and he knows we ate them, he's probably going to get angry."

This is a cunning streak I didn't know Nari had.

"Wow, you're worse than Youngsook!" I say to Nari.

"We still haven't been paid yet. Fuck him."

117. JOIN HANDS FOR PEACE

"*Annyeong haseyo,* Mr Park CEO!"

We all bow in unison before Mr Park. He's suddenly turned up in our gym, only a few minutes before dinner. I'm starving so I hope whatever he wants to tell us doesn't take too long. Ijun is standing next to him, playing with her phone, and looking bored out of her mind as usual. Mr Park on the other hand looks pleased, I assume this is going to be good news.

"I have a special announcement to make. I am pleased to report that Halcyon's international profile has been increasing. As a result Halcyon has been invited to perform at the prestigious JHFP festival in the United States. Naturally, we have accepted this opportunity for the group, to grow our audience internationally."

The whole group cheers, except Iseul who doesn't seem too impressed for some reason and just raises her eyebrows a bit. I'm not that impressed either actually, I don't know what this festival is or what it means for us. Mr Park clears his throat and continues.

"Of course, an increased international profile means increased global scrutiny of the group's activities. You will all need to be on your best behaviour in all settings, as our worldwide audience increases. Be aware that every speech, every movement you make, is measured and monitored, and act accordingly."

While Mr Park says this, he casts his eyes up and down over me for a moment. I know that he's doing that on purpose, to drive it into me that I have to behave. I shiver a little as he continues.

"Caitlin, please step forward."

Caitlin takes a step forward from our lineup.

"Since you are from America, and have the most fluent command of the English language in the group, while the group is in the United States for promotions, you will be the leader. Note that this time is only very short as we will only be in America for a few days, yet it is nevertheless critically important. You will be taking the lead and guiding the group through our American promotions."

Caitlin bows. "Thank you, Mr Park CEO!"

Mr Park motions for Caitlin to step back in line, Caitlin steps backward.

"The trip will require preparation as we will need to secure travel documents for all of you. You will all be advised when the time comes on what you need to do. In the meantime please do your best to preserve Halcyon's reputation on the international stage, and not squander the hard work that our team have undertaken to secure this opportunity."

Ijun gives Mr Park a dirty sideways glance, like he just insulted her. I wonder what that's about, as nothing he said seemed all that bad. Ijun then returns her gaze to her phone as Mr Park continues.

"I won't keep you any longer, as I know it is meal time. You are dismissed from gym for the day, please make yourselves available in the kitchen."

We all bow to Mr Park, who disappears into the admin area with Ijun trailing behind him. We file out through the hallway and into the kitchen. There are bowls of food on the table already waiting for us. I sit down and take a look at the contents of my bowl; half a boiled egg and a single lettuce leaf.

"Where's the meat?" says Shu.

"This is bullshit! They're cutting our meals again! This can't be real!" moans Youngsook.

"I think we're being punished for that pizza, he must have found out somehow," says Iseul.

I quickly start eating my half an egg before anyone has any ideas about taking it off me. Nari thumps the table with the palm of her hand to get Iseul's attention.

"Iseul, you're Little Miss Contraband, why don't you use your powers for something useful and start sourcing some actual food for us? Seeing as how our agency is too stingy to do it?"

"Nari, I thought you were all about making us starve just as much as Mr Park was?"

"Don't be dumb. Of course dieting is important and we can't overeat, but this here isn't dieting, this is literal starvation. This can't go on, this is ridiculous. We won't have energy to do our dance routines if we don't eat. We already don't have energy. I'm fed up with half of us collapsing on stage, collapsing in the gym, they don't care about our health. They just want us to be as skinny as possible regardless of what it does to us."

"Okay, so what do you want?"

"We're basically athletes, and I know what an athlete's diet is supposed to look like. I'll draw up a proper meal plan for us. Then I'll get you to shop for those things. It'll have to be all based on non-perishable stuff, that doesn't require refrigeration, things that we can hide in the dorm easily without them going bad or developing a strong scent. So no fresh meat or anything like that, but trust me it'll still be better than what we get at the moment. I'll do a list tonight."

"Okay. You realise that I may not be able to get everything easily."

"Given the things that you've proven you *can* get, I'm sure you'll find a way. It's not like I'm asking for the kind of things that Caitlin wants."

Caitlin starts laughing.

"Hey, marijuana is food too!"

Nari rolls her eyes.

"Not for any sane person."

"Hey I hate to change the subject here, because we all love food, but we're going to my country! This is going to be awesome!"

"What's the festival? Do you know it?" I ask Caitlin.

"Nope. I'm going to go look it up. Be right back!"

Caitlin picks her half-egg out of her bowl and leaves the room. Fifteen seconds later she returns, chewing her egg, phone in hand, and sits back down next to me. Caitlin starts reading from her phone screen.

"JHFP... Join Hands For Peace Festival... celebrating the convergence of technology, culture, activism, art, film, music and lifestyle... over a week in Los Angeles..."

"That's where you live, right?"

"Not quite, Los Angeles is the same state but it's kind of down south more. Let's have a look at who actually plays this thing..."

"I wonder what strings Mr Park pulled to get us this show. Probably something dirty," says Iseul.

Caitlin's eyes suddenly widen.

"Hey Redshift played it last year! They were the only Korean act on! Everyone else on the bill is a... well, actually I've never heard of these names? But they're not from Korea, that's pretty obvious. Oh, Lord Dajuan is playing it this year!"

"Who's he?" I ask.

"Jamaican guy, he plays reggae, he also does rock music too. That's someone I want to meet."

"So we're going to be like the token Korean act this year?" Nari asks.

"I guess."

"Well, presumably they know what they're getting."

Shu gets up out of her chair and starts looking over her shoulder at Caitlin's phone.

"Are those the other acts we are playing with?" Shu asks.

"Yeah, that's them."

"Oh. Wow, they all look so different from each other!" Shu seems fascinated by this for some reason.

"It looks to me like every artist is different from every other artist on purpose."

"Oh. Why?"

"I don't know. Maybe it's supposed to be like different artists of different types coming together to play a show, is like an analogy for different nations coming together for peace. I guess."

"Gosh, that's so smart!"

I can't help but roll my eyes at Shu. Nari instantly notices and smiles at me.

"Hey, does anyone think it's ironic that Hana is going to be performing at a peace festival?"

The whole room laughs at me.

"You're all assholes! I declare war on all of you!"

Caitlin suddenly drops her phone, pushes the table aside and straddles my chair. She's sitting on top of my legs, facing me. The dining chairs are small school chairs, they're not balanced, I can feel the chair wobbling.

"War is declared!" says Caitlin, smiling down at me.

"Are you going to get off me?"

"Not until you surrender!"

"Then I'll fight to the end!"

"Break it up, you two lesbians!" says Nari.

"Fuck off, I'm not mphh..."

143

Caitlin bends down and forcefully kisses me so I can't speak. I quickly give up trying and return the kiss. I then feel myself losing my balance as the chair tips over backwards. Caitlin quickly whips her hand behind my head and pushes it forward so I don't hit the back of my skull on the floor. Even when she's being stupid Caitlin can't help but show that she cares.

"You two clowns, stop wrecking things!"

"The furniture can take it!" says Caitlin.

"Maybe it can, but I don't think I can. Get up!"

"We'll get up when we're ready!"

I continue kissing Caitlin. I know we can't do this for long, Nari will break us up soon enough. I can hear her still complaining, but I've stopped listening.

118. SHOWROOM

"Look at this one Hana, it's so pretty and cute!"

Shu waves a bright yellow phone in my face. She starts playing with the hinge, flipping the phone open and shut repeatedly. The phone makes an annoying clapping noise.

"That's so stupid, why does it have buttons? It looks like my father's old phone."

"I think it's cute!"

Shu puts the ugly phone back on the long shiny jet-black display cabinet, which contains dozens of other phones in varying colours and shapes. We're in Hancel's Seoul regional office product showroom, waiting for the video camera crew to sort themselves out. The floors, walls, ceiling, and furniture here are all the same marble black design, and everyone on the crew is also in completely black suits. There are only two colourful items here; the rainbow selection of phones, and us two. Shu is wearing a red *qipao* with gold trim, and as much as I'm reluctant to admit it, the look actually suits her. I'm in my ugly purple True Miracle Entertainment branded gym tracksuit which I was given at the start of training.

It's starting to show serious signs of wear, but I'm sure the stylists will find something else to put me in soon. We're going to be shooting our advertisement for Hancel here today in just a moment.

"Hana?"

I turn around. A lady is looking at me, she's about my height and looks like she's in her late thirties. She's dressed in a black suit, the same as the rest of the film crew.

"It's me, Hana."

The lady looks me up and down. Another lady, slightly younger but slightly taller and dressed exactly the same way walks up next to her. They both start scanning their eyes over my body, sizing me up.

"Actually... she looks fine... what do you think?"

"I don't think we need to do the hair at all."

"It's scruffy but it'll work. The tracksuit is okay."

"Wait, look at that company logo."

"Oh... that's a company logo? Right, it has to go."

"So tacky, anyway."

"Horrible design. I think we'll just take the tracksuit top off and give her a shirt. The bottoms won't matter as they won't be in frame."

"What about a cardigan?"

"Do we have anything that looks cheap enough?"

"I think there's one in lost property. Any makeup?"

"Just colour correction. I mean, look at her."

The older lady walks right up to me, reaches out her right hand and holds my chin up, angling it around while she inspects my face. I instinctively flinch back.

"Oh girl, settle down, I won't hurt you... my, that skin is really blotchy, isn't it."

"There's a lot of redness under the eyes, isn't there?"

"A lot of redness in general. Definitely too dark. Please get a shirt for this girl and see if you can get that cardigan."

The younger lady leaves the room, while the older lady lets go of my face and just stares at me in silence, still sizing me up. I'm hating this bitch and hating being inspected like an object even more, but I have to maintain some composure and get through this, my livelihood depends on it. I try to breathe deeply and calm myself down. Thirty seconds later the younger lady returns.

"Catch."

Something soft hits me in the face before I have time to react, and then falls to the floor. I bend over and pick up the two pieces of clothing that the younger lady just threw at me.

"Get into those, quickly. We start in a minute."

"Where's the bathroom?"

"You need the bathroom?"

The younger lady rolls her eyes at me, and then looks at the older lady. They both then look at me in silence, stony-faced. Are they expecting me to change my top out here, in front of them and all this camera crew? That's definitely not happening. I just stare back at them.

"Down the hall, first on the left," says the older lady, finally, after about a thirty second delay of them both sizing me up some more for no apparent reason. What a couple of hateful bitches, I'd love to hit their stupid heads together and crack both their skulls open.

"Thanks," I say with the smallest amount of sincerity that I can get away with.

"Go on then," says the older lady.

I quickly leave the room.

"So unprofessional..." I hear the younger lady mutter under her breath, what a fucking cow. I follow their directions and enter the bathroom, which has the same jet-black shiny décor as everything else here. I unfold the clothes onto the sink; a crumpled white T-shirt and a light brown cardigan with frayed fabric. I quickly put the clothes on and walk back to the showroom where the two ladies are waiting for me. They both inspect me in the new clothes.

"Took your sweet time."

"A bit unkempt, isn't she?"

"Hana, go over to the man with the clipboard."

The older lady points to the other side of the room, where Shu is talking to a man. Happy to leave the two bitch ladies behind, I walk quickly over to where Shu is. As I get closer I hear that the man is talking to Shu in Mandarin. He takes one look at me, and then continues to talk to Shu and ignore me. I stand around waiting, this feels awkward. After a minute of conversation, Shu turns to me and smiles.

"Hana, he wants you over there!"

Shu points over to a corner of the room with a green backdrop and white lights. I walk over to the illuminated area and stand. The younger of the two stylist girls comes up to me with a makeup application sponge, and starts roughly padding my face. I flinch back a little.

"Hold still, young lady."

I try to stay still but can't help closing my eyes every time the brush hits my face. It's not as bad as when Marie does it but it's not much better. After about thirty seconds of making oddly strategic-looking thrusts at my cheeks with the applicator, she stops and hands me a mobile phone.

"Take this, and listen to the director."

"Okay, thank you."

I look at the phone, it's black and extremely thin. I hold down the button and turn the phone on. Instantly, the lady who gave me the phone walks up and grabs it back off me.

"I didn't say to turn it on! Listen to the director!"

She turns the phone back off and glares as she hands it back to me.

"I'm sorry, thank you." *Fuck off you rancid bitch.*

The stylist bitch walks away again. I stand there with the phone, and wait. Eventually the man who was talking to Shu walks up to behind the camera.

"Okay, roll the camera. No need for cuts, we'll edit later. Hana, why are you just standing there with a phone in your hand doing nothing?"

"I was told to stand here?"

The man gives me a massive eyeroll like I'm an idiot.

"We're selling phones here, do you actually have to be told to turn the phone on?"

"But..."

"Don't talk, Hana. Turn the phone on, please."

I sigh and turn the phone on. These fucking people are such assholes already. The screen flashes the Hancel logo and then slowly starts a boot up process.

"Once you get to the menu, please navigate to the settings and turn on developer mode. You can do this by tapping the IMEI number on the status page in the settings section."

What the fuck is he even talking about, and what the hell is an IMEI number? Thirty seconds later finally the phone menu displays. I look at the icons, they're all in Chinese. I don't know how to change the phone language over to Korean. I guess the cog might be the settings so I press it, and another page comes up, it's all buttons with Chinese characters next to them and no pictures to give a clue as to what any of the options do. To make matters worse the characters are also really small and hard to read, so even my very small amount of Chinese knowledge gained from the dorm language lessons that I barely paid attention to is useless here.

"I can barely read this?" I ask.

"Hana, don't talk! Just do your best."

"It's in Chinese? I can't..."

"Hana, what did I say?"

"But I can't read it?"

"Hana..."

The director stares at me angrily. I'd better not annoy him further. I guess I'll just have to try to figure out how this stupid phone interface works. I spend the next two minutes pressing random buttons containing bits of text that I can barely read to see what they do. Some buttons do nothing, others take me to other pages full of more Chinese characters on more buttons. I can't believe this bullshit, what a nightmare. I'm never going to be able to do this.

"Shu, go over and help. Camera, keep it rolling."

Shu walks up to me and smiles.

"Do you need some help, Hana?" Shu asks, politely.

"Yes," I reply, quietly. For once I'm relieved to see her. Shu looks at the screen.

"You've gone too far forward, go back twice."

I follow her instruction. I'm back at the first page.

"Okay, press that button there, then that one..." Shu points to the screen and I follow along. "...and that one there ... scroll down, there's your IMEI number! You can press that one now!"

I press the button and some text pops up. Shu smiles.

"Yay Hana, that's it!"

"Thanks!"

Shu gives me a wide *aegyo*-infused grin. I smile back weakly.

"Okay, cut! That was great, Shu, thank you! Hana, you can leave now, go and get changed. Shu, stay there and we'll do some more shots with you."

"That's it?" I ask.

"You can leave, Hana. Go."

"But don't you want..."

"Go now! Don't stand there, Hana!"

Fuck, why am I being rushed out of here so quickly? I feel like I should beg him for more of a shot at this, but I don't want to anger him again. I quickly walk off to the bathroom to get changed back into my tracksuit top. That wasn't much of a video shoot but at least it was over with quickly. They don't seem very impressed though, hopefully I didn't mess anything up too much. I stare into the bathroom mirror and try to stem my creeping anxiety as I think about my possible future status in the group.

119. SILVER HARVEST

It's late and I'm lying in bed. All the other girls are here doing the same, except Nari, who is probably in the gym I guess, working out because she's a masochist. Shu is asleep, snoring lightly, but the other girls are all awake. I'm staring at my phone, watching the text in the "girls" chat group fly by.

Astrid: how is the party plan coming along

Iseul: it's going to happen, soon

Amna: is it just us girls, or boys too?

Gyeongja: PARTY

Caitlin: boys too

Iseul: boys and lots of them

Youngsook: boys!

Gyeongja: no way I want girls night

Amna: as long as there's girls too it's cool

Gyeongja: GIRLS NIGHT GIRLS NIGHT

Iseul: too late the boys are already locked in

Sumire: I kind of want just us girls too

Youngsook: I'd like to "lock in" some boys

Gyeongja: NOT FAIR I WANT GIRLS NIGHT

Astrid: we could have two parties

Astrid: one for everyone, another for just us

Gyeongja: GIRLS NIGHT

I go to type something but then think better of it before I even decide what to write. I don't know if I even have the energy to participate in this chat. I decide to just continue to watch the scrolling text.

Iseul: we're pretty boy-deprived over here, sorry

Amna: We're only inviting boys from the whitelist, right?

Gyeongja: GIRLS NIGHT

Youngsook: actually two parties are a good idea, Iseul can you make our attendance happen at both?

Iseul: Amna – yes apart from the exclusions you girls insisted on

Iseul: Youngsook – we will find a way

Amna: Hey it's different rules for boyfriends

Gyeongja: GIRLS NIGHT

Iseul: don't worry, we have Hana, she will make sure that people behave, we'll hire security too

My phone suddenly vibrates. This means that I have a new private message. It's from Pearlfive's Sumire, who never messages me privately, but now has my number thanks to the "girls" chat group.

Sumire: Hi Hana, you're lesbian - did Yohan reach out to you?

Before I can even type back that I'm not a lesbian, Sumire sends through the chat an embedded video from a news website. I can tell before I even play it that it's

Yohan who is in the news again for something, because it has his picture in the thumbnail. It's definitely not unusual for him to be in the news, usually due to EB-K breaking sales records.

Me: yeah he did. what's this?

Sumire: He spoke to me briefly also. Thought you might be interested in this.

I press play on the video. A female news anchor speaks over footage of Yohan attending an event, surrounded by fans and the flashing of cameras.

Earlier this evening, Yohan attended a special preview screening for "The Love Complete", the new feature film by controversial director Han Leejung which is due to be released later this year. The premiere was not open to the general public, but was a closed screening for test audiences. It is understood that the film is still in the final stages of production and many elements are yet to be added. Given the controversial nature of Han Leejung's previous film "Silver Harvest", an adaptation of the infamous book about life during the Korean war, it has been widely speculated that the new film will have equally confronting subject matter, but the director has remained tight-lipped about the film's content.

The footage cuts to Yohan being questioned by a reporter who points a microphone at his face. Yohan's slicked-back hair is bleached blonde now and he's wearing sunglasses. The flashes from the cameras surrounding him blink across his dark lenses several times per second.

"Why did you attend the preview screening?"

"I was invited. As an entertainer, it is my job to please the public. I do not go where I am not welcomed."

"What did you think of the film? Can you tell us anything about it?"

"I can't discuss it. I wish I could!"

Yohan smiles confidently. The reporter looks nervous.

"Are... aren't you worried about your image, that people might consider your attendance inappropriate?"

"I was grateful to be invited. I think that turning down such a rare opportunity would have been a much more inappropriate action."

"Han Leejung is known for her controversial themes. Does this concern you, that you may be associated with this?"

Yohan pauses for a moment, like he's weighing his words carefully.

"I understand that people may feel conflicted about my attendance. I don't wish to invalidate the feelings of those who have deep convictions. I would ask those bothered by controversial themes to not see the film. However I also feel that people in creative fields should be able to explore subject matter freely without impingement or personal scrutiny. I apologise if my thoughts on this are a cause for concern."

I stop watching. I don't know this director or their work so I don't really know how to feel about this. Sumire seems to think this is important, so I guess she knows. I start texting her.

Me: what's the big deal with this film woman?

Sumire: you don't know Han Leejung?

Me: No?

Sumire: she's the most well-known lesbian film director in Korea. All her films are LGBT themed in some way.

Me: really?

Sumire: "Silver Harvest" isn't a big deal because it's set during the war, it's a big deal because it's about a gay couple having a relationship during the war. It was an even bigger deal when she chose to adapt it. Of course she toned it down a lot from the book but it was still way too much for most people.

Me: what about her new film?

Sumire: nobody knows what's in it yet. It's not an adaptation, it's her own screenplay this time. But if Yohan is supporting her, it means what he said to us is true, he's really looking to change things for LGBT people for real in this industry, it's not just talk.

Me: I don't know, he didn't say that much to the press about it?

Sumire: baby steps. He can't say much more than what he did, he's an idol, he'll be crucified, he'll lose contracts, everything. He's sticking his neck out as it is. Hey I'll send you some Silver Harvest stuff.

Me: Thanks but I don't have time to read a whole ass book?

Sumire: I mean the film. Just some clips.

Me: ok thanks

Sumire: you'll understand why it's such a big deal. Times will get better for us.

Me: you're lesbian?

Sumire: YES dummy why do you think Yohan talked to me at all

Me: sorry

Sumire: don't be sorry, anyway some clips incoming

I wait for a minute and a video clip comes through. I press play on the thumbnail. It's footage of two male actors dressed as soldiers, in some kind of dirt trench, they start embracing each other. At first the embrace just seems friendly but then they start making heavy eye contact and the music starts swelling, it's obvious where the scene is going to go. The two soldiers start kissing, then they both take off the rifles slung around their backs, and then start removing their shirts, still while kissing each other. I keep watching, expecting the scene to cut to something else but it just keeps going and going, as they start kissing each other's torsos. One of the men starts kissing further and further down the other man's chest, licking the other man's abdominal muscles as he goes, and I have to stop watching. It's so lurid and pornographic, it's making me cringe so hard, I really don't want to watch these two guys.

Me: I'm glad this exists but I don't want to see this

Sumire: too racy for you? Are you a prude?

Me: I just don't want to see guys doing this

Sumire: That's fair. I promise you'll like the next clip more, it touches on some of your interests I think

A second video clip comes through the chat and I press play. It's a scene in a hospital ward, there's a female nurse making a bed, pulling the covers over the feet of a man who is lying in the bed, eating a meal from a dinner tray balanced on his lap. Another female nurse appears and motions the man to lift his head up, he complies and she grabs the pillow from behind his head, exchanging it for a fresh, newer looking pillow which has plastic wrap on it. Suddenly the nurse pushes the pillow in her hands into the man's face, smothering him, while her other hand produces a knife and she repeatedly stabs him in the neck. As blood spurts up from his torso, the other nurse grabs his legs by the ankles, pushing them into the bed so he can't move. The sudden switch in tone of the scene makes my heart jump a little because there's no gradually building foreboding music or visual clues or anything like that to make me know anything like this was coming. Blood spatters onto the blue and white uniforms of the two nurses and pools on the mattress as the victim writhes in panic. Once the man stops struggling and moving about, the nurse with the pillow releases the pressure. She turns to the other nurse, and holds out her hand. The other nurse takes the offered hand gently, and they smile at each other. The video ends.

Me: Okay I'll admit that was good, but what was the point of that

Sumire: Guess you'll just have to watch all of it, or maybe read the book

Me: Like I have time?

Sumire: Each film by Han Leejung is more extreme than the last. The public are waiting to see where she'll go next. This is what Yohan is supporting.

Me: how does Yohan have an idol career
Sumire: men can get away with it
Me: men get away with a lot, don't they
Sumire: hey he's using his power for good. Embrace it

I put down the phone. I know Sumire is right. I don't know how I am going to do this yet, but somehow, I know I have to support Yohan.

120. PARTY SUPPLIES

We're sitting in language class, reading our English textbooks. We've been doing English every day since the American show was announced. Our language teacher Ms Kim is sitting at the front of the class, wearing headphones, and reading on her laptop, ignoring us as she always does. She's such a crap teacher, she doesn't actually teach us anything at all, she just sits there like the stupid bitch that she is, she reminds me of the equally useless relief teachers at my school. As usual us girls are passing notes between each other because we're bored, and Ms Kim doesn't even try to stop us anymore as long as we don't do it too openly. I guess after the fight we got into last time, she decided that it wasn't worth the effort to try to discipline us. I wait for the note to come around in my direction. Eventually I feel the familiar feeling of a paper plane hitting me on the back of my neck. At least with my hair shorter, the planes don't get stuck there anymore, the only benefit of the shorter hairstyle that I can think of. I pick up the plane from the floor and take a look at the heading from Iseul.

Time to shop - remember, party soon. So let's get ourselves some party supplies!

I look at the responses from the other girls. The note has clearly done a couple rounds of circulation before it's reached me, as there's writing all over it. Youngsook has written *condoms, lube.* Underneath this Iseul has written *you're a dirty bitch*, and under this Youngsook has responded with *takes one to know one*. Shu has written *vuvuzela*. What the hell is that? Iseul has responded with *it's a party at night we can't be noisy* and Shu has responded with something in Mandarin that I can't read, and has drawn a smiley face next to it. Nari has written *need a new resistance band, the one I was using broke, also a door anchor strap for resistance bands and protein powder, running out. Also when you do your food run for us can you pay attention to the macros please. Carbs and sugar in single digits per one hundred grams, thanks.* Iseul has responded with *I said party supplies, you are the most boring bitch on Earth* and Nari has responded with *I'm not even going to your stupid party but since you're shopping can you get this stuff or not?* Caitlin has drawn a picture of some cubes in some sort of tray, and the number *420* underneath. I know from the number that this is definitely something to do with drugs but I'm not sure what. Iseul has replied *that's very hard to get here, will see what I can do.* No further response from Caitlin. I start thinking about what I want, but I've never even been to a party like this, I don't even know what to expect. I start thinking about how lame that is, and what my life has been like up until this point. Being stuck with these girls isn't always much fun and sure gets annoying, but talking to them has made me realise that I've missed out on so much of life that other people get to experience. My thoughts are interrupted by Caitlin.

"Ms Kim, can I ask something?"

Ms Kim doesn't react, I guess her headphones are up too loud. Caitlin raises her hand and waves it to try and get Ms Kim's attention.

"Ms Kim?"

Still no reaction. Sighing, Caitlin gets up from her seat, walks up to Ms Kim's desk and waves her hand in the space between Ms Kim's eyes and her laptop screen. Ms Kim looks up at Caitlin and glares.

"What is it?"

"Ms Kim, have you read this textbook?"

"Yes, of course."

"Have you seen what's on page eighty-seven?"

Caitlin has the English textbook in her other hand. She opens the textbook up and shows it to Ms Kim, who looks over the page briefly.

"What about it?"

"What about it? *What about it?* Are you serious?"

"I don't see anything wrong. Sit back down."

"Ms Kim, look! Just look at the page! You can't have *that* in a textbook!"

Ms Kim just stares at Caitlin and says nothing.

"Ms Kim, you're the English teacher, you don't see anything wrong with this? Seriously?"

"No, I do not. Sit back down and continue your study, Caitlin."

"Do you even know English at all? If you did you would know that this is both incorrect English usage and completely unacceptable as material to be training us with. I mean, we're supposed to go over there and make the company look good and *this* is what you're using?"

"I will not be lectured to by a *gyopo,* especially a junior! Sit down!"

Caitlin turns to us.

"Hey everyone, just so you know, just disregard the conversation on page eighty-seven, okay? If any of us talk like that when we're in America we'll get the entire group in serious trouble..."

"Really?" asks Shu.

"Yeah, we'd be so screwed. Our careers in America would be over. Maybe tear that whole page out of the book just to be safe..."

Ms Kim gets out of her chair and slaps Caitlin across the face. The whole room gasps in shock.

"None of you are tearing a damn thing out of the textbooks! Sit down and behave!"

Caitlin stares at Ms Kim, looking hurt and surprised. I don't think she thought Ms Kim would do something like that. Caitlin then snatches Ms Kim's laptop off the desk and tucks it under her arm, then walks around the desk so she has a physical barrier between her and Ms Kim.

"Hey, nice laptop!"

"GIVE THAT BACK!"

Caitlin doesn't say anything.

"GIVE THAT BACK RIGHT NOW!"

Ms Kim makes a grab for the laptop. Her grip only half connects but it's enough to bump the laptop out of Caitlin's hands. The laptop falls to the floor, in front of Iseul's desk. I stand there in shock, not sure how to react to this whole situation when Iseul quickly ducks under the desk and grabs the laptop.

"GIVE THAT BACK!" shouts Ms Kim.

We all look at Iseul, who sits back down with the laptop on her desk and starts laughing.

"Hey I wonder what's on this that's so fascinating that you couldn't be bothered teaching us properly..."

Iseul opens the laptop up and looks at the screen. Ms Kim walks up to Iseul and tries to grab the laptop again, but Iseul anticipates the movement and holds the laptop out of reach with one hand. With her other hand, Iseul whips a pocket knife out of her tracksuit pants and waves it at Ms Kim, who backs away. Iseul starts giggling.

"Uh-uh!"

"You wouldn't dare!"

"No I wouldn't. But I bet Hana would!"

Iseul stands up and waves the handle of the knife in my direction. I get up from my desk and take the knife. Iseul is right, I'd gladly cut Ms Kim's stupid face just to make a point. I hold the knife out in front of me, in Ms Kim's general direction, even though I'm probably a bit too far away from her to be threatening. Iseul keeps laughing while examining Ms Kim's laptop.

"Oh wow, you're a bit disgusting. What a dirty bitch you are! You'd better hope that I don't tell anyone about what's on here!"

"Come on, that's enough!" says Nari.

Nari snatches the laptop out of Iseul's hands. Nari then looks at me.

"Put the knife down, idiot."

I guess the fun is over. For physical strength I'm no match for Nari, she'll make me put the knife down if I don't do it on my own. Sighing, I give the knife back to Iseul. Nari hands the laptop back to Ms Kim.

"Here's your laptop. Your teaching is garbage. Why can't you just listen to feedback? It's not like you..."

Ms Kim doesn't let Nari finish her sentence, and storms out of the room without a word, slamming the door behind her. Nari sighs, and then looks to me and Iseul.

"You two are both fucked in the head!"

"Yeah, like you're so great," says Iseul, playing with the pocket knife.

"Give that knife here. I'm confiscating it."

"No, it's mine, sorry."

"I don't want you pulling another dumb little stunt like that ever again."

"I don't care what you want, you can't have it."

Nari makes a grab for Iseul's knife. Iseul draws her hand away but Nari is too fast and grabs onto Iseul's wrist.

"Let go."

"No!"

Iseul struggles but can't get out of Nari's grip, Nari is way stronger.

"Come on, let go, or I'll make you let go."

"Screw off!"

"Fine."

Nari keeps hold of Iseul's wrist and walks around her desk, twisting Iseul's arm behind her back in the process. Iseul grunts in pain and instantly drops the knife on the floor, which Nari picks up. Nari looks at Iseul, smugly.

"Happy now?"

Iseul nurses her arm in her lap.

"That hurt! You dumb fucking bitch! Do you know how easily I can get another knife?"

"I'll confiscate that one too!"

"Then don't expect your fucking shopping!"

"I can live without it!"

Nari smiles. She's enjoying putting Iseul in her place. I don't like Nari's bossiness much, but I don't like Iseul much either, so this is good to see. Iseul is still nursing her arm.

"Fuck, this fucking hurts! What did you do to me?"

"I was being pretty gentle. I can arrange for you to be in way more pain than this. How about you never do something like that ever again?"

Iseul doesn't say anything. Nari continues.

"I'm not trying to give you a hard time, I'm just trying to help us and look after the group, after all our interests. Our interests aren't in making trouble for ourselves like this. I understand that she's not a good teacher and she acted rudely but we have to take the high ground and act like reasonable people. I don't care what your background is, there's no excuse..."

"Nari, on second thoughts why don't you come back here and twist my arm some more, it's less painful than your fucking lecture!"

Everybody laughs at Nari. To my surprise, Nari is laughing as well.

"Hey Iseul, here you go."

Nari folds the knife up and throws it gently to Iseul, who catches it. Iseul stares at Nari like she doesn't know what to say. Nari smiles back.

"On second thoughts, you might as well have the knife back. You're right, you'll just get another one. Besides, you're useless with it anyway!"

Iseul's face is red, she doesn't like being humiliated like this.

"Bitch, what would you know?"

"Don't embarrass yourself further by trying to act tough. It won't work out well for you. Just get our party supplies like a good girl."

Iseul sits back in her chair and doesn't say anything else. Watching Nari humiliate Iseul is a glorious thing.

121. DGT

"Spin around for me, Shu!"

"Okay! I will spin!"

"Faster, keep going!"

All of us girls are sitting on stools at the far wall of the DGT photography studio. Only Caitlin and Shu are here to be photographed, but Mr Park has made us all go, for some reason, who the fuck knows why but I guess it's good to not be in the dorms for a while. Mr Park hasn't come with us, instead the photographer is looking after us for today. She's a short lady called Min who looks about fifty years old, she has thick glasses and long bright red hair stretching down almost to her knees. Right now Min is taking rapid-fire photos of Shu, while making her do all sorts of strange things. Shu is wearing a pale pink ballerina dress paired with big black knee-high boots that have massive square heels, the outfit looks weird and docsn't go together at all. The rest of us are just in our casual gym clothes although I'm sure Caitlin will be made to wear something different later when it's her turn to get photos taken. Shu spins around clumsily as instructed by Min and starts giggling.

"I can't twirl in these things, I'm going to fall over!"

"It doesn't matter! You're doing great, cutie!"

"These boots are huge! Do people really wear boots like this... ow!"

Shu trips over her own feet as she spins around and lands knees-first on the tiled floor of the studio, breaking her fall with her hands. Min isn't bothered and keeps snapping photos at the rate of about one per second.

"Look this way, Shu!"

"Okay!"

Min crouches down next to Shu and keeps snapping pictures as Shu looks into the camera.

"Are you good to get up? Do you need help?"

"I think I can do it on my own!"

"Okay, I've got something for you..."

Shu gradually wobbles back to her feet, while Min stands up and wanders over to a box in the far corner of the room. She picks something out of the box and passes it to Shu, a skipping rope.

"You want me to skip?"

"Yes!"

"In these boots?"

"Don't worry, you don't have to be good at it. It'll be fine. Just do your best!"

Shu starts skipping slowly while Min resumes taking photos.

"Go faster! Go as fast as possible!"

"Really?"

"Try to go faster than your own heartbeat!"

"My heart's going pretty fast, though?"

"That's fine!"

"Oh wow, okay! I will go very fast!"

Shu increases the pace of her skipping but only manages to do a few skips before catching the rope under her boot.

"Don't get discouraged Shu, just try again! Let's go! Pretend that you're in a skipping race!"

Shu keeps trying to skip quickly but she can't quite do it, she starts giggling again. Iseul is sitting next to me, I look over at her, she seems amused by what's going on.

"Wow, this is weird," says Iseul.

"What?" I ask.

"This is such a different vibe to when my dad takes photos. This looks like it's actually going to be fun."

"She seems more professional. I wish she could do photos for all of us. Why can't we have her instead of your loser dad."

"Dad gives Mr Park the 'family' rate, that's why. Also he likes to humiliate me."

Nari gets out of her seat and walks up to me and Iseul. She's got a copy of DGT Magazine in her hands. She opens up one of the middle pages and then hands me the magazine.

"Check this out, Hana."

I take a look at the page Nari has opened. It's Ora from Pearlfive. She's dressed in a black corset dress and is carrying a riding crop, she glares at the camera with a domineering grin. It's a great photo, made even better by the lighting which is moody and dark. It really captures what is attractive about her.

"Oh wow, this looks amazing."

"Keep turning, there's more."

I flip over the page, and there's a picture of Gyeongja. She's wearing a puffy pale blue doll-like dress, and is lying face up on a bed. I count eight fluffy white cats on the bed with her, including one on her lap. Gyeongja's expression is hard to read, her and the cat on her lap are both staring at the camera together.

"Gyeongja as a crazy cat lady kind of makes sense. How did she get the cat and her staring together like that?" I ask.

"Who knows. She's good, right?"

I turn the next page and there's Mia, the only girl in the group I haven't met or had any communication with. She has shoulder length blonde hair and is wearing a bright yellow T-shirt and blue jeans, the photo looks like it's taken while she's in mid-air, but there's no motion blur, it's clean and crisp. She smiles happily at the camera against a bright background.

"Fuck, I hate her," says Iseul as she looks over my shoulder.

"You know Mia?" I ask.

"That bitch is a waste of space. Have to admit, good photo though."

I turn the page again, there's a picture of Sumire. She has her usual short hair in a quiff and is wearing tight

172

camouflage gear with lots of straps. She's holding out a police baton while kicking towards the camera with her feet. It's a stunning picture.

"That's the girl who kicked your ass in fencing, right?" Iseul says to Nari.

Nari looks at the page and laughs.

"She's not so tough. I'll get her next time."

"These photos are all amazing," I say to Nari.

"Min took them all. She's a real pro, hey."

Suddenly I hear applause. I look over at Min and Shu, they're both clapping.

"Okay, we're done here for the moment! We'll pick it up a bit later. Shu, you can take a break, freshen up a bit. Caitlin, come over here, I need to do some planning!"

Caitlin gets out of her chair and walks over to Min, while Shu clomps off to the bathroom in her chunky heels.

"Where do you want me?" asks Caitlin.

"Nowhere yet. I'm just trying to decide a concept."

"Sure."

Min starts circling around Caitlin as she stands there, looking her up and down from all angles.

"How are you finding being an idol, Caitlin?"

"It's alright. Not much food, not much socialising, not much boys. Okay apart from that."

"Are you popular with boys?"

Caitlin smiles.

"Some of them!"

"I'll bet it's more than just some! Hey, just turn your face to the side a little."

"Okay."

"You know... I think I'd like to do a couples shoot with you. We need a boy though."

"Oh. There are no boys here though, right?"

"Use Hana! She'll be the boy!" says Iseul.

"Of course! Hana!" adds Youngsook.

"Hanaaaaaa!" yells Shu, from the bathroom next door. She can obviously hear us from in there.

Min looks over at me, she looks thoughtful but I don't know what she's thinking. I can feel my face turning bright red. Everyone starts laughing.

"Okay. Hana, come over here to Caitlin and just stand next to her."

I walk up and stand by Caitlin's side. Min starts looking at us both, up and down.

"Hana, how do you feel?"

I don't know what she means. What a question. Why does she care how I feel? Isn't she a photographer?

"What?"

"I mean... about being the boy. Doing a couples thing with Caitlin. Are you okay with that?"

I look at Caitlin, she smiles at me and grabs me around the waist, drawing me softly into her. I hold my breath as she gently pushes her torso up against mine and looks down into my eyes. I nod in response to Min, but while looking at Caitlin.

"Definitely okay?" asks Caitlin, while stroking my hair. I flinch but only a little.

"Yes," I respond quietly. I feel blood rushing around my body faster. It's been so long since I've been able to be close to Caitlin properly. Being Caitlin's partner for a photoshoot definitely won't require any acting ability at all, that's for sure.

"Okay. I think I've got it. Girls, wait here, just amuse yourselves for a minute, I'll be back before you know it."

Min wanders off to another room and closes the door.

"This is your dream shoot, Hana!" yells Youngsook.

The rest of the group start laughing.

"Fuck off! Stop making me blush!" I reply.

"Hey I'll take your mind off it," says Caitlin.

"Oh?"

Caitlin leans in and starts kissing me on the lips, gently. At first I'm hesitant because we're in front of all the others, I can hear them hollering and cheering, it's shameful. After a few seconds the feelings of warmth from Caitlin's lips take over my body, I decide that I don't care, and start kissing her back, more passionately. Caitlin increases the pressure to match the tempo of my lips against hers, while squeezing her hands around my waist tightly, drawing me into her. We're interrupted by Min clearing her throat.

"Hate to interrupt the acting rehearsal, but I've got something for you."

Fuck, I didn't think she'd be back so quickly. We stop kissing and look at her awkwardly, expecting to be in trouble. She's smiling at both of us, she doesn't even seem to mind. She's holding out a small cardboard box. In it are several pairs of eyeglasses.

"Hana, try on a pair."

I pick a random pair of glasses from the box and put them on my face.

"I can't see anything! Everything's blurry as hell!" I complain.

Min laughs.

"The glasses are not for *you* to see, they're for others to see *you*. I don't like those ones anyway, not the right frame for your face. Try another one."

I put the glasses back in the box and try on a different pair. Again my vision becomes a total blur.

"No, not for you either. I think we need some different frame types, I think that maybe the type that I have on would work, but there's none in the box like that. Let's try my glasses on you."

Min takes off the thick glasses she's wearing on her own face, and puts them on mine. My vision isn't blurry in these at all, I can see really well in them. I look at Caitlin.

"How do I look?" I ask.

"Cute!"

"Hey, you look good too..."

I keep staring at Caitlin. Her face is so pretty, I've never seen it look this good before. Everything about her face is so crisp. Caitlin has the most subtle row of freckles across her cheeks and the bridge of her nose that I've never even noticed before.

"Look at me," says Min.

I turn to look at Min. She also looks really crisp and defined. It's the glasses, it has to be. I try to process my thoughts. I need glasses. I've never had glasses before. How do I get glasses? I don't even know.

"Hey that suits your face really well. Hana, you're upset. Are you okay?"

"Where did you get these?"

I take the glasses off my face. Min suddenly looks a bit blurry. I turn to Caitlin, she also looks blurry. Everything looks murky and weird now. How have I been putting up with this all this time? Min gently removes the glasses from my hand.

"Hana, I can't give you my glasses, because I need them, I'm pretty much blind without them, so I can't take photos without them. But, I have a second pair, they're at home so I have to go and get them, and you can wear those while we do the shoot. They're exactly the same."

"Okay," I reply.

Min speaks up a little louder so everyone in the room can hear.

"My place isn't far, I'll be about half an hour. While I'm gone, I want you and Caitlin to go into the wardrobe room together, that's the door right there next to the bathroom. Hana, you are to pick out a plain black button-up shirt and black jacket and pants for yourself, from the men's section, that's aisle C, they're labelled up the top. There's a lot of choices in that rack, and they're sorted by size, just anything that roughly fits will do, it can be a little loose, it doesn't have to be an exact fit. Dress for comfort. Caitlin, there's a specific dress that I want you to wear, aisle D, number 167, it will be tight but it will fit you,

Hana will help you get into it. You'll find the accessories for it in a box underneath the rack that's also tagged 167, put all that stuff on, except the earrings, which won't suit you, forget those. Everything else is fine. It won't take you anywhere near half an hour to get that stuff on but I'm sure you two can find a way to amuse yourselves, just don't wreck anything."

I hear the others laughing. I stare at Caitlin, who grins back at me. I feel my face going red again. I can't believe Min is openly just giving us permission to do what we want, this is crazy. I hear the other girls talking under their breath.

"The rest of you... here, someone, take this."

Min holds out a card. Nari gets out of her seat and grabs it.

"There's a sushi bar next door to the entrance of the building. Go down there with the other girls, show the staff this card, get sushi for everyone, eat it down there, come back here in half an hour. Tell them to put it on my tab. Don't forget to bring some sushi back up here for me, Hana, and Caitlin. I'll be starving when I get back so bring a lot, got it?"

"Got it. Is there any..."

Min cuts Nari off. "No limit, I don't care what you get. Just eat and don't be shy about it."

Nari bows.

"Thank you, Min!"

"Right, I'm out of here. Back soon."

We all go to bow but before we can do anything Min has already run out of the door. Caitlin grabs my hand.

"Orders are orders. Come with me!"

I take Caitlin's hand and we walk briskly over to the wardrobe room. As soon as we're in the room I close the door behind us as I don't want any of the others looking in, but as I close it I see them all filing out quickly down the stairs anyway. I guess they're more worried about food than about what we're up to. I turn around and look at the room, it's huge, with massive rows upon rows of clothes hanging up on racks, all neatly sorted.

"There's a lot of clothes here," I say.

Caitlin turns around and presses her body gently against mine.

"To try on these clothes, we first have to remove the clothes we have on, right?"

"It's important to do things in order."

Caitlin's left arm wraps around my waist, while her right hand starts playing with the buttons around my collarbone. She smiles at me, her face so close that the tip of her nose brushes gently against mine, and walks my body slightly backward so I'm pinned up against the door. I feel my heartbeat racing.

"You've always got buttons."

"I like buttons."

"I can tell. That time we got to go shopping, all the tops you bought, they all had buttons on the front."

"It's just what I've always had. It makes me feel more comfortable."

"Your style is cute. I hope undoing them doesn't make you feel too strange, but we've got clothes to try on."

"It's what has to be done."

Caitlin leans in and kisses me, more passionately before, this time with the knowledge that for once we won't be interrupted. I return Caitlin's kisses as she starts working the buttons of my shirt loose. I feel my heart pounding through my chest as Caitlin removes her own T-shirt with one swift arm movement and presses her torso against mine. I've missed her touch, missed the rare freedom to be with her, so much.

122. AMERICAN ENGLISH

"Where's Ms Kim, our language teacher?" Nari asks.

Ijun is sitting where Ms Kim usually sits to take our language class. She's playing with her phone with one hand, with her other hand she points to the chairs.

"Sit."

We all sit down in the classroom chairs and face Ijun silently. She's still playing with her phone. We all know better than to interrupt her phone time so we just wait. After about a minute Ijun mutters something under her breath and puts the phone down.

"Ms Kim isn't working for us anymore."

"Why not?" asks Shu.

"She found another job and left with no notice. I'm going to supervise your language classes from now on."

I nervously look around the room. I see Iseul and Youngsook both nervously look back at me. I guess this means no more passing notes, I might actually have to start concentrating on lessons. This is going to be a drag.

"We don't get another teacher?" asks Shu.

"You can teach yourselves. Caitlin, you know English fluently?"

"Yes, I do," Caitlin replies.

"Great, you can come up the front here, and pick up the exercise book from where you left off last time. The others need to get the English stuff under their belts. You can teach them, and me, also."

Ijun stands up, walks over to the desk next to mine and sits down, facing Caitlin. Now Ijun is the student and Caitlin is the teacher. It's so weird to have her sitting next to me. She's younger than me but she has the power to cancel my career in an instant. I nervously straighten my back a little. Ijun leans over to me.

"Open the exercise book, I'll follow along. Caitlin, what page are we on?"

"Page eighty-seven. But about that..."

I open the book up and Ijun peers over at the page. It's a conversation between two people in English. It seems advanced, I have no idea what it says. Caitlin continues.

"...we were talking to Ms Kim about this before she left. It's not proper English that we should be using. We would get in trouble if we used it in America."

"Like, a controversy?" Ijun asks.

"Yes."

"Then this is a good learning experience. We should study this so we know what not to say. Get someone to translate the passage."

"I'll do it! I'm good at English!" says Shu.

Caitlin nods in Shu's direction.

"Sure, give it your best shot."

"Okay, there's two people, they are friends having a conversation! Person one says: 'What is up, you are a black person!' Person two says: 'Hello, you are also a black person, what is wrong with you?' Person one then says: 'I am very high like a poop!' Person two then says 'There is no poop, but I was... released from a prison?' I don't think it makes sense, but was I close?"

Caitlin looks at Shu for a few seconds, like she's not quite sure what to say. I think she's trying to stop herself from laughing. Ijun turns to Caitlin.

"It's not quite right, is it?"

"Actually, that wasn't too bad!"

"It's a weird conversation!"

"It's a very stereotypical and racist depiction once you understand it fully, that's part of the problem with it. We can't talk like that. Shu, how did you know that the word in the first two sentences was referring to black people?"

Shu takes a deep breath.

"Well, in Tianjin there's a restaurant called Seven Duckling, it's very popular, and celebrities like movie stars often eat there when they go to the city. We used to get a lot of tourism, and then we had the pandemic, and then people were worried about cleanliness, so they put up a sign on the door for a while and it was in Mandarin but also in English too for foreigners, and it said 'no black people are allowed in the restaurant', and they used that same English word for black people that's in the book!"

Caitlin looks shocked.

"Really? They are that racist?"

"Actually no, that's not right. I remember now, it was 'no black people or dogs are allowed in the restaurant', that's correct! So I know the English word for 'dogs' too!"

Caitlin gasps. She looks even more shocked.

"What the hell? How did they get away with that?"

"They didn't! It was a big controversy! I never went there but I know about the sign because it got in the news overseas, and then because of that, it got in the news back in Tianjin because the reporters here were talking about the news overseas, and then they had to change the sign because foreigners thought that the restaurant were being racist."

"Well they *were* being racist!"

"I thought it was a bit mean too! What's wrong with black people and dogs?"

Caitlin looks like she's about to say something and then stops herself. She's speechless for a moment before eventually continuing.

"Okay, look, everyone just know that the word there for black people, you can't *ever* say that word in America. We will get cancelled overseas for that, at best. We could even get attacked for saying it. It's a very racist word."

"Oh. So is the conversation racist?" asks Shu.

"Well, the two people aren't being racist to each other, they're actually being friendly."

"But how can they be friendly with a racist word?"

"Well because they're both black, they can say it."

"They can be racist to each other?"

"It's not racist if they say it. Look, just trust me on this one, we don't ever want to say that. I'm not even going to say it now. None of you are allowed to say that word, *ever,* okay? Not even when it's just us. Notice how I'm avoiding saying it right now? You should all do that."

Iseul chuckles. "Why are you so precious about it in front of us?"

"I just want us to get into good habits, that's all."

Ijun nods.

"Everyone, that's actually a very good idea. You don't want to get comfortable with a bad word that could cause us problems in another country and then it slips out at the wrong time. That could easily happen as you have a lot of language study to do, you could get confused. Everyone, no saying it *ever*, okay? Or you are in trouble if you do."

We all nod. Iseul mutters something under her breath that I can't quite hear. Caitlin glares at Iseul.

"Iseul! Just trust me on this, please! If we say that in America we will have every black fan think we're a bunch of racist assholes! They won't even give us a chance! There's a lot of black people in America who like Korean music, we don't want to alienate them!"

"I trust you, I just think it's dumb."

"Well it's not your culture, you wouldn't get it. There's a big power imbalance between black and non-black people in America, black people are a lot poorer for instance, and they had slavery..."

"So that's our fault? We have to pander to their feelings, just because they don't make as much money as the richest people in the richest country in the world, and because they had slavery once? While in the meantime *we're* the actual slaves, because our agency doesn't pay us?"

"We're *guests* in their country, so yes we do have to follow their rules! It doesn't matter if you don't agree! Your dumb ass doesn't have to understand it, just do it!"

"Whatever."

"Don't be like 'whatever', this is important. It's like, taking your shoes off indoors, right? We do it but in other countries they think that's stupid that we get upset, but it's offensive to us."

"But that's just practical, it's so you protect the floor and don't track dirt into your house. That just means people in other countries are dumb and grotty. Which is probably why the Seven Duckling wouldn't let..."

"Iseul, I think you're missing the point a little!"

I can see Caitlin is getting really annoyed at Iseul now. Ijun clears her throat.

"Iseul, Caitlin's the expert, just do what she says and don't argue. It's important that we avoid controversy."

"I agree!" says Nari.

"Good, thank you!" replies Caitlin, settling down a bit.

"We'll all be good, and I'll back you up on that all the way, I won't let anyone use it. I wouldn't chance our careers on something like this. I've sure I've never said that word anyway, except when singing along to songs..."

"Well, you can get in trouble for that, too."

Nari raises her eyebrows.

"Really?"

"Yeah."

Youngsook puts her hand up.

"You know, recently I recorded a cover song in the studio, I just sort of tried to do the English phonetically, but maybe it had that word in there? I'm not sure, I'd have to go back and check it."

"Have you uploaded it anywhere yet?"

"No."

"You should check and delete it if you have to. If those recordings get out to the American fans..."

"So I can't sing that song?"

"Just don't sing that word."

"Are you serious?"

"YES!"

"Okay, I'll bleep it out."

"No, you can't do that either, because then they'll know you *definitely* sung it."

"So I can't sing it, but I also can't *censor* it?"

"You can't sing it or *indicate that you possibly sung it.*"

"But why do they put it in a song, if they don't want people to sing it?"

"They can sing it to each other, but we can't. It's like they're reclaiming the word. It's like, taking the power of it to demean and offend away."

"Well that's obviously not working out very well, is it? I mean, if they won't let anyone else use it, they must still feel pretty demeaned by it, so it's clearly got plenty of power left, maybe even more power than before..."

Caitlin's starting to get more and more irritated.

"Look Youngsook, fuck... how would you like it if I called you a ching-chong slope bitch nip fat slug? Huh?"

"Well, I wouldn't like that, I'd be upset, of course."

"Well it's about on the same offensiveness level, okay?"

"Right, okay."

"So, you get it?"

"Yeah sure, but... why would I put that *in a song?*"

"Oh fuck me, we're going around in circles. I can't handle this. Hana, just back me up here. You wouldn't see a reason to use the word, would you? Please just say 'no' for me."

I think about it.

"Well, I guess not?"

"What do you mean you *guess* not?"

"I mean, I wouldn't use it normally, but you say it upsets people?"

"YES!"

"Well, what if I *wanted* to upset someone? Then that word would be the perfect choice, wouldn't it? I mean, I wouldn't use it with someone I *liked*, but there's a lot of people who deserve to be upset, because they suck..."

"We're supposed to be idols, Hana!"

"But what if someone's insulting me and being rude? Why can't I use it then and be rude back? Can't I use it in self-defence?"

Caitlin holds her head in her hands.

"Oh my god, I can't trust any of you clowns!"

Ijun waves her phone hand to get everyone's attention.

"Let's stop talking about this now. Obviously there are some differences in how it's used but we don't need to understand all the nuances of this and that, we just need to know the word isn't to be used by us. If you can't understand it, then don't say it, and just let Caitlin do all the talking when you're in America."

"Thank you, Ijun!" says Caitlin. "When are we going to America again?"

"Two weeks. Summer Soak first, then America straight after that."

"Oh, no. I'm not doing Summer Soak," says Iseul.

"Yes you are," replies Ijun, who has suddenly gone back to playing with her phone.

"No, I'm not!"

Ijun keeps playing with her phone, not saying anything in response to Iseul.

"Ijun, please."

Ijun continues to say nothing. I can tell she's annoyed.

"You know I can't let people see my tattoo..."

Ijun slams her phone hard onto the table.

"Do you think we don't know that, idiot?"

Ijun's harsh words and the bang of her phone on the table surface right next to me both make me shiver. She's normally so placid. Iseul starts to say something but Ijun continues.

"You are really pissing me off right now! You always want to get special treatment! Just be grateful for your position! You are doing the show and that is all!"

Iseul looks like she wants to say something but is holding her tongue. Damn, I guess if even nepo baby Iseul can't get out of this awful Summer Soak show, I sure won't be able to. Ijun turns to Caitlin.

"Caitlin, please continue through the book. You're doing well. I know that we are ignorant, but that's why we have you, to educate us. The rest of you, don't argue with Caitlin, I'm sure there are many other important rules for dealing with Americans and speaking American English, you don't have long to learn everything you need to know. Oh... and Iseul?"

"Yes?"

Ijun holds up her phone. The screen detaches from the phone's body and falls onto the desk in two pieces.

"Put me on your list for a new phone, please."

123. THE PARTY

"So where are we?" I ask Caitlin.

"This is Astrid's house. How do you not know that? Didn't you read about where the party was in the chat?"

"I can't keep up with that damn chat group."

I'm in the back of the van with the other girls, except Nari, who has decided that she wants nothing to do with the party because she's boring. Iseul's courier "Jane" and the gun dealer who is always with her are in the driver's cabin, they've just pulled the van up in front of a large house, after a boring hour-long drive where we've had to change vehicles twice.

"It's huge! Coming through, don't rip my party dress!" says Shu as she climbs through the van awkwardly in her red and gold *qipao* and slides open the side door. The rest of us are dressed casually but Shu has gone all-out with the formal wear for some unknown reason.

We all file out after Shu and stand in the parking lot, looking up at the house, a two-story mansion with a boxy, modern design.

"How does Astrid afford this?" Youngsook asks.

"Rich parents," replies Iseul.

"Let's go and meet everyone!" says Shu, running off to a lane on one side of the house, decorated with coloured balloons.

We all follow Shu around the side of the house, which opens up into a large backyard. It's crowded here. There are a few wooden tables where people are sitting around, talking, drinking *soju*, and smoking cigarettes. There's also someone cleaning a barbeque here, unfortunately there's no food on yet. Beyond the tables is a large pool, where there's about half a dozen boys paddling around and chatting. On the other side of the pool I recognise my first familiar face, which is Petal, the security guard who sometimes works for us. She doesn't notice me, she's busy keeping an eye on the partygoers in the pool.

"Fuck yes! There's a pool here! I've missed the water so much!" says Caitlin.

"You can swim?" I ask.

"Yeah, I've been swimming since forever! I'll just go and put my party stuff inside, then the pool is mine! Actually, can you do it for me?"

Caitlin's carrying a backpack, she hands it to me.

"In here there's a tray of brownies that I brought for the guests. Can you give them to Astrid? There's a sign that goes with them, don't forget to give her that too. The sign is very important. Be gentle with the bag because the brownies are a bit fragile."

"What's a brownie?"

"It's like a little cake."

"Okay. What does Astrid look like?"

"Like her avatar in the chat group."

"That weird pink photo? That's actually her?"

Caitlin points to the glass rear wall of the house, beyond which is a lounge room and kitchen. There's a tall girl in a pink dress with dead straight blonde hair talking to some guests by the kitchen bench, it's definitely Astrid. She does in fact look a lot like her chat avatar.

"Okay, I'll give them to her."

"Thanks! Look after my stuff!"

Caitlin turns and walks away toward the pool, she seems really keen to get in there. I unzip the backpack and start looking for her swimwear, which she's obviously going to need. It must be in here somewhere, but I can't find anything in here apart from a plastic bag which just seems to have that tray in it.

"Hey, Caitlin, don't you have..."

I look up at Caitlin who has stripped off her T-shirt and skirt, and is standing on the edge of the pool in her underwear. She smiles back at me and dives in, making a big splash. All the boys around the pool area immediately start cheering. Caitlin surfaces a few seconds later and immediately starts talking to a guy who I don't recognise, I can't hear their conversation. While she's talking, she removes her wet underwear and throws it so it's together with her other clothing. The boys around the pool all seem very interested in this.

"Your girlfriend looks happy!" says Youngsook.

"Do you think I should be worried?" I ask.

"No, there's security here. Nothing bad will happen. I'm going inside though, I can't compete with this. If I want to meet boys I have to be where naked Caitlin isn't."

I start thinking about Petal, our sometimes security guard. She's always looked out for us girls, I remember her smacking down boys who crossed a line during our fan meetings. Youngsook is right, I shouldn't worry.

"I have to meet Astrid anyway, I'll come with you."

I follow Youngsook through the sliding glass doors into the lounge room and kitchen area. Iseul is already here, she's talking to a group of three guys that I don't recognise. I can't see Shu anywhere, who knows where she went but it's a relief to not have her near me for once.

"Oh fuck, there's Troy!"

Youngsook looks at a tall, muscular boy dressed only in his bathers and a towel, who has just entered the lounge room from behind us. I guess he just got out of the pool. Youngsook's eyes nearly burst out of her skull as he walks past us.

"Hana, look!"

"I don't care?"

"How do I approach him, Hana?"

"How the fuck should I know? Just tell him you like his dancing or something."

"Thanks, you're a genius, Hana! Bye now!"

Troy disappears somewhere down a hallway and Youngsook follows him. I guess I'd better get this stuff over with. I walk up to Astrid, but she's distracted by some other people. I notice that one of them is Ora, as soon as I look at her she locks eyes with mine. Ora is dressed in a black formal dress, she looks stunning. My heart suddenly shoots up into my throat.

"Oh, hey baby!"

Everyone turns to look at me. This is awkward.

"Hi, Ora. Hey, Astrid, I've got..."

Before I can say anything else Ora walks up to me and gives me a hug. I stop speaking as I lose my train of thought and my mouth becomes full of her black hair. I drop Caitlin's bag at my feet. Ora then holds me softly around my waist and looks into my eyes.

"I've missed you babe!"

I don't know what to say to this. "I've missed you too?" No, not really true. "I want you to get your hands off me?" Actually that's not true either. I just stand there looking into Ora's eyes, feeling stupid while she smiles at me. Ora then breaks the tension by turning me around so I'm facing Astrid.

"Hey Hana, this is Astrid! Astrid, meet Hana!"

I smile awkwardly. "Hi, Astrid, it's me, Hana!"

Astrid smiles at me.

"Hi Hana! It's good to finally meet you!"

Astrid walks forward and gives me a very brief and polite hug.

"I've got something for you, from Caitlin."

"Oh, the brownies?"

"Yes, that's them!"

"Just pop them on the kitchen bench and I'll get a plate for them!"

"Sure."

I open up Caitlin's backpack and take out the plastic bag. Inside the bag is the brownie tray, a bunch of cakes in neat rows. There's also another smaller plastic bag here, it's Caitlin's marijuana bag. Trust her to bring weed with her. I take the tray out and leave her drugs in the backpack. I don't think anyone saw them. Astrid puts a plate down on the bench.

"Just empty the brownies out onto this, then you can put the tray back in the bag so you don't lose it."

I tip the tray upside down and the brownies fall out. I'm hungry so I quickly grab a brownie to eat for myself and take a big bite, because there's a lot of people here and there aren't that many brownies so I'm sure these will be gone soon. I notice that a folded white piece of paper has also fallen out, this must be the sign that Caitlin was talking about. I unfold the paper and read the sign:

WARNING: CONTAINS "MAGIC"

"What's that say?" asks Astrid.

I show the sign to her.

"Ah, very important. Put them on the coffee table in the lounge with the sign upright, make sure it's visible. People need to know that."

I carry the plate over to the lounge and put it on the table, leaving the sign facing up on top of them as directed. I realise that the brownie actually tastes disgusting, it looks like chocolate, and it kind of tastes like chocolate at first too, but then there's this weird lingering aftertaste that I just can't place. It's like I'm eating lawn clippings or something. What kind of taste is that?

Oh no. *Of course.* Fuck, I'm so stupid.

I go back to the kitchen, quickly stuff Caitlin's tray back into her backpack and then run outside to where Caitlin is, by the pool. I might not have much time. She's still talking to that guy. I run up and kneel down by the edge of the pool. Caitlin turns to me and smiles.

"Hi, Hana! What's up?"

"Caitlin... what's in those brownies? Is it what I think?"

"Why? Did you eat one?"

"I ate part of one."

Caitlin starts laughing.

"Yeah. It's probably exactly what you think! Didn't you read my sign?"

"I did, but... a bit too late. I'm sorry, I saw food and I was hungry! Will I be okay?"

"Well, eating brownies isn't the same as smoking it. It's like a smoother high, but it's longer."

"How long?"

"I don't know, it depends. Maybe twelve hours?"

"Twelve hours? Oh my god, I'll die!"

"Don't panic. It might actually work for you better this way. People who don't like smoking sometimes get a better feeling from edibles. You might enjoy it. You'll find out soon! If something happens and you panic, just find me or one of the other girls, okay? I'll look after you if I need to."

"Okay."

"Don't stress! You can come and swim with me in the pool if you like!"

"Yeah, come swim in the pool!" says the guy she's with.

I'm nowhere near confident enough to just strip down and get in the pool the way Caitlin did. Especially with boys around, there's no way that could happen. How she has that kind of confidence I don't fucking know, but I sure don't.

"I'd rather not," I reply.

"Then you should probably sit down a bit and try to relax. Just keep your mind off it for now, if you had enough to get high, trust me, you'll know."

"Okay, that's an idea. I'll go back inside. Thanks!"

"That's okay. We're all right here."

Caitlin resumes talking to the guy she's with. I get up and walk back inside. Nobody's sitting on the couches so I take a free couch. I'm not that interested in talking to anyone here, so I'll just sit for a while. I look at the television in front of the couches, it's playing an image of a fireplace, which is weird and also boring. I get out my phone and start looking at messages.

"HANAAAAAAAAAAAA!"

I look up. It's Gyeongja. She's standing in front of me, dressed in exactly the same black hanbok that she wore last time I saw her, at that funeral. She sits down next to me and puts her arms around me, squeezing me tightly and putting her head against my shoulder. The sudden physical contact makes me jump a little.

"Hana! Hana Hana Hana! It's good to meet you again! I'm so happy to meet you again!"

"Hi, Gyeongja."

"I'm so happy to meet you! It's good to meet you!"

"Yes, we have established this..."

"Hana! I'm so happy to meet you! Have you killed any more people yet?"

I look around in a panic. I don't think anyone else is paying attention to us. Gyeongja continues.

"Because I have a list, you see! I want lots of people to die! Do you think you can do it for me? It's so good to meet you again! I'm so happy to meet you again!"

"We shouldn't talk about it here..." I whisper.

"Why not?"

Gyeongja finally stops squeezing me around the waist. I take a few seconds to get my breath back.

"There's lots of people here I don't know..."

"We can get to know them!"

"Yes but they might tell the police..."

"Oh. Yes. Well, we can use a code! How about when we want someone to die, we use a different word?"

"Like what?"

"I don't know?"

I just think of the first thing that comes to my head.

"Okay, we'll say we want them to 'get in the pool'. How about that?"

"That sounds great! There's lots of people who I'd like to see get in the pool! It's so good to meet you again! I'm so happy to see you! Have you seen your advert?"

"What advert?"

"You are in an advert for Hancel! With Shu!"

"Oh... yes, I was. No, I haven't seen it."

"Just search yourself and Hancel, you'll find it!"

I have my phone in my hand already so I search for the advert, it comes up immediately along with several articles about the advert. I press play on the video. It's a Chinese advert, fortunately it has Korean subtitles so I can follow along. I watch as the male narrator speaks in a deep voice.

The Hancel X870 – the future of phones has arrived.

There's an image of the phone rotating on a stand.

Classic lines, timeless aesthetics.

Shu is wearing a red and gold *qipao* and is seen holding the phone. I realise that it's the same outfit that she's wearing at the party right now. The scene changes, and Shu is now wearing a black suit and talking on the phone while looking into the distance, against a modern cityscape background.

Durable, without compromising elegance or style.

Shu wears a ballet dress and does a dance move which is filmed in slow motion, over a black background. I recognise the dance as the pre-chorus of the "Love Carousel" routine that I recently helped her with. While spinning between the poses, Shu reaches out a hand and gracefully grabs the phone, catching it in mid-air.

Powerful, yet so simple anybody can use it.

Shu is shown stepping me through how to use the phone. The camera zooms up on my relieved face as I realise which button generates the IMEI number, and then zooms up on Shu's face, smiling. The actual phone screen isn't shown here, so viewers wouldn't know what she was getting me to do, or that the entire interface was in Chinese. Shu gives the camera a thumbs up.

The phone you deserve, with the style you want.

A shot of Shu, standing still and smiling to the camera, next to another rotating image of the phone. The phone rotates and cycles through various colour options. With each new colour option shown, Shu is wearing a different coloured *qipao* to match the phone. On the final colour, which is red, Shu pumps her fist in the air and jumps.

Hancel - experience tomorrow today.

Another image of Shu smiling, she holds the phone up to her face and winks at the camera. I've seen enough. I scroll down and look at the video's comments, but they're mostly in Chinese so I don't know what they're saying. I keep scrolling down looking for Korean comments, after a while I find a few.

They sure did Hana dirty

Hana doesn't like Shu, check out her body language, she flinches away just a little when Shu comes close

"Anybody can use it, even a dumbass Korean" is what they're really saying, this ad is so racist

Is Hana a good actress or is she really so dumb that she does not know how to use a phone

Another Hancel fail, but Shu is pretty

Chinese junk by Chinese zoo monkeys, fuck off out of our country with your inferior products and stop riding on our idol pop to sell your junk

These two have no chemistry at all

Hancel's phones suck but Shu is in this commercial and she's my bias so I have to buy one now, I'll give it to my grandmother though, I don't want to use it

Hana looks stupid and the phone is stupid too so they're a good match, nobody buys Hancel

"What do you think?" asks Gyeongja.

"I think everyone at Hancel should get in the pool."

"Hana! It's so great to see you again!"

Gyeongja squeezes me tighter. I suddenly feel strange, like it's kind of funny. I'm not sure. Gyeongja is very weird. I guess I'm weird too, although what's weird really? I try to think of what to say to her. It's good that she is here but she is odd. I suddenly realise that my thoughts are racing and fragmenting. It must be the brownies. Everything's going fast in my head. This is worse than last time I was stoned. I don't know what to say. How do I say this to someone? I should say something to someone.

"What is it, Hana? You look upset!"

That's Gyeongja talking. How does she know that I'm upset? Oh, I'm crying, I just noticed. How did I not know that? How can I cry and not know?

"Hana?"

I need to say something to Gyeongja, but I don't know what. What do I say to Gyeongja? She's so strange, I guess she's kind of funny. But then maybe that isn't funny, that it's kind of funny. Wait, I need to tell her something, but why? I've forgotten why. Oh, that's right, I'm... I guess I'm freaking out. Help me. Oh my god.

"Hana?"

How do I fix this? I should get Caitlin. That's right. Caitlin said to talk to her. Caitlin will know what to do.

"Gyeongja... this is going to sound odd, but... can you get Caitlin please?"

"Okay Hana! What do I tell her?"

That's a good question. How do I explain it. I guess Caitlin will know what to do. Caitlin will know what to do. I just have to keep telling myself that, to trust her.

"Tell her to come here. She will know what to do."

Gyeongja gets up and walks off. Where is she going? Oh that's right, she's going to get Caitlin. There's a boy. Why is there a boy here?

"Hi, Hana! I'm Sunmin!"

Who the fuck? Who is this boy? Why is he here? Can he fuck off? I just stare at him.

"Hana, I just wanted to introduce myself! I always thought you were the prettiest in your group! So I had to come and say hello to you!"

Oh great, he's making a move. Maybe it's because Gyeongja is gone? Why is he here? Where is Caitlin?

"Hana, are you okay?" he asks.

Fuck this. I can't stand this. Where is Caitlin?

"No I'm not okay! Fuck off! Leave me alone!"

Sunmin kneels down in front of me.

"I'm so sorry to bother, Hana, I just..."

"Get the *fuck* out of my face!"

Sunmin backs away, bowing. Caitlin appears.

"Hana?"

I don't know what to say. I'm so happy to see Caitlin but I'm also so miserable.

"Hana, you're crying?"

Am I crying? That's right, I was crying before. I guess I'm still crying now. I guess it makes sense. I wonder where the guy went, I hope he doesn't come back. Caitlin is so nice. I'm so happy she's here, but I'm not happy because I can't think.

"It's started... it's like, really quick. Help me?"

Caitlin sits next to me on the couch and puts her arms around me. I start crying into her shirt. Her shoulder feels nice. I just realised she was in the pool.

"I'm sorry I got you out of the pool..."

"It's okay, Hana. I'm here."

"I'm sorry!"

"It's okay, Hana!"

Caitlin squeezes me tightly. I feel my heart skip a beat, but in a weird sudden way, not like normally. It feels strange. Maybe I have a heart problem? Maybe it's a medical emergency? It feels a little painful? I should tell Caitlin this.

"My heart feels funny, like it's skipping beats. I think I might need to go to hospital, it might be an emergency?"

Caitlin laughs and smiles at me.

"Don't be silly. You're not going to have a heart attack. Nobody in the history of the world has died from eating dope brownies. You're just stressed out because of your headspace right now. Here, let's breathe together."

Caitlin grabs my hand and puts it under her T-shirt, against her ribcage.

"Feel my chest expand and contract, and time your breathing, so you breathe when I do, okay?"

"Okay. You're not wearing underwear?"

"It was still wet. Don't worry about that. Just breathe."

Caitlin starts breathing slowly and I breathe along with her. It's helping, a little. I keep breathing along with Caitlin, she strokes my hair as we breathe together deeply on the couch and I try to control my crying and my mind. I'm so lucky to have her in my life.

124. PREPARATION

I'm in the agency bathroom, I've just finished getting changed and I'm looking at myself in the mirror above the sink. Under my eyes I'm really dark and swollen from crying a lot last night at the party and I have a slight headache. I think I'm still a little bit high, it's hard to be sure. After some sleep, the pace of my thoughts has finally slowed down to the point where it's not upsetting and I can interact with people without feeling weird. It's just as well that we don't have any training today, instead we're preparing to go on a van trip to the Summer Soak festival, so that will buy me some time to calm down more and rest my head. I'm wearing blue denim shorts cut off at the upper thigh and a white midriff-exposing T-shirt, this is my costume for the event. Of course this outfit has been picked out by the agency, I wouldn't wear something like this anywhere by choice. I should go back to the dorm room so the next person can come in here and get changed.

"Hurry up in there, stop daydreaming!"

It's Iseul's voice, yelling from the other side of the door. I grab the rest of my clothes and exit the bathroom. As soon as I open the door Iseul pushes past me and walks straight in.

"Took your time. Hey, Hana..."

"What?"

Iseul turns around and looks me up and down.

"That's actually a good outfit. Looks good on you."

"Okay...er, thanks?"

"Hey it's better than what I'm going to have to wear."

"What have they got you in?"

"Some bullshit. Anyway leave me alone, I don't want you staring at me getting changed, lesbian."

Iseul is annoying me right now but my head is still tender and I don't have the energy to fight her. I ignore her and walk into the dorms. The other girls are sitting on their beds, packing their gear, and getting ready, except Shu who is lying down, asleep for some reason. Everyone else has already changed into their outfits. Youngsook has a similar outfit to mine, while Shu, Nari, and Caitlin all have threadbare green bikini-type clothes. I get into my bunk and lie down, hoping to get some relaxation in before the long van trip.

"Hey Hana, take one."

Nari holds out a plastic tub next to me, I sit up, reach inside it, and grab a stick of some weird black sinewy substance.

"What is this stuff?"

"I told you all that I was going to improve our food supply here, and I mean it. We need energy to do all these performances. I don't want us collapsing on stage again."

I put the black thing in my mouth and chew on it, it's sweet and spicy, it tastes good. The strong flavours make me feel more alert, distracting me a little from my headache.

"Okay, but what is it?"

"It's *yukpo*. Take a second stick and hide it, eat it in the van right before we get to the venue, or earlier if you need to. It's important that we don't get caught with food so swallow it quickly if you think you might get busted."

I nod and take a second stick, then lie back down on the bed. I'm ready to go but I don't have anything left to pack so I grab my phone from under the pillow and take a look at the "girls" chat group to kill some time.

Gyeongja: party was stupid, when is girls night

Astrid: we'll work it out

Gyeongja: GIRLS NIGHT

Amna: hey isn't Pearlfive going back to Music Train tomorrow?

Ora: two days

Gyeongja: GIRLS NIGHT

I don't feel like engaging with this chat, it's exhausting to follow and I'll worry that my head will start hurting more. I put my phone down and stare at the bottom of the bunk above my head. I then hear the dorm door open.

"This outfit is bullshit!"

It's Iseul's voice, I lift my head up to look at her. Looks like she's scored the same skimpy green bikini-style outfit that Caitlin, Nari, and Shu all got. Iseul turns around and shows her back tattoo to all of us.

"The fucking CEO knows I can't wear this! There's no coverage at all! What the fuck am I going to do?"

"Just don't ask Ijun that question," Nari laughs.

"Youngsook and Hana, how come I have to wear a bikini and you two get the semi-decent outfit?"

Youngsook shrugs at Iseul.

"Don't get shitty with me, I didn't request anything. Maybe if you'd been a bit less of an annoying pest about it to Ijun, she might've worked something out..."

"Oh, screw off! It's not my fault, I can't go showing this tattoo. I should have your outfit, at least I'd get some coverage. This space at the back here needs to be filled!"

"You had some space at the back filled last night, so I hear."

"What?"

Youngsook starts laughing.

"I heard you had two guys at once."

Iseul looks annoyed. I think Youngsook has hit a nerve.

"That's not true! Shut up."

"Just what I heard."

"What would you know?"

"Three people on the mattress has a lot of inertia. The whole lounge room area could hear you getting pounded upstairs. I thought the ceiling was going to cave in."

"You were chasing boys the entire night! How did you even have time to hear shit?"

"At least I waited until one cock was finished inside me before I let the next one in!"

I can hear Caitlin giggling in the bunk above mine, she thinks this is hilarious. I don't really care about this conversation, but it's funny to see Iseul get increasingly annoyed by Youngsook.

"Cut it out, you two. We have to get moving soon, try to be serious for once," says Nari.

Nari's trying to defuse the argument but Youngsook doesn't care, she just starts laughing more.

"Give me another *yukpo* and I'll shut up."

"No. You're too heavy and you've already had one stick, no more for you."

"You're just jealous because when you change your tampon the moths fly out."

Nari stares at Youngsook, and says nothing but just gives her an unimpressed glare. Meanwhile Caitlin is laughing so much that she's nearly falling out of her bunk. Youngsook continues.

"How long has it been since anything else has been up there? You should have come to the party. Next time come along, we'll organise an 'Iseul Special' for you!"

Iseul throws a pillow at Youngsook's head, which misses and lands on the floor next to Nari. Seeing that Nari is distracted, Youngsook quickly grabs the plastic tub of *yukpo* sticks out of Nari's hand and runs out of the dorm.

"Thanks for the food, nice knowing you!" shouts Youngsook as she runs off.

Nari runs off and chases Youngsook down the corridor.

"Give that back! I'll catch you!" Nari screams.

"See you around sometime!" laughs Youngsook.

Nari and Youngsook quickly run out of earshot. Now that I can't hear them anymore, I notice that Caitlin is still laughing.

"Hey Shu, you're up!" says Caitlin between giggles.

I turn to look at Shu who is sitting up in her bed, stretching her arms out and yawning.

"I've been ready for ages! Is it time to go yet?"

"Mr Park will get us soon."

"So, not yet?"

"Not just yet."

"Oh great, I can sleep more!"

Shu lies back down in her bed. I watch her trying to get to sleep, about half a minute later I can hear her lightly snoring. I don't like to admit that I'm envious of anything about this annoying Chinese bitch but her ability to sleep on cue is supernatural, I really do wish I could do that.

125. SUMMER SOAK

"We are Halcyon! *Annyeong-haseyo-Halcyon-imnida!*"

We all bow at ninety degrees to the audience, in our ridiculous tiny outfits. I put one hand in front of my chest as I bow, so people holding phones and cameras can't point their lenses down my neckline, and put the other hand on my headset earpiece so it doesn't fall out of my ear. The headset microphones are not switched on, but as usual the earpieces still work so the sound crew can talk to us. Nari has the only working microphone, which is hand-held and covered in a clear film and a fuzzy tip, she addresses the audience.

"It's great to be here at Summer Soak! We are so happy to see you, are you happy to see us?"

Some mild cheering comes from the crowd, as a few jets of water randomly fly up from the fans at the front of the stage. I look out at the people who are watching us, a lot of them are dressed similar to how we are. It also seems that every second audience member has a high-powered water pistol of some kind.

"That was a pretty pathetic effort. Come on, you can do better than that! Are you happy to see us?"

Another mild cheer. The crowd don't seem to be very excited. Nari puts her microphone down and turns to us.

"What can we do, team, to make this crowd care?"

"I've got an idea!" says Caitlin, playing with one of her bikini straps.

"Anything but that!" replies Nari.

"Let's just go straight into a song!" says Shu. "They might like us more after we show what we can do! We can do the introductions later, once they decide they like us!"

"We can't just change the order. The sound engineer won't like it."

"They don't have a choice. If we say we're going to sing they'll have to start playing the music no matter what! Or we'll just stand there and wait!"

Nari thinks about it for a few seconds and nods.

"Okay, let's try that, I'll skip the introduction and then we'll go straight into 'Love Light' and if the techs don't like it, too bad."

Nari turns back to the audience and brings the microphone back up to her lips.

"We're going to skip the introductions for now, and just go straight into a song. We hope that's okay with you! When you're mfff..."

A massive jet of water sprayed by a fan in the front row hits Nari right in the face. Nari coughs a little, spitting water out of her mouth. The audience laughs and then cheers a little louder than before. Iseul walks up and gives the audience member a squirt back with a large water cannon that she's wearing over the top of her bikini outfit, shaped like a rifle. The water rifle connects via a hose to two large scuba-style water tanks that Iseul is wearing on her back, our CEO's idea to cover up her back tattoo, that he only revealed to us a few seconds before we went on stage. I guess he wanted to make Iseul sweat for the longest possible time, what an asshole. Nari addresses the audience again.

"Come on people, please behave, after all we're professionals here. As I was saying, we're going to..."

A whole bunch of fans instantly unload their water pistols onto Nari's face, stopping her from talking once again. Nari squints and tries to block the water sprays with her hands but there's just too many of them. The audience lets out a big cheer as she squints and coughs.

"Okay, we seem to be under attack here! Halcyon girls, we're officially declaring war on this audience! We need to fight back against this oppression! Hana and Shu, go to the water cannons! Your mission is to drown anyone who stops us from speaking or performing, okay?"

There are two big water cannons flanking the stage. I run over to the cannon closest to my side, it's basically a large hose mounted onto a huge metal tripod. There are two big handles to control the nozzle direction, a large silver lever on the side, and a label:

WARNING: this device can cause serious injury, do not aim at the face or eyes.

I don't see any other controls so I guess the lever is what I use to make the water come out.

"Don't be shy! Take no prisoners!" says Nari.

I point the cannon to the front of the stage and pull the lever. Water rushes out of the hose with such force that it takes me by surprise. My first jet of water hits Nari straight in the side of the head, the audience cheers again, louder than before.

"Hey, watch for the collateral damage!" shouts Nari.

I redirect the spray onto the audience, and start moving the hose around, trying to hit as many audience members in the face as possible. The audience fights back, drenching me with their pistols. Every few seconds I also spray Nari's body a little bit with water, and the audience respond with more cheers each time. I look over at the other side of the stage, Shu is just randomly spraying water everywhere, seemingly trying to get the jet of water as high and as far as possible out into the audience for no particular reason I can think of.

"Okay, that's enough!"

I stop squirting people at the front of the stage and watch Nari.

"Okay, we're going to sing 'Love Light' now. Cheer for us, or else we'll drench you!"

The audience cheers loudly and squirt more water in Nari's direction. Nari makes a gesture to the people in the sound booth and the music starts up, it looks like Shu's plan worked.

You came into my room, and gave me your heart / I know why you're here, and what you want to do / Time is precious, and I can feel your soul aching / Let's make the most of us, let me take care of you

There's no dance routine for this song, so Nari, Youngsook and Caitlin all just wander the stage aimlessly while pretending to sing the song, while myself and Shu stay on the cannons. Iseul isn't even pretending to sing, she's just running around at the front of the stage occasionally squirting random people. I'm sure our lip-syncing doesn't look very convincing but I don't think anyone in this audience cares.

There's no need to rationalise our love / The meeting of our hearts is its own reward

That was my line in the song but I think someone else mimed it, or maybe they didn't, whatever. I notice Caitlin running over to me, holding her hands in front of her chest while laughing. She turns around and I see what's happened, the straps at the back of her bikini top have come undone, so she's keeping her bikini in place with her hands. Caitlin might be laughing but she obviously needs my help. I quickly let go of the water cannon and run around behind her to do up the straps. As I do her up, the audience starts hollering and we both become soaked with water from all directions.

I'll turn the switch / I'll shine the love light / It's automatic, fantastic / We will always be together / As long as you wish it / As long as you want it

I give Caitlin a quick tap on the back to indicate that she's good to go, she gets the message and starts walking around the stage again, doing various suggestive poses to match the song's theme as she mimes the words. I notice some of the audience members are trying to get my attention and gesturing to Caitlin at the same time, I think they want me to shoot her with the water cannon. We're both completely soaked anyway so I figure I might as well, and let fly with a burst of water at her body, also trying to get all the other girls in the same spray. The jet takes Caitlin by surprise and she starts laughing even harder as she slips around on the stage. I then receive a massive jet to the face myself; Shu has noticed me spraying the other girls and has decided to get revenge on behalf of the team. The force of the water is too much, I squint and lose my grip on the cannon. The audience roars with laughter.

You came into my heart, and stole my soul / Now you're gone, and I don't know what to do / Time is precious, and I can feel my heart yearning / For the time that we next meet, let me take care of you

Is anyone even listening to our rubbish song at this point? Nari motions for Iseul to attack me with her water rifle, she starts squirting me as well. I get back on the cannon and swivel it around so I can hit Iseul in the face with it, but it's hard to aim because Shu keeps spraying me in the head and it's interfering with my vision. The audience cheering gets louder and louder, they are loving the chaos on stage. I think at this point the entire group has given up on even trying to mime the song. I look down and realise that I'm so drenched that my white top is almost completely transparent and I might as well be up here in just my underwear. No wonder the audience are making such a noise whenever I get hit. What a bunch of assholes. I point my water cannon back in the direction of the audience, looking for any men who are looking at me, so I can squirt them in the eyes and hopefully take out an eyeball. I start thinking about how much better it would be if this gun fired something other than water. Bullets are the obvious choice, but then maybe some kind of acid would be even better. I smile as I think about the idiots in the crowd dissolving away in a puddle of green fluid, the acid burning their flesh and filling the air with toxic smoke. If only the reality of this stupid event could keep pace with my imagination.

126. ARRIVAL

"Ladies and gentlemen, Seoul Airlines welcomes you to Los Angeles International Airport. The local time is six twenty-five in the evening and the temperature is thirty-one degrees Celsius with moderate south-westerly winds. For your safety and the safety of those around you, please remain seated with your..."

"Oh thank fuck. I thought we were about to die!"

I relax my grip around Caitlin's waist, who I've been holding onto for the last fifteen minutes during the descent. Caitlin smiles and strokes my hair as our plane rolls steadily across the tarmac.

"Hey Hana, congratulations on surviving your first flight! How do you feel?"

The motion of her hand makes me flinch a little. Caitlin notices this straight away.

"You still don't like your hair this way, do you?"

"I'm not used to it."

"The shoulder length look suits you. I know why you don't like it, but you really should consider keeping it. Not only does it look cute, but forcing yourself to go

219

without the longer hair might also force you to deal with like, trauma and things, you know?"

"I don't want to deal with trauma though. I could just grow my hair again and not worry about it."

"Well, that's if the agency lets you."

I sigh. I know Caitlin is right. There's no guarantee that the company will ever let me grow my hair out. I should at least try to get more comfortable with the shorter style.

"Hey, we've got Internet back, right?"

"Yeah but use my phone if you want to look at stuff. Yours won't be set up for roaming in the States."

Caitlin hands me her mobile phone. I immediately go to the 'girls' chat group, and hold the phone up so we can both see it.

Me: we've landed!

Sumire: congratulations

Astrid: kick ass for us over there

Gyeongja: hey is Hana around?

I guess I'd better reply.

Me: it's Hana, I'm on Caitlin's phone as she has roaming for the US or something and I don't

Gyeongja: YAY HANAAAAAAAAAAAA

Ora: Hana, Gyeongja has had a hard time.

Me: what's up?

Ora: we did Music Train last night. That asshole PD assaulted Gyeongja.

Me: Gyeongja are you ok?

Gyeongja: MR JEONG NEEDS TO GET IN THE POOL

Caitlin looks at me strangely but I'm too focused on the chat to really react.

Me: you're okay though?

Shu: I'm so sorry, Gyeongja! He's a bad person!

Gyeongja: IN THE POOL! IN THE POOL!

Ora: she's alright for now, just a bit shaken. We don't want to go back though. I won't say what he did or repeat what he said, but it will be worse next time. He made some threats

Gyeongja: IN THE POOL!

Me: what a prick. he did the same shit with me both times I've been on that show

Sumire: it's because Gyeongja is the maknae and so is Hana. That's his thing, assaulting the youngest

Ora: right

Gyeongja: IN THE POOL!

Shu: It's true! He looked at me really weird, until he found out Hana was the maknae. Then he just looked at Hana and ignored the rest of us!

Ora: you know, while I personally wouldn't advocate or encourage harm towards any individual, if something unpleasant happened to a certain PD just by sheer circumstance, there would be very few tears shed by Pearlfive as a group. Just saying

Sumire: except Mia, I bet she would cry

Ora: Mia's not in the chat group for a reason

Astrid: Come on, Mia's not that bad

Sumire: yes she is

Astrid: okay, yes she is

Ora: anyway take care Hana let us know how it all goes over there

Gyeongja: GOOD LUCK HANAAAAAAAAAA

Ora: say hi to Caitlin, don't do anything I wouldn't do

Me: so do whatever, then

Ora: pretty much

Caitlin taps me on the shoulder and stands up.

"Hey we're getting out now. Come on, let's go."

Everyone gets out of their seats and immediately clogs the aisle while they fish their bags out of the overhead compartments. I can't move anywhere or even stand up because of all the people and their huge bags. I suppose I could push my way through but I really don't like dealing with queues and people squished together, it reminds me of school cafeteria line. I look up at Caitlin.

"I'll wait. I'll go when it's safe."

"It's not unsafe, just crowded. Come on."

"You can go if you like. I'll come out later."

"Okay, see you in the terminal."

Caitlin zips out into the aisle, grabs her suitcase from the overhead locker and somehow manages to disappear from view. I'm not following her just yet, I'll wait until the crowd has mostly moved along. I feel a vibration in my hand and realise that I still have a tight grip on Caitlin's phone. I look at the screen, Caitlin has received a message from someone called Jerome, who has an avatar of a young muscular man with dark skin in bathing trunks, standing by a beach with a surfboard. I wonder if he really looks like that or if that's just some random photo of a surfer. I'm bored so I take a look at the message, it's all in English so I can't understand it, and it's half emojis of fruit for some reason. I scroll back a little through the history of Jerome and Caitlin's texts. All the messages are going one way, Caitlin hasn't replied to any of them. Another vibration. A new message, from Shu.

Shu: Where are you and Hana? We're almost at immigration!

I'd better get moving. I quickly stand up and move out to the aisle, which is easy to do as the crowd has thinned out a bit now. I look in the overhead locker for my bag, it's slid right to the back during the flight, or maybe the other passengers bumped it back there when they were getting their own bags out. I stretch out my free hand but I can't reach it. Shit, this is going to make me late. I stretch out my hand again, this time jumping up at the same time to try and get some extra reach and still no luck. Suddenly I flinch back as I feel someone touching me from behind. A tall man reaches his arm over, grabs my bag and puts it down by my feet. I look up at him, he's maybe about ten years older than me, absolutely huge, well over six feet, I'm not sure which country he's from but he doesn't look Korean. I should thank him, he didn't have to do that.

"*Kamsa-hamnida!*" I say, bowing as I grab my suitcase and quickly move away from him and down the aisle. I'm trying to be fast as I'm conscious that I'm clogging up everyone's progress off the plane. I don't know why I care about this, but I do.

"*Anieyo!*" I hear him respond from somewhere behind me, in a perfect Seoul accent.

I keep walking quickly, I have to catch up to the others. I don't really know where I'm going and there's lots of signs here that I can't read, but everyone's moving in the same direction so I just follow the crowd down the aisle, through a bridge into the terminal, and then into a corralled section of floorspace.

"Hana!"

It's Shu's voice. I look around, and see Shu jumping up and down, waving her arms in the far corner of the room. The other girls and Mr Park are all with her, waiting in a cordoned-off line, flanked by airport security. I quickly walk over to Caitlin and hand her phone back.

"Sorry I'm late! I couldn't reach my bag!"

Caitlin smiles at me.

"Don't worry about it, you didn't miss much except us standing around. Oh, hey..."

We're suddenly waved forward by the security guards, to a desk, where a man in uniform sits opposite us in front of a laptop. I notice immediately that he's Korean.

"Travel documents please," he says to us, smiling.

Mr Park hands a stack of passports over to the man, who opens and inspects each one. I guess he's the immigration officer. As he opens each passport, he starts looking at each one of us, matching us up to our passports. He starts smiling more and more, until he gets to Caitlin's.

His smile then evaporates and he suddenly has a concerned look.

"What brings you to LA?" he asks the group.

"We're on tour!" says Shu.

Mr Park gives Shu a subtle nudge on the back with his hand. Shu clears her throat and straightens her posture.

"What sort of tour?" the man asks.

"We're... touring the country! On a holiday!"

"Seeing the sights?"

"Yes! Lots of... things to see!"

The man then looks at Caitlin.

"Okay, so why are *you* with them?"

Caitlin smiles.

"Same reason. I'm with the girls!"

The man sighs and then starts typing something on his laptop while looking at our documentation. We sit in silence for a couple minutes as his eyes flick back and forth between the screen, our faces, and our paperwork. Eventually he turns the screen around so it's facing us. There's a video on there. It's us, performing at Summer Soak festival.

"Touring the country? What for, exactly?" he asks.

"We like the beach! LA has the best beaches!" says Shu.

The man rolls his eyes.

"I'd just like to point out that lying to an immigration officer carries serious penalties."

The man swivels his laptop around and starts typing more, then after a few seconds shows us the screen again. It's an advert for the Join Hands For Peace festival, the reason why we're here. A photo flashes up of our group, with all of us clearly visible in it. The man touches the screen and freezes it at that moment.

"Just seeing the sights?"

"Yes... like the sights of... a concert! But I didn't lie! We do like the beach a lot!" says Shu.

The immigration officer starts laughing at us. At least he has a sense of humour.

"Nice try, but your visas are not correct, we can't let you into the country. Except for... here, Caitlin Hamilton, your paperwork is fine, because you're a United States citizen, you are allowed to come in. The rest of you are all getting on board the next plane back to Seoul."

"We're a team. I'm staying with the girls," says Caitlin, as she puts one arm lightly around my waist.

"If you want to stay with them, you have to pay for your flight. They will be deported at no cost, but since your travel back to Seoul is voluntary, you have to pay."

"Fine."

"You also realise that if you stay with them, this could affect your future travel to the United States?"

Caitlin looks at me.

"Does this mean that you might never be able to come back here?" I ask.

Caitlin wraps her other arm around me and brings her face up to mine.

"There's nothing left for me back in Oakland."

I try to think of something to say but Caitlin stops my train of thought by planting her lips on mine and giving me a long, passionate kiss.

"I'm with you, okay?" Caitlin whispers.

"Okay," I reply back.

"Break it up, you two!" says Mr Park.

We immediately sigh and separate from each other.

"I understand," Caitlin says to the immigration officer.

"Well, good luck to you two," he says back, nodding.

I suddenly feel like I want to cry, I feel the tears rushing forth. I grab Caitlin's hand tightly, she accepts it and squeezes mine back, even tighter.

127. EXCUSES

"So, what excuse do you girls have?"

We're all lined up in the gym, in our tracksuits, after just having arrived back at the dorms from our American trip that wasn't. We haven't even gone into the dorms or unpacked our bags yet. We know Mr Park is angry at us because of the visa situation. We didn't know the visas were incorrect however, he's the idiot who put in the applications, all we did was have our photos taken and sign where he told us to, and lie at the immigration gate, like he also told us to. What would I even know about a visa application anyway? Mr Park scans back and forth between us, waiting for someone to speak. It's not going to be me, unless he specifically asks for me. I've already nearly been thrown out of the group once, I'm not risking that again. Ijun is standing next to him, playing with her new phone that Iseul got for her two days ago, she doesn't seem remotely interested in what's going on. Iseul clears her throat, it looks like she's about to speak. There's no way Iseul the group nepo baby is going to get thrown out so I'm glad she's stepping up, as she has the least to lose out of all of us.

"Mr Park CEO, about the visas..."

"This is not about the visas!" Mr Park snaps back.

It's not about the visas? Then what the hell is he so angry for? What did we even do wrong this time? Iseul is silent, she clearly doesn't know what to say next. We all look at each other, checking to see if anyone else in the line-up has anything other than a look of confusion on their face. Mr Park takes a deep breath. This isn't good.

"I see that you are all very intent on playing dumb. Everyone bring your bags and empty them out, in front of me, right here. Do it now."

Mr Park points to the space in front of his feet, on the gym floor. We all carry our luggage over from the far wall into the centre of the room and start unloading the contents neatly in front of his feet – it's just clothing, shoes, and mundane miscellaneous stuff.

"Faster, I haven't got all day!"

Mr Park grabs Youngsook's suitcase out of her hand, and tips it upside down, spraying clothes all over the floor, and then throwing the suitcase off to the side of the gym.

"Come on, step it up, lazybones! We wouldn't want to accidentally lose a precious kilojoule, would we?"

Youngsook steps back into the line-up, Mr Park having done her job for her. I can see that she's trying to hold back tears. I quickly empty my bag and slide it away, and the others do the same. Within a few seconds the floor is covered in clothes.

"Ijun, go through that pile."

Ijun continues to play with her phone. Two seconds later, Mr Park grabs Ijun's phone out of her hand and throws it against the gym wall. The phone shatters into half a dozen plastic pieces. Ijun's face immediately turns bitter, she stares at Mr Park.

"That was brand new! You just broke it!"

"It'll be you who is broken in a minute if you don't get down on your knees and *go through that pile of clothes!*"

Ijun quickly kneels down and starts sorting through the clothes.

"What am I looking for?"

"Anything but clothing!"

After about a minute Ijun has sorted through the pile, and made three smaller piles out of it; a pile of clothes, another smaller pile of shoes, and a third pile with all the other items; some toiletries, three novels, two magazines with the Seoul Airlines logo on them, Iseul's electronic tablet, a thigh resistance band, a pink plush toy, and a wristwatch. Surely he's not this upset because a couple of the girls stole magazines from the plane?

"Ijun, get up. Go search the dorms."

"For what?"

"Anything that shouldn't be there."

Ijun gets on her feet and walks out of the room into the hallway, slamming the door behind her. Mr Park stares at us in silence. I can hear the sound of Ijun opening and closing the bunk drawers loudly, it's obvious that she's venting her frustration by making as much noise as she possibly can. I suddenly realise what Mr Park has sent Ijun to look for. We left all our contraband food in the dorms. I start shivering. Ijun's going to come back with all that stuff and Mr Park is going to tear strips off of all of us as soon as he knows we're not sticking to the agency diet. I look at the faces of the other girls, they look nervous, I think they've also realised what's going on. After a minute of banging, Ijun walks back into the gym.

"There's nothing there," says Ijun.

Mr Park gives Ijun a cynical look. Ijun continues.

"There's nothing there! Except a bong! And drugs!"

"I doubt that."

"I checked everything!"

"That was too fast to check everything."

"It was easy because their clothes are here in the gym and that's all they have! There's nothing there, I swear!"

Mr Park stares at Ijun and raises his eyebrows. It's obvious that he doesn't believe her, and neither do I. We had so much food we're not supposed to have in those drawers. I can't believe that Ijun is lying to cover our asses. That, or something else happened, which would be weird. Ijun stares back at Mr Park defiantly.

"Are you calling me a liar? I don't lie unlike some people! Do you want to go and look for yourself? Huh?"

"Then do you want to explain how these girls are still incapable of losing any weight whatsoever even though we've cut their meals down to practically nothing?"

"So you admit that their diet isn't sufficient? What do you want them doing, passing out even more than they already do? Do you have any idea how we look to the public and the fans when our group collapses on stage repeatedly? Do you know who deals with that? Do you know how sick I am of waiting by hospital beds?"

"Don't change the subject."

"Why not? The subject needs changing!"

"I'm not having this discussion here, come into my office."

Mr Park and Ijun start walking away, still arguing with each other as they walk over to the admin door.

"I have to mop up the online mess every day! And no-one's buying it! What do I say to the one thousandth person who says 'TME need to treat the girls better', have you thought of that? What do you want me to write back, 'no fucking shit'? Is that what you want?"

"That's not a comment even worthy of a response."

"If I don't respond, we look like criminals!"

"If you do respond you add fuel to the fire. The public have no view of what goes on inside here, nor should they have it. Why aren't you ignoring negative feedback?"

"You're the one who put me in charge of public relations. Am I in charge or not? I'm supposed to not relate to the public now?"

"You have to pick your moment."

"Sounds like shit to me!"

"Ijun..."

"The fans smell shit at this agency and so do I! I also know exactly which asshole it's coming out of!"

Ijun turns to us just before she disappears through the admin door.

"Girls, no training, do whatever the *fuck* you want today, I don't give a fuck! Our CEO Mr Park Shit Ass is a fuc... ow!"

Mr Park grabs Ijun by her hair and the door to the office slams shut. Ijun and Mr Park then both start screaming at each other from behind the door. I can't make out any of it because they're both screaming at the same time and not listening to each other, so it's just a lot of yelling. I then hear another door slam, which is no doubt their office door. They're screaming so loud that I can still hear their muffled yelling, interrupted by bursts of furniture moving around and the sound of unknown things breaking. A shiver goes down my body each time I hear a loud furniture sound. We all look at each other.

"He's going to kill her," says Nari.

"Maybe she's going to kill him," says Iseul.

"I don't like her chances, he's way stronger. She'd need some outside help."

"Quiet Nari, don't give Hana ideas like that."

Too late, Iseul. I've had that idea for a long time.

128. GUARDIAN ANGEL

"Hey Hana, come up here."

"I'd love to, but I'm scared. You come down here."

"No. Come on, you can do it. It's only a bunk bed, you're not going to fall off and die, I promise."

"I'm afraid of heights!"

"You were just in a plane!"

"That's different, I can't fall off a plane! Also I had no choice! I have a choice about this!"

"Come on. I've got something to show you."

"What is it?"

"Not telling. I'll show you what it is when you get up here. But you'll like it."

I sigh and crawl out of my bunk bed. I gradually ascend the precarious-looking mini ladder on the side of Caitlin's bunk, and climb up into her bed. Caitlin grabs my arm to help me up, and then slides over to where the bed meets the wall to clear a spot for me.

"Can I lie on the side by the wall? This is scary."

Caitlin smiles.

"No, you can't! Don't worry, I got you. Just lie here next to me."

I sigh and slide up next to Caitlin, and she wraps her arm around me to secure me in place.

"Okay, I guess I can handle this. It's kind of cozy."

"You two don't get any ideas, you aren't allowed to be doing any lesbian shit in here," says Nari.

"We weren't going to, but now that you've given me ideas, hey Hana do you wanna do some lesbian shit?"

"Why Caitlin, sure!" I reply.

Caitlin gives me a wink, which means the trolling of Nari is about to commence.

"You know I've got some strap-ons now, and a neat new DP dildo... or I would if someone hadn't removed all our stuff from the dorms..."

"Shut up, Caitlin!" says Nari.

"How about *you* shut up and stop being a bitch? We're allowed to lie together and just chill, fuck. You asked for it by being an asshole."

"Hey it's not like you two haven't got it on in here before, our paranoia isn't without reason!"

"And *we will again* if you don't stop bringing it up whenever we get within three metres of each other!"

"What the hell is a DP dildo?" I ask Caitlin.

"A dildo for DPs."

"But what's DP?"

"Double penetration."

"What's that?"

"Okay, so let me describe in detail what happens during a double penetration..."

Caitlin suddenly gets hit in the face by a flying pillow, an accurate and firm throw that could only have come from Nari.

"I said *no lesbian shit!* Oh my god, can you two behave for once in your lives?"

Caitlin, me and Youngsook all start laughing at Nari's reaction.

"You know they're trolling you, right? The more you react in that homophobic way, the more they'll do it!" says Youngsook.

"It's not homophobic to just want to relax in bed late at night and not hear these two talking about sex. Is it too much to ask?"

I ignore Nari and keep talking to Caitlin.

"What did you want to show me? Not the dildo..."

"No, silly. This."

Caitlin slides a magazine out from under her bed covers. It's one of the flight magazines from the plane. She opens it up and starts flipping through the pages.

"Couldn't you have just thrown this down to my bunk? Why did I have to come up here?"

"I want to see your reaction. Here, read."

Caitlin opens up a magazine page. It's an interview with Yohan of EB-K. Caitlin points to a paragraph in the middle of the interview. I squint at the letters and start reading.

Interviewer: Despite your status as an idol, you've been very outspoken about support for the film "The Love Complete", and now it's been rumoured that you're taking a role in the post-production?

Yohan: I don't know what "taking a role" means exactly, before claiming such a term, I would want to understand its meaning more precisely. But due to my musical background, director Han Leejung asked me about who I would like to see on the soundtrack, as some parts of the soundtrack and sound design are not finalised yet. I suggested some talented people.

Interviewer: May we ask who?

Yohan: I can't talk about aspects that are not finalised, but I gave Han Leejung a list of people who I feel would find the film especially relevant to their interests.

Interviewer: Not even a clue?

Yohan: I have been meeting several new people lately as part of a project to protect the wellbeing of performers in this industry that are at a natural disadvantage. I would like to see some of those performers in roles such as this. I will have more details on that to share soon.

Interviewer: What type of disadvantages can affect performers heavily?

Yohan: Those that are innate to our bodies and our selves, our true selves. We cannot control everything about our existence, but there is an expectation to put on a certain homogenic face to the public regardless. This can make people feel pressured, and while the public deserves the best product, performers also deserve to have their physical and emotional labour acknowledged and respected. It's a serious issue, and there are serious health impacts. I hope I can do well to increase the quality of life for performers in our idol system who find themselves at a disadvantage. To this end, I have a special plan to make this world better for struggling artists.

I turn and look at Caitlin.

"Sorry but I don't even understand what this fucking shit means? What is he even saying?"

Caitlin laughs.

"He's choosing his words carefully, but what he's basically saying is that Han Leejung asked him 'what singers should I use for my new lesbian as shit movie?' and his reply was 'here's a list of some people I met recently who are actual lesbians and they also sing a bit, why not use one of those'. So since you met him recently, and you're like the most obvious lesbian ever, you're probably one of the people he put forward. I'm sure there weren't that many. So your chance of picking up something here is really good."

"But I can't sing? Like, at all?"

"Hasn't stopped you here yet, has it?"

"I guess not. Will he be mad though, or her, if they find out I'm basically talentless?"

Youngsook snorts.

"Don't worry, they have machines for talent now!"

"Does he know absolutely for sure that you're lesbian?" Caitlin asks.

"I'm n..."

Caitlin raises her eyebrow at me. I sigh.

"I'm sorry, it's just habit! Yes. Yes he does."

"Then it's you. I bet it's you. You'll get a call soon."

The dorm door opens. I peer over the edge of Caitlin's bed. Ijun is standing in the doorway, wearing her usual black and red school uniform, and carrying a large plastic garbage bag.

"*Sillyehamnida...*"

"Hi Ijun!" says Shu, waving annoyingly.

"Are you okay?" Iseul asks.

Ijun ignores Iseul's question. She puts the garbage bag on the floor of the dorm.

"These are everyone's things."

"You had them?" Youngsook asks.

"Oh wow! You're our guardian angel!" says Shu.

We all bow in Ijun's direction.

"I did a cleanout while you were all on the flight. Mr Park talked about doing a raid of the dorm room just before he left but didn't have time and said he'd do it when he got back because he knows you are all sneaking food. I didn't think he meant straight away, but I thought I'd better do it to be careful you know because..."

Ijun suddenly puts her head down and starts crying. Iseul jumps down from her bunk and approaches Ijun, seemingly to comfort her, but Ijun takes a step backward toward the doorway. Iseul stops. Ijun just continues to stand there and cry. This is awkward, nobody seems to know what to do. Eventually Ijun starts talking through her tears, with great effort.

"You will... find nothing is missing. Youngsook, I put the camera for you in the... bag with all the other stuff. There are recordings on it. They are important! Play them for all the girls, in the order I made them! And only the girls! Don't get caught! In this room only! And once you know, don't tell! Then, delete everything, straight away!"

"Okay, thanks Ijun. I will!" says Youngsook.

"Then record an apology video for the travel debacle, because the American fans are upset. We should explain ourselves to them."

"What should I say?"

"I don't know. Just apologise. Try not to blame any one individual, make it look sincere. You don't all have to be in the video. Get Shu to do it. Everybody likes Shu, she's impossible for people to hate."

I beg to differ. Shu does a little salute.

"Yes Ijun, I will apologise! You can trust me!"

Ijun takes a shaky step forward and looks at Iseul.

"If you want to help me, or make me feel better, just get me another phone. Make sure you get a case with it. I... will thank you for doing this only."

"You know I will. What sort?"

"Anything new and good, just not another Hancel. Their phones are a total trash pile!"

Shu starts giggling, and so do I. Ijun smiles just a little at us both, before turning around and leaving the room without another word.

129. IJUN'S VIDEOS

"Well, that was more awkward than usual," says Nari.

Youngsook grabs the bag that Ijun left on the floor.

"I'm getting the camera out, then you can all just pass the bag around. I don't have anything else that will be in there for me."

"What, no hidden food? You?" asks Nari.

"I ate it all already!"

"No wonder you're fat!"

"I've had enough body shaming from the CEO today, don't *you* start! I'm starving right now if it makes you feel any better!"

"Fine, just get the camera out."

Youngsook fishes out the camera and starts it up, while Shu takes the bag off her and starts poking around in it.

"Put the camera on my bunk, so we can all watch," says Nari.

Youngsook plays with the camera for about a minute before standing it on the edge of Nari's bunk and pointing the built-in screen so we can see it. I slide over to the ladder and very carefully make my way down to the floor from Caitlin's bunk, so I can see the camera screen. Everyone ignores the bag and crowds around the camera.

"There's some video files on here that aren't usually here. I'm a little scared, but here we go. They're all just labelled with the default timestamps that the camera generates so we can easily watch them in order. This is the first one."

Youngsook plays the file. It's Ijun, pointing the camera at herself while she's sitting at one of the desks in the open-plan office part of the administration area. She has her normal blank expression. She stares at the camera for a few seconds, then takes an eyeliner pencil from the desk and does her makeup for a few more seconds. She then reaches for the camera and turns it off.

"Well, that was anticlimactic. Why is she showing us her makeup routine?" says Youngsook.

"Play the next file. She said we need to see all of them. Maybe it will make sense once we see more," says Nari.

Youngsook plays the next video. The screen shows a room. It's the dining room that also doubles as the teaching room we use for lessons. The camera zooms up on one of the corners of the room, where there is a vent. Then the footage cuts out.

"Okay. Ijun is weird," says Youngsook.

"This means something. Keep going," says Nari.

Youngsook starts up the next piece of footage. It's footage of one of the two toilet bowls in our communal bathroom. It's zoomed out enough so we can tell which toilet it is – it's the toilet cubicle closest to the door, not the one closest to the wall. I literally never use this cubicle, I always use the wall one because it's further away. The footage zooms into the bowl and then stops.

"Oh no," says Iseul.

"What?" says Nari.

"I think I've worked out what this is."

"What?"

"I don't want to say until I'm sure. I really hope I'm wrong. Just play the next one, Youngsook."

Youngsook plays the next video. It's the mixing desk in the recording room, the one that our audio engineer Mr Nam uses. The camera zooms up on the right side of the desk.

"OH NO! I fucking knew it! I *fucking knew it!* That fucking asshole pervert! Fuck!" screams Iseul.

"Shit, I've worked it out too!" says Nari.

The rest of us look at Iseul.

"Dummies, she's showing us where the…"

Nari puts her hand over Iseul's mouth.

"Keep your voice down. For all we know, there's a camera in here, too."

"No there isn't, she said we could watch this in here. That means there's not a camera in here."

"Okay, but we need to know where the rest of them are. Youngsook, just keep playing the videos until we've seen them all, okay? I know we're all emotional, and we have every right to be angry, but let's save the commentary for after. We need to know what we're dealing with first."

I finally understand. I look at the others, I think they all get it too now. Ijun is showing us visually where all the CEO's hidden cameras are located in our building.

"Ijun's an angel. She's our guardian – she's looking out for us!" says Shu. For once I think she's absolutely right.

Youngsook plays the next video. It's a video of the "sick room", the small closet with the mattress in it, the one that I got locked inside as punishment on one of my first days here. The camera zooms up on that weird random shelf in the room, that I could never figure out the reason for, that has tiny black studs embedded into it. I wondered what those were when I first saw them, now I know. Caitlin taps me on the arm, I look at her. I know exactly what she's thinking. We were interrupted in that room together, and then we were punished. That's how Mr Park caught us, how he knew what we were up to, he could see. The video then cuts out.

"Keep going!" says Nari.

Youngsook plays the next video. It's the gym space. The camera zooms up on the fire extinguisher on the floor on the far wall of the gym. The footage then cuts out.

"Damn I hope there's no more," says Youngsook.

Youngsook plays the next video. It's back to the open plan office in the admin area. Ijun is walking around with the camera, nobody else is around. She zooms up on a random desk, which has a page-per-month calendar on it. She then turns the month over, so it shows the next month. The camera then cuts out.

"Okay, I get this one. She's going to show us where we can expect cameras to be added soon," says Nari.

Youngsook plays the next video. It's our dorm room. It doesn't zoom up on anywhere specific, and only flashes up for a second and then the video ends.

"Oh great, that fucking pervert," says Iseul.

"I guess she doesn't know exactly where the camera will be added, just that it will be," says Nari. "How much more of these videos are there?"

"Unfortunately for us, there's quite a few more," says Youngsook.

"Okay, keep it rolling. Let's get through them."

Youngsook starts the next video. Ijun is staring at the camera again, in the open plan office. She stares for a few seconds at the camera, then she gets an earring and holds it up to her ear, like she's inviting us to check how it looks. She then reaches out and stops the video.

"Okay, I really don't get that one," says Nari.

"Microphones. She's going to show us where the CEO can hear our conversations," says Youngsook.

"Right. Of course."

Youngsook starts another video. It's Ijun again, this time she's in the gym, by the fire extinguisher. She points the camera at her face for a couple seconds, and then points it at the fire evacuation plan on the wall above the extinguisher. With one hand she holds the camera and with the other she starts scribbling over the fire plan with a red marker, making heart shapes and crosses on the map, like she's trying to make it look pretty. When she's done, she steadies the camera on the map for a while. Every room has multiple little hearts in it. Every room also has at least one little cross in it, with the exception of the dorm room, the open plan office area, and Mr Park's office, which have none. The camera then shakes around for a few seconds before refocusing on the fire plan. Ijun now has a green marker in her other hand. She starts drawing more hearts in green, and some small circles as well. Once again the hearts are randomly distributed, but the circles are only in the dorm room, and the yard area outside the gym. The video then cuts out.

"Well. That's good to know," says Nari.

Youngsook starts the next video. It's the same calendar footage as before. It lasts only a few seconds.

"I think it'll be dorms next, because where else could he put them? There's nowhere else left, and I don't see why he'd bug the offices," says Youngsook.

"Not outside?" says Nari.

"Too difficult to mic up an outside area, the sound will just drift away. You need specialist microphones and they're large, not the kind you can hide, also you need to point the microphone exactly at the sound source because shotgun microphones have a special hypercardioid style polar pattern called a lobar patten, which is..."

"Okay okay, I trust you on that, I don't need a science lecture," says Nari, cutting Youngsook off.

"I can't believe that perverted fuck has microphones in the toilets. What a pig," says Iseul.

Youngsook plays the next video which shows the fire plan, with the same circles and crosses. Ijun draws a little cross at the dorms and Mr Park's office. The video then cuts out.

"Okay, so I was wrong, he's going to be bugging his own office, how weird," says Youngsook.

"Maybe that's so he can blackmail visitors or if we say something compromising in there, he has a record of it. We have to be careful what we say in there from now on," says Iseul.

"There's only two more videos, so it can't get too much worse than this."

Youngsook plays the next video. Ijun is standing in a concrete corridor, next to another fire extinguisher.

"Where is this?" asks Shu.

"Under the building," says Caitlin.

Again Ijun zooms up on the emergency evacuation floor plan that sits on the wall above the extinguisher. She draws some hearts and then puts a green circle around the entire plan, obviously indicating that the entire basement is safe. The video cuts out.

"Well, that's no good to us, we're not allowed down there anyway," says Iseul.

"Maybe that will change somehow now that we've established Ijun is on our side," says Caitlin.

Youngsook plays the last video. Ijun is standing in Mr Park's office, facing the camera which seems like it might be on a tripod this time. Behind her is Mr Park's desk. Ijun starts doing a dance routine. There's no music, but I recognise it immediately as the first part of the "Show Me Love" dance. After about half a minute of doing the initial dance steps, Ijun stops, like she's forgotten the next step in the routine. She holds one hand out stiffly, and does some weird movement with the other hand, which isn't how the dance goes, it's like she's trying to get back into the groove somehow but can't remember the next motion. After about ten seconds of repeating this movement, she walks up to the camera and turns it off.

"What was that?" Iseul asks.

We all look at each other.

"Maybe she's trying to show us our dance but forgot a step?" I ask.

Nari shakes her head.

"That's a completely different motion. Why would she do that?"

"I don't know? I mean why couldn't she just tell us what she means then, instead of making a video for all this stuff? She could have literally just told us all this now?"

"Well it's a lot more helpful to show us than tell us where something like a camera location is. Those videos are so useful, they pinpoint the locations exactly, that's what we need to know. *Molka* cameras are microscopic and verbal descriptions can be ambiguous."

"Yeah but that stuff at the end...?"

"Think about how she's made this. She's made the footage in such a way that if Mr Park picked up that camera and started asking questions, or even if he saw Ijun while she was filming, she could maybe explain it away as random camera tests and bored doodles. That last thing, if someone found her doing that, they'd just think she was trying to learn our dance and failing. I feel like there's something important there she's trying to tell us."

"But why not say it?"

"I don't know. Maybe it's too risky to say, if there's a chance that Mr Park hears?"

Shu puts her hand up.

"Maybe she was miming driving a car? She looked like her left hand was on top of a steering wheel and the right hand was shifting gears? Maybe she's upset about not being allowed to drive the van?"

Nari looks uncertain about Shu's theory.

"I don't know. Ijun doesn't seem to be the kind of person who would care about something like that. I'm pretty sure she's not even legal driving age yet anyway."

"I know, I know! The right hand that does that funny downward motion, it looked like a cat's paw! It's like when a cat is trying to get your attention! Maybe she wants to have a kitten and the CEO won't let her?"

Nari chuckles a little.

"I hope that's what it is, because that's kind of cute! Maybe we'll figure it out later, it might come to one of us. For now let's focus on what we know for sure."

"We know for sure that the CEO is a piece of shit, and we're completely fucked for any sort of privacy in this place," says Iseul.

"Okay, so let's think. We have to keep any personal conversations that we don't want Mr Park overhearing in the dorms, or outside in the yard area. Eventually we won't be able to use the dorms either but we're okay for now. When that new camera goes into the dorms, we need to find out where exactly. I suspect Ijun will find a way to tell us. It'll no doubt go in during a time when we're not around, so each time we come back in here, let's be wary and look for anything odd. We should always assume we're being filmed until we can confirm that we're not. Once it's in, maybe we can find a way to block it without it looking deliberate so at least there won't be our pyjama footage all over the dark web or wherever these things are going. And Caitlin and Hana, now you have an extra reason to rein in your lesbian nonsense."

I sigh. Nari unfortunately has a good point this time.

"What about that disgusting toilet camera?" says Iseul.

"Use the other toilet."

"You know he'll suspect something if we all start exclusively using the other cubicle."

"I know. Not sure what to do about that yet. We can just get into the habit of blocking the camera with enough paper, or cleaning the toilet very thoroughly and breaking the camera in the process, but I don't know how durable those cameras are or if you can even break them easily."

"You know, I thought I hated my father more than Mr Park, but now I'm not so sure."

"Your father might be one of the people watching Mr Park's videos."

"I don't even want to think about that shit."

130. APOLOGY

"Okay so do it in Korean first, and then we can do it in English straight after. How's your English, Shu?"

"Pretty good!"

"Okay, good. Caitlin will correct you if needed."

"Okay, I'm ready!"

Shu smiles directly at the camera and straightens up her posture on the gym floor. The rest of us are sitting in a semi-circle around Youngsook, who holds the camera.

"Don't smile for this, Shu. It's an apology video, you can't be smiling."

"But don't the fans want to see me being happy?"

"Well normally yes, but the fans are upset. If you look happy then they can't relate to you. They might also think that you're not sincere."

"Oh, okay. I'll frown and look sad."

Shu puts on a frowning face, it looks so stupid. Youngsook sighs.

"Shouldn't I frown?" Shu asks.

"No, just have a flat expression, like you're tired of life or something. You know, like the one Ijun has all the time. Try to mimic her."

Shu adopts a flat expression and stares at the camera.

"Is this okay?"

"Yes, that's very good! Okay, I've started the camera, start your apology."

Shu does a bow at ninety degrees and looks at the camera.

"*Annyeong-haseyo-Shu-imnida!* On behalf of all of Halcyon I would just like to apologise to all fans for the outcome of our non-appearance at the show at the Join Hands For Peace festival. Sorry, Youngsook, I jumbled that up a little..."

"It's okay, just backtrack and then keep going, Ijun will edit it."

"Okay... we apologise to all fans for not attending the Join Hands For Peace festival. It wasn't our fault because our CEO got the wrong visas and so they wouldn't let us into the country..."

"Stop. It sounds like you're blaming the CEO instead of taking responsibility."

"But... it's his fault?"

"I know, but... we still have to look like we're taking responsibility."

"But we're not the ones who were responsible?"

"Yes, I know, Shu... just do it again. You can't have 'it wasn't our fault' in an apology, that's not really an apology at all."

"Oh, okay."

Shu clears her throat.

"We apologise to all fans for not attending the Join Hands For Peace festival. It was definitely our fault because we didn't get the visas right..."

"Stop!"

"What?"

"Shu, you don't need to say that either. It's already an apology, so the idea that it's our fault is assumed. It's kind of built into the sentence. Just skip over that bit and talk about being sorry more. That's what the fans want to hear. Don't even mention the visa thing, the fans already know what happened."

"Okay then... we apologise to all fans for not attending the Join Hands For Peace festival. We are very sorry to all the people who we upset by not attending. Especially all the black people!"

Caitlin starts laughing.

"Shu, you can't say that! Why are you even putting that in there?"

"I just wanted to apologise to the black people too?"

"But they'll feel singled out. It'll come off as racist."

"Yes, but you told us that there was a power imbalance and black people in America were poorer and had slavery and stuff, so if I give them a special apology won't that make them feel a bit better because they are poor? I'm just trying to do the right thing culturally..."

"The effort is appreciated, but it doesn't actually quite work like that. It'll just sound weird."

"Oh. Really?"

"Yes. Just trust me on this one."

"Gosh, there's so many rules to follow when talking to Americans... what would we do without you, Caitlin?"

"You'd probably get the group cancelled, that's what you'd do!"

"Don't worry, we'll edit that part out," says Youngsook, while readying the camera for Shu to continue. Shu clears her throat and steadies herself again.

"We are very deeply sorry about it. You can get a refund of the ticket at your place of purchase..."

Youngsook puts the camera down.

"That's wrong, Shu. They can't actually get a refund."

"They can't?"

"No."

"Why not?"

"Because there were other acts at the show besides us, and they still would have been able to see those acts."

"Do they at least get a partial refund? Like there were six acts before and now there's only five so don't they get one sixth of the money back?"

"No, unfortunately not."

"Oh. That's not very good."

"No it's not. Now you know why we have to do this apology video."

"Okay, that makes sense. I'll do that bit again."

Youngsook brings the camera back up to eye level.

"We are very deeply sorry about it, especially because you can't get a refund..."

"Oh my god, stop."

"That was wrong?"

"It was right. Just... don't even mention refunds, Shu."

"Why not?"

"It will feel like you're rubbing salt into the wound."

"But don't they need to know?"

"They already know."

"But how do they know when *I* didn't even know?"

"It's printed on the back of the ticket for them. It would also be in the terms and conditions when they buy their tickets online. You don't have a ticket and didn't try to buy one so you wouldn't know."

"Oh. Then how do *you* know?"

"I've bought tickets to events before, Shu."

"Oh, okay... I'll start again from that bit. We are very deeply sorry about disappointing all our fans like this. Please accept our deepest apologies. We will learn from this experience and reflect and return with a more mature image of ourselves for you. Please expect us fondly as we bring to you more activities in the future."

Shu bows at ninety degrees again. Everyone applauds.

"That last bit was good, Shu!" says Youngsook.

"I can't believe we finally got through it," says Iseul.

Shu starts jumping up and down.

"Yay! I hope they like us again!"

"These spoiled rich Americans had better appreciate all this pandering," says Iseul.

"Says the nepo baby," replies Caitlin, smiling.

"Screw off, *gyopo*. Go raid daddy's credit card."

"Don't talk too tough, baby's first gangster!"

"Oh my god, do you wanna die?"

"Oh relax. Your fake *iljin* act doesn't work on anyone with a brain."

"Quit it you two, or I'll take you both outside and deal with you both!" says Nari.

Caitlin doesn't say anything more but just smiles at Iseul, while Iseul just grimaces. It's always good to see snooty bitch Iseul lose an argument and that's been happening a lot lately. I hope this trend continues.

131. IDOL ENQUIRY

"Hello everyone and welcome to another episode of Idol Enquiry! I'm Lim Hoona and I'll be your host for tonight! Everyone please give a warm welcome to our special guests tonight, Halcyon!"

We walk up to the stage, stand in our usual lineup and bow to the television audience, who politely applaud.

"We are Halcyon! *Annyeong-haseyo-Halcyon-imnida!*"

There are three black leather couches set aside for us on the stage. We take a seat on the couches, with two of us on each couch. Our lineup order means that I'm sharing the middle couch with Nari. The couches are extremely comfortable, softer than the beds in the dorms, I sink into the soft leather and sigh. The host for the show, Lim Hoona, is a man who looks like he's in his thirties, he is wearing a black suit and tie. We're all in our "Show Me Love" formal dress-style outfits, and we're wearing black clip-on microphones which is nice because it means we don't have to play microphone relay and can talk more naturally. Hoona gestures to Shu, who is bouncing up and down on the lounge cushion for some reason.

"Do you like our furniture, Shu?"

"It's squishy!"

Shu giggles as she bounces around while sitting on the couch. I'm so glad that I'm not sitting next to her for this.

"Idols always seem to like our furniture for some reason."

"It's because we don't get nice furniture! Can we take this back to our dorm? I promise we'll look after it!"

"We do actually need to interview other groups..."

"No! Don't interview other groups! Just us!"

Shu keeps bouncing away like an idiot. Everyone's laughing at her, they seem to think this is really amusing.

"Iseul are you okay, being on the same couch?" asks Hoona.

"Actually the bouncing doesn't really carry across. You've got good separation here between the seats..."

Nari clears her throat.

"Hey, can I just say something?"

"Go ahead Nari," Hoona replies.

"So we've done a few of these shows now, and this is the first one we've been on where the host actually knows our names in advance. I think that's very professional and deserves a round of applause, don't you?"

Nari motions to the television audience and they all start clapping and cheering.

"They invite you on but they don't know you?"

"They always ask us to introduce ourselves. They're being polite but it's just a transparent way for them to refresh their memory about who they're really talking to."

"You know, this is why we're called 'Idol Enquiry', it's because we actually do the enquiry part first!"

"I see! Please teach the others!"

"No, we don't want them to do it as good as us. We just want to be better so we can get their ratings."

The audience laughs. I look out into the inky blackness of the crowd, there's probably about a hundred people there but it's hard to tell because the television lighting is so strong, I can't really see anyone properly. I shift my sitting position a little so I'm a bit more diagonal. This couch is so comfortable, I could go to sleep on it. We need something like this back at the agency, if we have to put up with hidden cameras we should at least get a nice couch. I'm sure a nice couch wouldn't break Mr Park's wallet as much as all his fucking hidden cameras did.

"Hana?"

Hoona is trying to get my attention.

"Oh, hi."

"Just waiting for your response, Hana."

"Sorry, I missed the question."

"As we were saying, you and Shu were on a commercial together and it's been really popular?"

What is he talking about? I don't remember this being the topic? Did I fall asleep for a moment or something? I'd better get back on track.

"Oh, you mean that Hancel one?"

"Yes. It's gone viral in China. I was just wondering how that has affected you."

"I had no idea."

"You do remember that you did a commercial, right?"

The audience starts giggling.

"I know that it's a thing that exists, and that I was in it, but, you know, we don't really get time to do things like watch television. We don't have a television anyway."

"Yes we do," says Youngsook.

"Oh we have that screen in the gym... but I thought it was for dance practice. Can we get television on it?"

"Hana, that thing *is* a television."

The audience laughs.

"I mean television *channels,* silly."

"Hana, you don't need television channels, there's this thing called 'the Internet' and you can plug a television into it and it can do all sorts of things."

"Like, when do I get the chance to ever do that? How do you even plug that thing in?"

"With an Internet cable."

"Our agency has an Internet cable? Where?"

"Or you can use wi-fi."

"That thing has wi-fi?"

Youngsook turns to Hoona and sighs.

"Hana's lovely, but she's a lot of work."

More giggling from the audience, they're laughing it up just because I don't know things. It's embarrassing. Hoona looks back to me.

"Hana, it was actually your performance that made it go viral, how you looked so confused by that phone. That was the key viral moment that was shared in China, and that people commented on."

"That's because I was really confused by the phone."

Shu raises her hand.

"The phone text was in Chinese, and Hana can't read Chinese that well, so she needed some help."

"That's not really made clear in the ad," Hoona says.

"No, it isn't. They were very sneaky with editing!"

Shu is sticking up for my reputation. She doesn't have to do this, but I guess I appreciate it. It really annoys me that Shu is underneath her annoying exterior actually a good person, because it means that I can't justify anything other than being nice back to her. What a drag.

"Hana?"

Oh, Hoona is talking to me again.

"Oh, hi there."

The audience giggles a little.

"Hana, I wonder if you have ever been diagnosed for ADD?"

"What's ADD?"

"Attention deficit disorder."

"I don't know what that means."

"Really? They don't teach you that in school?"

"Maybe they did, I don't remember, I probably wasn't listening at the time."

Roars of laughter from the audience.

"I guess that confirms it! Anyway we'll go back to your commercial – you see, because of your ADD, I'm now changing topics quickly to keep you interested..."

"Thank you for accommodating my serious health condition that I only found out about ten seconds ago and that you still haven't explained to me."

"If I went into a big explanation I very much doubt that you would listen to all of it."

"Actually that's true, I wouldn't, I'd get bored. Hey, how did you know that?"

"Because you have ADD."

"What's ADD again? I forgot."

"We're going in circles a bit, let's try to stay on track... I imagine an endorsement like that makes quite a bit of money?"

"Yes, so I'm told."

"So you haven't been paid?"

I turn to look at Nari.

"Have we been paid yet for this? You were going to ask Mr Park CEO about it?"

"We're still waiting on an answer," says Nari, smiling awkwardly.

"So how much money have you and the others made, as individuals, through Halcyon so far, from all your activities?" asks Hoona.

All of us suddenly laugh.

"None!" says Nari. "Mr Park CEO, we're still waiting! Please don't forget us! I still need to have that meeting with you! Don't you forget! Don't brush me off again!"

"I made ten thousand *won* so far!" says Shu.

The entire group gasps and turns to look at Shu. It's hardly any money but the fact she made anything at all is still amazing, it puts her ahead of all of us.

"Ten thousand *won* – no way? How?" Iseul asks.

"A fan sent a note to me in the mail!"

"That's group income, you have to share that with us!"

Shu gets out her phone. Iseul tries to make Shu put it away but Shu holds the phone away so Iseul can't reach.

"You're not supposed to get your phone out during an interview! This is a professional operation here! We'll get marched out the door!"

"I'm working out ten thousand won split six ways! I can't do that in my head!" Shu punches some numbers and shows her phone screen to Iseul. "Look, it's one six six six, dot, six six six six six six... oh, if I scroll along there's even more sixes, it's six six six six six, six six six, six six... how am I supposed to work out all of these sixes without a phone calculator? Anyway you can't have it."

"Why not?"

"It's a fan gift!"

"Then why did you calculate it six ways if you're not going to split it six ways?"

"I just wanted you to know how much money you are not going to be getting! They're my sixes, all of them!"

Shu smiles at Iseul and puts her phone down. The audience laughs.

"Shu, since you're the richest member of the group, how are you going to spend your wealth?" asks Hoona.

"Well, I was going to buy some fried chicken. I think I could get a nice bucket for ten thousand *won*, but we're not allowed to eat fried chicken because we have to diet. So I'm going to use the note as a bookmark, and then later when I'm not on a diet I'll buy the fried chicken then!"

"That's some willpower! Is dieting difficult?"

"No, it's very easy. You just don't eat, and that way no food goes in. However I'm worried, because of inflation."

"Inflation?"

"What if the price of even a small bucket of chicken exceeds ten thousand *won* soon? Should I invest my money instead, so my currency doesn't devalue and I can still afford the chicken later?"

"You could invest in a stock."

"I'll invest in chicken stock! That way the chicken will pay for itself!"

The audience laughs again. I really don't want to be here. I hope I don't get asked too many more questions and can just relax on this couch without bother. I sink into the black leather and try to remain as low-key as possible.

132. LOVE CALL

Gyeongja: GIRLS NIGHT
*   Astrid: We are organising it. Be patient.*
*   Gyeongja: GIRLS NIGHT*
*   Gyeongja: GIRLS NIGHT*
*   Gyeongja: GIRLS NIGHT*
*   Gyeongja: GIRLS NIGHT*
*   Amna: oh my lord have mercy*
*   Gyeongja: GIRLS NIGHT*
*   Gyeongja: GIRLS NIGHT*
*   Gyeongja: GIRLS NIGHT*

It's late at night and I'm in bed, staring at the 'girls' group chat. It's insane and impossible to follow as always, mostly due to Gyeongja spamming the same phrases over and over, but the mind-numbing repetition of it does sometimes help with insomnia. Whatever minimal amount of sleep benefit I was receiving from trying to follow this nonsense is suddenly interrupted by Nari opening the dorm door.

"What fucking bullshit!" Nari yells as she jumps up into her bunk bed.

"What's up?" asks Caitlin.

"I just had a meeting with Mr Park and it was the worst ever. What do you want first; the bad news, the even worse news, or the shit news?"

"Whatever."

"Okay, firstly, he won't pay us, or let me see any financial information at all. I've been asking him to see financial records for months now. Today, after stringing me along for ages, he finally said it's not happening."

"Why?"

"He said that it's not in the contract that he has to disclose anything until the contract term ends, so he won't, but that we still haven't made money yet. Which I'm sure is bullshit."

"Could be real," says Iseul.

"No way."

"Sure it can. All he has to do to put us back into debt again is spend more on music videos."

"I don't know if you've noticed, but our videos aren't exactly world-class productions."

"They still cost more than you think. Anyway he's got dozens of ways he can move money around to make us look like we don't earn. We'll never be out of debt, I guarantee it."

"Maybe you're right. There has to be a way forward though."

"He doesn't care about laws. He'll get away with what he can get away with. Trust me."

"Anyway, the second thing is, my interview with the fitness publication got cancelled. He said it was too much of a risk and not relevant to career advancement so he just turned it down on my behalf, without even asking me!"

"Well that sucks," says Caitlin.

"Oh no!" says Shu. "You were really looking forward to that!"

"Yeah well... I guess I'm not now."

"What's the last piece of bad news?" Shu asks.

Nari turns to look at me.

"He wants us to do Music Train again."

My heart sinks deep into my chest. Not Music Train, not again. Last time I got lucky and Yohan bailed me out before the gross Music Train PD Mr Jeong could molest me, I'm certain I won't get that lucky again. He made threats, too. I'm definitely going to be sexually assaulted again – at best.

"I'm so sorry, Hana. Oh and he wants to see you in his office next, I told him I'd tell you, so just go in there when you're ready."

"Any idea why?" I ask.

Nari shakes her head.

"He didn't give anything away. He's not in a great mood though, so don't expect anything good."

"Should we come in with Hana?" Iseul asks.

"No, he wanted to see her alone. I don't know what that means, if it's good or bad. But probably bad. Anyway, we'll talk after you come out."

I guess I'd better face whatever my fate is. I climb out of bed and walk out of the dorm, towards Mr Park's office. I'm not going to get changed out of my pyjamas or try to put on a good impression because I'm sure whatever news I get is going to just make me want to go straight back to bed and cry. Eventually I reach his office, he's behind his desk, in his big chair, leaning back. Ijun stands next to him, playing with her new phone, she doesn't look up at me. I take a seat in the chair opposite Mr Park.

"You wanted to see me?" I ask.

"Yes."

"Am I in trouble?"

"That depends on you."

"I'd rather know if I was in trouble."

"What do you think you might be in trouble for?"

"I don't know?"

"Is there something you want to tell me?"

Oh wow. I wasn't prepared for him to flip the question around like this. I really shouldn't have asked.

"Look, I don't *want* to be in..."

"Firstly, Hana. Some good news. The Hancel contract was a success. I know you're already aware of the spread of the advert as it's come up in interviews. The amount of financial compensation we received for your appearance was significant, and it will lead to future opportunities and even more profit."

I wasn't expecting to be congratulated. I suppose I should look grateful, given that I was going to get kicked out if this didn't work out for me. I bow in my chair.

"Thank you, Mr Park CEO."

"Just ensure that you display good behaviour and do not say anything to jeopardise the contract. Is that understood?"

"Understood, Mr Park CEO."

"Secondly, I've been contacted by a representative for Liangu Pictures. They want you to contribute vocals to a song for Han Leejung's new film, called... Ijun?"

"The Love Complete," says Ijun, not looking up.

"So, Hana, we are working this out currently between ourselves and the film company. We do understand that Han Leejung is a filmmaker who has a questionable reputation, so we have some reservations..."

"Just say yes," Ijun interjects, not looking up.

Mr Park stops addressing me and turns to Ijun.

"Ijun! Put your phone away and look at me!"

Ijun lowers her phone. I guess she doesn't want to get it smashed again.

"Ijun, do you enjoy constantly trying to undermine my authority as CEO?"

"But Han Leejung is huge! She's so big she is even known internationally! It's a no-brainer! This is one of the world's greatest filmmakers right now making a love call – to *us!* What's there to even discuss?"

"We still need to negotiate..."

"Mr Park CEO... even if we *weren't* being paid for this, it would be worth doing, just for the exposure! But they're offering seriously good money for this, just for one feature with one singer!"

Mr Park says nothing and just glares. Ijun doesn't seem to even care, she continues.

"Yohan from EB-K is involved in this. *Yohan!* And he's apparently doing a whole bunch of his own work on the soundtrack for *nothing!* Yet they're paying *us!* How are you even *thinking* about turning this down? Do you have any idea what a ridiculous position you're taking?"

Mr Park spends a bit more time glaring at Ijun and then turns back to look at me.

"I'll let you know the outcome of negotiations."

Ijun starts walking out of the room.

"You'd better say yes."

Ijun leaves the room and slams the door behind her.

"Come back here, young lady!"

"SCREW OFF!" Ijun screams from the other side of the door while walking away.

Mr Park turns back to me.

"Thirdly, and I'll make this very quick. I'm sure that Nari told you about Music Train."

"She did."

"You are to do everything Mr Jeong says, without exception. I expect total compliance. Is that clear?"

I stare at Mr Park. He knows how Mr Jeong assaulted me, and Mr Park never took my side or did anything about the assaults at the venue, or at the restaurant on our non-consensual "date" which I'm sure Mr Park arranged purely to suck up to that asshole. He blamed me all the way and is now happy to just throw me straight back into the ring to be assaulted another time. He knows this will happen. What true pieces of disgusting shit they both are.

"Is that crystal clear, Hana?"

"Yes it is, Mr Park CEO."

Looks like luck won't be on my side this time. I might just have to try and make my own luck.

133. DAEBAK

"I want the same one."

"Same as last time?"

"Yes!"

"I don't have that one here right now."

"But I didn't even get to shoot it last time!"

It's night and I'm in the back of the van with Jane and the gun dealer, we're parked in some unknown location, an underground parking garage somewhere. The gun dealer is sitting in the van and Jane sits next to him. They're both wearing their usual all-black clothing and face masks. The dealer has his suitcase open in front of me, with four guns to choose from. Three of them are revolvers, and the other one is a big shiny silver one that looks way too big for me to even hold.

"Are you sure that you don't want anything you see here?" the dealer asks.

"I like the big silver one! Does it fire full auto?"

"It would break your hand if it did."

"Then no, I guess I don't want that one."

"You definitely don't want a revolver either?"

"Not full auto, also too few bullets."

"Actually the big silver gun doesn't hold all that many bullets either."

"Oh. So how quickly can you get the gun that I want?"

"It all depends. When do you need it by?"

"I'm going back on Music Train in two weeks from today. It definitely *has* to be before then."

The gun dealer looks at Jane.

"That could be pushing it," says Jane.

"What's the issue?" the dealer asks.

"It just depends on the other client's job. I mean, if we're lucky and everything goes smoothly, we'll have it by next week for sure, but... well, you know how it is."

The dealer nods and looks back at me.

"If we can't get it, are you happy with something else?"

"Like what?"

"It won't be any of the ones in this box. It'll be like the gun you had the first time, that, or something very similar to it in operation. Whatever it is, we'll make sure it's not too difficult for you to use."

"It'll have to do. I can't do this after Music Train, it has to be before."

"What else do you need? Will one magazine do?"

"I don't really know how to reload, so it will have to."

"I can teach you, it's not very difficult."

"The gun isn't here though?"

"I'll show you with my own gun. They have similar mechanisms. Not exactly the same, but close enough for you to get the idea. Whatever gun you end up with, this will be the procedure, the only difference is the release button isn't always in exactly the same place."

The gun dealer takes a black pistol out from his jacket, and does a series of sliding movements with it that are way too fast for me to follow along with. After a few seconds he hands it to me. I grab the pistol by the grip and hold it up, it has a sleek, finely polished look.

"Wow, this is nice."

"Careful where you wave that thing! It's not loaded, but even so, don't point it at any humans."

"But pointing it at humans is the general idea, right?"

"Yes, just not the humans with you right now."

"Okay, so where do I point it?"

"Point it over there, we'll pretend that's your target."

The dealer points to the corner of the van behind him, and I aim the pistol in that direction.

"Now on the left of the handle, there's a button, near where your thumb is, on the pistol grip. Press that in. While you push that in, put your other hand under the gun, to grab the base of the magazine and pull it out."

I push the button in and pull on the base of the handle with my other hand, the magazine easily drops down into my palm.

"Very good, first try. You're very coordinated."

"All that dance practice has to be good for something."

"Now put the magazine back in again, we'll just pretend it's a new magazine that's already loaded. Slide it back into the handle and you should feel it catch."

"Do I need to do the button again?"

"No. If you do it right, it'll just lock itself in place."

I slide the magazine back into the handle and it falls straight out again.

"Firmer than that. Don't be shy about it. Also you're waving the gun all over the place. Keep the gun pointed at the far corner while you do this, that's your target. Always aim at the target."

I point the gun back at the corner, and push the magazine in harder. This time the magazine stays in place with a small click.

"Much better, very good. Now remember that there won't be a bullet in the chamber so you need to push back the sliding part at the top, which brings a bullet up."

I slide back the top part and hold it.

"You need to let go again once you slide it back."

"Okay. Sorry, it's been a while."

I release the sliding part and it jumps forward back to where it was.

"Good. Of course there's no bullet because the gun isn't loaded, but that's the general idea. That's the simplest way to do a reload."

"There's more than one way?"

"Yes. There are other ways that are more efficient but they also have more moving parts to memorise how to use, and they differ more between gun types. Since we don't have access to anywhere you can practice, or the gun you'll be using at this moment, it's best to keep it simple. In a panic situation you're not going to quickly remember details like that."

"Yeah, I learned that last time."

"Now just be aware, although this might seem simple, executing a reload quickly enough to be useful in a fight is actually difficult to do without a lot of training. If you run dry and you're under threat, you're better off retreating to safety first, and worrying about reloading your gun second. Not that I think you'll be fired upon, but there may still be threats so just don't try anything fancy. Lightning fast reloads are for trained soldiers and computer games only, so just go slow. Slow is smooth, smooth is fast."

"So slow is fast?"

"Well, yes and no."

"So slow is fast and yes is no as well? Is up also down?"

Jane taps the dealer on the shoulder, I can tell that under the mask she's smiling.

"Oh, Hana... let's just move on! Why don't we recap and discuss the plan."

"Fine. So Hana, you're getting a pistol, with a silencer, two loaded magazines with hollow point bullets, and if we can get it for you in time, the 'fun switch', is that correct?"

"Yes. Wait, why are my bullets hollow?"

"Your bullets have always been hollow."

"Why can't I have solid bullets?"

"Hollow points are better. They do more damage."

"Really?"

"A solid bullet will often just go straight through your target and out the other side. This means it will go straight through a lot of other things too. That's not good because all bullets end up somewhere, you want your bullets penetrating into what you're shooting at, and into as few other materials as possible. Hollow bullets are designed to fragment inside the target and stay there. Not only do you get less risk of shooting someone else by accident, but if you do land a shot on your intended target, the bullet will expand inside their body and slice up whatever it passes into. If you can make an accurate hit to a vital organ, there's no chance that your target will survive."

"*Daebak.*"

Jane starts laughing at the dealer.

"You're the best salesman, I swear. You know what your customers want!"

"Speaking of customers, Iseul paid already, right?"

"Of course. She's never late."

"Why can't all our customers be like her. She's such a good girl."

I can't keep a straight face at this.

"That's the first time I've heard anyone say those words about Iseul!"

Jane laughs.

"Well, good is relative! She's good to us. Not so sure about her being good for an idol pop group, but I guess that's your problem, not ours!"

134. VISION

"Hana, how is that?"

"Worse."

The optometrist, a lady in her forties called Sunae, changes over the lens in the weird metal eye machine thing I'm staring into.

"How about now?" she asks.

"A little better. Not much."

"Can you read the line fourth from the top?"

I stare through the lens at the rows of letters on the far wall. The text in each of the rows gets smaller with every descending line.

"I can do the first three lines. It's blurry after that."

"Okay, let's swap again. We can get it a lot better."

Another lens goes into the machine.

"Oh my god."

"Better?"

"That's so sharp."

"How many lines?"

"Seven."

"Read out the letters on line seven for me."

"*Bi, Mi, Eung*... a fish? Is that really a fish?"

"Very good."

"Then the number six."

"Good. Now, hold still, we're going to add the other lens that we did before. This should get you up to nine or ten."

"Really? That low?"

"Line eleven is normal vision at your age."

"People can really read row eleven? Without glasses?"

Sunae extends part of the lens holder machine, which has a metal frame that goes over my other eye. Sunae waves to Caitlin, who is sitting on a chair on the other side of the room, next to the eye chart.

"Come over to where Hana is sitting, can you see line eleven on that chart?"

Caitlin gets up and walks over to where I'm sitting, then turns around and looks at the chart.

"I can do all the rows except the bottom two."

Sunae chuckles.

"Nice, that's the twelfth line, which means you have 1.2 vision. Can you read it for me?"

"*Eung, Giyeok, Mi,* a tractor, three."

"Very impressive Caitlin."

"Is 1.2 the same as 20/20?"

"1.2 is 20/17. That's better than 20/20. Now take a set and stop showing off in front of your lady friend."

Caitlin laughs and sits back down on the other side of the room. Sunae slides a lens into the other frame. I look at the chart again. It's even sharper than before.

"I can do row ten. Pretty sure."

"Read it out."

"*Siot, Bi, Eung,* a bird, the number eight."

"Wait."

Sunae does another lens change.

"No, that's worse. It's blurrier now."

"Okay. Wait some more."

Another change. It's back to how it was before.

"Read row ten again."

"*Siot, Bi, Mi,* a bird, the number eight. Wait, that didn't change, did it?"

"You were correct that time. Can you do row eleven?"

Row eleven is harder to see, I start squinting.

"*Eung... Bi...*"

"Stop. No, you can't. That's okay. Ten is pretty good."

Sunae slides the machine away from my face. Everything goes blurry again. I'm really noticing now how much I can't see.

"Oh wow, it's so obvious now how much my eyes really suck."

"You'll notice a big difference when you get your glasses. Now, you were certain that you wanted glasses and not contacts?"

"It has to be glasses."

"Mr Park might not be happy. He might not let you wear them. You know what he's like about the look of the group," says Caitlin.

"I can't have a lens touching my eye. Just the thought of it is so weird, it freaks me out. I can't stand things that touch my eye. It just... I don't know. I'd rather be blind."

Sunae smiles.

"Well, guess that makes the decision easy. Do you want any lens coatings?"

"What lens coatings can I get?"

"We do blue light, UV, or scratch resistance. Blue light is for if you stare at screens a lot, it'll stop you getting eyestrain by filtering out blue light from monitors. UV is for blocking out ultraviolet sun rays."

"How good is the scratch resistance?"

"You still have to treat them carefully, but it will make your glasses more durable to normal wear and tear, for instance, if you drop them a lot, or if you have them in a bag and they rub up against metal objects."

"I'll just get the scratch resistance. I don't really look at screens or go outdoors that much, but I'll probably drop them and bump them around all the time."

"Very good."

"So can I have them now? I've already picked out the frames."

"We have to make the lenses first!"

"Can't I just have the lenses from the machine?"

"We have to cut lenses for each pair of glasses that we do, so that they fit into the frames."

"Oh. How long does that take?"

"Since you only want scratch resistance, we can have them ready in a week."

"That's good. I've got some important stuff coming up very soon and I'm really going to need to see well."

"Oh. What are you doing?"

Fuck, why does this nosy bitch have to ask me that? I obviously can't tell her that I'm going to murder some piece of shit soon and it might help my job go a bit smoother if I can actually see him before I shoot, so I'd better make up some bullshit.

"I'm going to be on a... television show, and there's like a person, and I have to look at him from far away so I can coordinate... um, shots."

Technically not a lie.

"Which show?"

"It's... um..."

"Music Train," Caitlin interjects, coming to my rescue.

"Oh, Music Train. I know that show. My son likes to watch that when he can. Maybe he'll be watching if he's not busy studying. Anyway the glasses will be two hundred thousand *won*, just order at the front."

We both stand up and bow to Sunae.

"*Annyeonghi gyeseyo!*"

Sunae bows back.

"*Annyeonghi gaseyo!*"

As we walk through to the front, I look at Caitlin, who is paying for this.

"Can you even afford that?"

"Yeah, it's fine."

"Where are you getting the money from?"

"My parents send it. I guarantee you it's not from being an idol. Come on, let's go order these glasses. You need to be able to see stuff. We can go clothes shopping after this, as long as we don't get recognised too much. We both need new clothes badly. Also I want to go to the sex toy shop again, that place had some cool stuff and now I have more money, so..."

"No way. We are *not* going to the sex toy shop!"

"Why not? Afraid of having too much fun?"

"It's not that... if we get seen in there, we'll get kicked out of the group!"

"Who says we'll be seen? We'll buy some hoodies and sunglasses, it'll be fine."

"I don't know relaxed the music press are in America but it's not like that here. Seriously, you can't go in there now that you're known. Controversies kill groups here. Also, it's shameful anyway. Maybe you don't have any shame, but I do. I don't want to be embarrassed."

Caitlin sighs.

"Okay, I get it. I guess I'll be ordering online."

"I feel strange about you paying for all this anyway."

"Don't. You look good in those frames, and I like dressing you up, so it's a gift for me too, really. It's not even that much money anyway."

"Yes it is!"

"It really isn't. Besides, we rarely get to sneak out like this, so the money my parents send over just builds up over time."

"Seriously? So how rich *are* you? You just get money from your parents?"

Caitlin smiles and slaps me lightly on the behind.

"Never you mind! Rich enough to take care of you, don't worry about it. Anyway I'll go and pay now, mind your business! Asking about where I get money is rude!"

I stare around the shop and look at more frames while Caitlin fixes up the money at the register. My vision doesn't seem that bad anymore, but I'm sure that's just because I've gotten used to my normal way of seeing again. I wonder how long my vision has been broken for, months or years, maybe? Perhaps this is why I wasn't ever doing that well in school, I just couldn't see anything? Why didn't anyone ever tell me? Maybe my mother knew and didn't say anything because she didn't want to spend the money? Or maybe she just didn't even know or care? She has glasses too and has had them since forever, surely she would have suspected that I might also need them? I haven't spoken to my mother in a long time, I've been too scared to ring her, and she hasn't rung me recently either. I wonder why she's been so quiet lately? I don't want to think about her right now. I keep looking at the frames in the shop display and do my best to forget about my mother's existence.

135. THE LOVE COMPLETE

Look at me and smile
I was so thankful for you
Coming into focus
The love complete

The place where we walked
New flowers bloom
Shapes in the distant sky
The love complete

Let us meet again
When we see tomorrow
Walk along a flower path
The love complete

I'm standing in front of a microphone in a studio recording room, wearing headphones, and reading the lyrics sheet that was placed on the music stand in front of me a few minutes ago. This room isn't the one that my group usually records in, I've been taken to a different studio that's owned by the film company. This is good because it means that I don't have to work with Mr Nam, our creepy studio engineer who has written and recorded all of our other songs so far. Instead there's a different man behind the control desk, he has a beard and looks foreign, he hasn't said anything to me yet. Ijun is in the control room with the man, the other girls are not here, they're all back at the dorms. I scan over the lyric sheet again. It doesn't have any markings about what is a verse or a chorus, which is strange. I'm not sure how I feel about the weird lyrics but I suppose anything is better than the crap Mr Nam writes for us to sing.

"Hello... Hana, can you hear me?"

A voice in my headphones. I look over at the control room window and nod at the man behind the desk.

"Yes!"

"Hello Hana, I'm Jorgen, I'm the engineer on this project. How has your day been so far?"

What a question.

"I did some classes and gym, and then I came here?"

"I mean, are you feeling okay, Hana? Are you excited to be working on this project?"

"I don't know, I guess? I just do what I'm told. I mean, it's definitely an honour to be chosen, but I don't know why I was picked. I'm sure there are better singers than me that they could have used."

Jorgen smiles and laughs a little.

"Okay, that's fine. Don't worry about your singing, I'll coach you through it. For now I'm just going to play the track into your headphones, okay? It has a guide vocal on it. You don't have to sing it yet, just listen to how the guide vocal and the instruments go, and try to get a feel for how the song should be sung."

"Sure, I'm ready!"

The instrumental starts in my headphones. It's just a piano, nothing else. This song has a really slow feel, it's nothing like anything that my group normally does. The singing eventually comes in, it's very soft, just singing a few syllables at a time. It doesn't seem too demanding, which is good, I feel like I might actually be able to sing this without messing it up. The song continues on and comes to a part where an acoustic guitar joins the piano and they play together, with no vocal.

"Is there any more?" I ask.

"Just keep listening," Jorgen replies.

The guide vocal comes back, singing a bit higher than before. I sing a few notes and try to match the pitch of the singer on the recording, but I can't do it. I'm not sure how I'm going to go with this recording. I guess Jorgen will work out a way to make it sound good with electronics or something, like Mr Nam did. Eventually the track comes to an end.

"How do you feel about that? Got the idea?

"I think so. The end is a bit high for me though?"

"Don't worry about it. Let's do a take with you singing along to the guide track and... Hana?"

"Yes?"

"Hana, are you okay?"

It's Ijun's voice.

"I... think so?"

I look up. Ijun is here. I'm not in the recording room anymore, I'm in the control room, lying on a couch. What just happened? I was in the recording room just seconds ago? I look around, Jorgen isn't here, only Ijun.

"Hana, you passed out, so Jorgen brought you in here. He's gone to get you some food and drink. Did you eat anything today?"

"No... there was no lunch. The others had dinner but I had to come here. Usually I eat something in my room but I wasn't given any time?"

"You mean the snacks that Iseul sneaks in?"

"Yeah."

"I can't hide that stuff from Mr Park CEO forever."

"What am I supposed to do then, just starve and die?"

I hear the control room door open. Jorgen comes into the room and hands Ijun a drink and a plastic bag before sitting down in his control room chair.

"Thank you, Jorgen. Hana, sit up and have this."

I gradually sit up on the couch, I feel a little dizzy. Ijun sits next to me and passes the drink to me, I take a sip. It tastes sweet and fruity. Ijun then passes over a cardboard box and some disposable chopsticks. I open the box, and the condensed steam from the *bibimpap* inside wafts over my face. I start eating quickly just in case she gets the idea of taking the food away again.

"Will she be okay?" Jorgen ask Ijun.

"Yes. She just needs to eat. This happens all the time."

"Your company can't afford to feed her?"

"We can afford it. They're just dieting."

"Must be some diet."

"Our CEO deems it necessary."

"Hana doesn't exactly need to lose weight."

"Even I need to lose weight according to our CEO."

Jorgen doesn't seem to know what to say to that, and wheels his chair back over to his desk to get the track ready or whatever. I'm not sure how to react to it either so I just don't say anything and keep eating. It's becoming clear to me that Ijun and Mr Park don't always get along, but I'm not exactly sure by how much. Are they mortal enemies or just a couple who fight sometimes? I don't know. At least Jorgen seems like a reasonable person, it was nice of him to get me the food and drink, he didn't have to do that, and Mr Nam sure wouldn't have done that. I wish we had more reasonable people like Jorgen back at our agency, but we don't, so I guess I'll just have to endure it there until I no longer have to.

136. GIRLS NIGHT

"Hana, you look amazing here!"

All the members of the 'girls' chat group are sitting around the lounge room of Astrid's house. Besides myself, Caitlin, Iseul, Shu and Youngsook are all here from our group. Gyeongja, Ora and Sumire are here from Pearlfive. Also here are Astrid and Amna, neither of whom I know much about, but this is the first time I've met Amna in person, a tall foreign girl from I'm not sure where, who has skin even darker than the surfer guy in Caitlin's phone, she's like the mirror image of Astrid. I'd probably know more about them if I actually paid attention to the chat group I guess. We've separated ourselves into two groups. Caitlin is smoking weed on one side of the lounge room, and Iseul, Youngsook, Ora, Astrid and Sumire are all sitting with her, passing the bong around between them and blowing smoke everywhere. The rest of us who don't smoke, which besides myself is Shu, Amna and Gyeongja, are sitting together and chatting on the other side of the room. Amna has a copy of the latest DGT magazine which just came out, it has the pictures of Shu and also the ones of Caitlin with me.

"That's my favourite!" says Shu, pointing to the photo that Amna has the magazine turned open to. In the picture I'm standing facing the camera, wearing a black suit and Min's thick glasses, Caitlin wears a red dress and whispers something into my ear. My eyes are turned away from Caitlin, our faces are half obscured by darkness and we cast long shadows on the wall behind us. It is actually an excellent looking photo, I even like the way that I look in it, which is unusual for any photo that I see of myself.

"What did Caitlin whisper in your ear to get that look out of you?" Amna asks.

"I can't tell you that," I reply.

"Oh. I see."

"Seriously, I'm not saying."

"You don't need to. Just look at your expression. Your cheeks are red and you're completely embarrassed. You're embarrassed right now, too!"

Amna starts laughing at me. This is not cool.

"Can we just turn the page?"

"Fine, fine."

Fortunately Amna drops the topic and turns the page, to a couple pictures of Shu. One is of her spinning around in the ballet dress and boots that the photographer Min made her wear, the other is of her in the same outfit, but on the floor after she fell over. In both photographs, Shu is captured mid-laugh. We all stare at the photos, they are really good actually, but since they're of Shu I'm not going to say how good they are, somebody else can be the first one to say it.

"Wow, what great photos!" says Gyeongja.

"Thanks," says Shu.

"Lixin will like these," says Amna.

"No he won't, I dumped him at the party."

"Really?"

"He just wouldn't stop drinking. He gets nasty and mean when he drinks, I don't like it!"

"You could have told me about it, you know I would have been happy to sort him out," I say to Shu.

"It didn't seem worth it. He's not going to change, he just doesn't want to. I'm not going to waste my energy on him anymore. I can do better!"

"What great photos! What do you think of Shu's photos, Hana?" Gyeongja asks.

How do I say exactly what I honestly think, but also without throwing Shu a compliment?

"The photographer Min was very professional. It was good to work with her. Usually we have our photos taken by Gisang, he's..."

Immediately both Gyeongja and Amna gasp.

"Gisang's horrible!" says Amna.

"I've heard he's a bad person!" says Gyeongja.

Amna nods.

"Mmm, he definitely is. You should have heard the things he said to me. He's not good. Not good at all."

"You worked with him?" I ask.

"Only once. Never again."

"I wish we didn't have to work with him ever again."

"Was he inappropriate?"

"Yes!" me and Shu say, at exactly the same time.

"Shu broke his camera equipment, and made it look like an accident. He hasn't been back working with us since," I add.

"Yay for Shu!" says Gyeongja.

The three of us applaud Shu for a few seconds. Shu takes a bow in front of us. I have to admit that was a good move on her part.

"I want someone to break Mr Jeong's equipment," says Gyeongja.

"Refresh my memory... Mr Jeong?" asks Amna.

Amna's lucky, she obviously hasn't met him yet. I'd better fill her in.

"The producer/director for Music Train."

"Oh *him*. Right. Oh yes. A disgusting man."

Okay, so she probably *has* met him.

"How do you know him?" I ask.

"White Iris was on that show once."

I guess that's her group. I don't want to ask if it is or not because I feel like I should know this already.

"He left you alone?"

"Yeah he ignored me, but he did try it on with some of the others in the group. Guess I'm not his type."

"I want someone to break Mr Jeong's equipment," says Gyeongja.

"Throw it in the pool," I reply.

"In the pool!" says Gyeongja, smiling.

"Who do you think is worse, Gisang or Mr Jeong?" Shu asks.

Amna thinks about the question for about ten seconds before answering.

"I think Mr Jeong is worse. Gisang just says disgusting stuff and he'll have wandering hands sometimes, but it's all on the surface, yes it's horrible but at least you know what you're dealing with. It's always the same. Except maybe with his daughter over there, I think maybe she deals with more than the rest of us." Amna motions with her head in Iseul's direction. "She's got all kinds of issues, it's Gisang's fault no doubt, god help her. Mr Jeong is sneakier though, he'll put up a front of being this good person in front of the corporate types but as soon as it's just the girls and the lower tier staff... let's just say there's more than one reason why the really big groups don't do Music Train."

"We have to do Music Train again soon. I'd really like to meet Mr Jeong before the event though."

"Ask Astrid about that."

"She can help?"

"She probably has his details. Astrid collects the details of everyone, she's a real socialite."

Amna suddenly whistles and waves to Astrid.

"Hey, Astrid! Come over here!"

"Give me just a moment!" Astrid yells from the other side of the room.

I look over at Astrid, she has Caitlin's bong in her hand. She quickly lights up the bong and takes a hit. She then blows the smoke across the room, passes the bong back to Caitlin and walks over from where she was sitting.

"Hey there... what's going on?"

"Hana wants to ask you something."

"In private," I add.

Amna starts laughing.

"I'll stay no more about it!"

Astrid smiles at me.

"Come with me, Hana."

Astrid reaches out her hand, gesturing for me to follow her. I get up and walk with her through the lounge room, down the house's main hallway, up some stairs and into a dark bedroom.

"Hana, how photo-sensitive are you?"

"I don't like bright lights much."

"I'm glad I asked. The light's coming on, it'll get very bright in here so watch your eyes, just a warning."

I cover my eyes with one hand as Astrid flicks a switch and her room lights up. I uncover my eyes slowly and I instantly see what she means; literally almost everything in the entire room is bright pink. The walls, ceiling and carpet are pink and she has a pink ceiling fan. In the middle is a pink double bed with pink and white covers, covered in pink plush toys. A pink bedside mirror cabinet has a ton of beauty products on them, all pink, besides this is a pink desk and a pink wardrobe. The only things not pink here are some of the books in a small bookcase in the far corner of the room, but even half of those are pink and most of the rest have been put in spine-first.

"Sit down," Astrid says, motioning to the bed.

I sit nervously on the edge of the bed, I feel uneasy, like I'm somehow interfering with the pinkness just by being here. Astrid sits next to me. I should try and make this as quick as I can.

"Amna said you had Mr Jeong's contact details?"

Astrid starts laughing.

"Ooh. Oh my. Yes, I do. I'll gladly give you that!"

Astrid walks over to her mirror cabinet and opens a drawer in it. She instantly closes it again and rejoins me at the foot of the bed, with a card in her hand.

"This is his business card. You didn't get it from me."

I take the card out of Astrid's hand and inspect it. It has his name, his business title, and an email address... but something's missing.

"There's no phone number?" I ask.

"Flip it over."

I turn the card over. There's a phone number written in red ink, and a message:

Astrid, call me - anytime.

A shiver runs across my whole body.

"Okay, that's disturbing."

"Yeah, he's a pig. Although I shouldn't say that. I think pigs are cute."

"Don't tell me he assaulted you also."

"Thankfully, no. He tried flirting with me, but our CEO saw what was happening and she improvised an excuse for our group to leave early, bless her. Mr Jeong insisted on giving me his card on my way out the door."

"You have a female CEO?"

"Don't be too envious, it's not so great having a boss who is emotionally intelligent. It means we can't get away with much. Still, she's very good with stuff like this."

"I still wish I had your CEO in charge of my group. Ours actually told me the other day that I have to do 'everything Mr Jeong says without exception', he actually made a special point of mentioning that."

"Real talk for a moment, I promise nobody's listening."

"Okay?"

Astrid hesitates for a moment before speaking.

"How has your CEO managed to cheat death for so long? Like, with *you* around?"

"Well if he happened to have an accident or something, I would be the obvious suspect, wouldn't I?"

"I don't know, would you?"

"There's been several witnesses to his mistreatment of me. So it's not like I could just deal with him and get away with it, you know. The police would question people and the trail would come back to me, and I'm not good at lying to the police."

"White lies are a life skill you should learn, especially given what you do."

"I try, I just seem to be bad at it."

"But you're confident you can deal with Mr Jeong?"

"I think he has probably tried to have his way with half of the female idol *maknae* population of Korea, he would have so many enemies by now."

"I think all the big bosses in our line of work have a lot of enemies."

"I have to deal with Mr Jeong. It's not even like I *want* to, although I probably *do* want to..."

Astrid starts giggling at me.

"Probably?"

"Okay, okay... I *definitely* do want to but also I just *have* to. This is more urgent than worrying about my own boss."

"Why?"

"My CEO Mr Park hasn't laid a hand on me yet, at least not in that way, so while he *is* disgusting, the situation isn't critical. He's only endangered me indirectly. Maybe I can just ride it out, I don't know. Whereas Mr Jeong has already... tried to do stuff, with both me and Gyeongja. I have to stop him quickly. I can't let him touch her again, she already went through hell with her old boss."

"Yeah she sure did. I've known her for a few years, she's changed a lot, and not in a good way."

"Do you think I'm doing the right thing?"

"It's not the sort of thing I would do... but I'm glad you're doing it. If he got busted, we'd have to all get dragged through court to testify, and relive all of what we went through, and for what purpose? These creeps will do five years in jail at the most, but most people who get caught don't do any jail time at all. We can't rely on the criminal justice system in this country. It's so stupid and conservative here."

"If there was another way to stop it, I'd stop it, but men only respect violence. If I want them to stop, I have to speak in the language that they understand."

"Just know that all the girls, we do understand, we have your back. All of us in the chat group, we appreciate what you're doing. Even though we obviously can't say that."

"Thank you. I might need to contact you about this in a few days. You can keep a secret, right?"

Astrid smiles.

"Of course I can, my warrior queen!"

137. NEWS

"Hey Hana, are you still wasting your life in that shitty pop group of yours?"

"Yes."

It's night, I'm in the yard, sitting on the metal bench and talking on the phone to Sooae. It's good to catch up with her, I haven't spoken to her in a while. Her caustic sense of humour always makes me smile.

"Just asking because our singer just left my group. Do you wanna replace her?"

"No way. She probably left your group because your music is shit."

I can hear Sooae laughing on the other end of the line.

"So it should suit you then. You have no fucking talent. You'll fit right in!"

"But your music sucks! Why would I join just to do music that I don't like, that doesn't even make any sense?"

"It's still better than what you're doing now."

"Okay I don't deny that our songs are garbage but I'm under contract. It doesn't say anywhere in my contract that I'm allowed to join shit groups that just make noise. At least people actually listen to our rubbish music."

"Only because they're mentally deficient."

"Okay, you've got me there. I have no comeback for that. Our fans are fuckheads."

Sooae laughs.

"Hey we've got to catch up sometime."

"Yeah I know. It's difficult to arrange."

"Should I arrange it through Caitlin?"

"You're in touch with Caitlin?"

"Yeah, of course!"

"How did I not know this?"

"Caitlin's cool. We talk every now and then."

I think about this for a few seconds.

"Tell me she's not working there, in the brothel where you work. You did mention that before, I know it was a joke, but..."

"Don't be silly, Hana."

"That wasn't a denial."

"Oh, relax! She's not working here. I mean it. Which is a real shame for me because some of the bitches here... they're a real pain in my ass sometimes, you know? I'd prefer it heaps more to work with Caitlin, she's way more chill. Plus she always has weed. Speaking of which, have you been smoking? You're paranoid."

"She just has a lot of money lately, that's all."

"A girl like Caitlin will always have a lot of money."

"What does that mean?"

"Look, if you're that fucking paranoid about it, why don't you ask *her* about it?"

"I did!"

"And what did she say?"

"She said she has rich parents."

"Well she's from the States and she can afford to fuck off to Korea and join your crappy idol group on a whim so that's probably true. What the fuck are you even worried about, you idiot?"

I hear the sliding door to the gym open and look up. Caitlin is coming out here. She looks oddly glum.

"Hey Sooae, I've got to go. Caitlin's coming out here, I think something bad has happened."

"Okay, say hi for me, look after her okay? You're on a good thing with her, don't you dare fuck it up."

"Thanks. Bye."

I hang up the phone and Caitlin sits next to me. She looks like she's holding back tears. It's unusual for Caitlin to be upset about anything, she's always so calm.

"What's wrong?"

"I'm so sorry, Hana. Look."

Caitlin points her phone at me. It's showing a news article. She's holding it too close so I grab her phone and adjust the distance from my face so I can read the screen.

EB-K's Yohan has been found dead.

According to a police statement, Yohan was found unconscious inside his parked car in Itaewon, Seoul.

He was immediately rushed to the hospital while resuscitation was attempted, but was pronounced dead on arrival.

Police suspect suicide to be the cause of death, due to items found at the scene which have not yet been disclosed to the media.

Stay tuned for further updates to this rapidly developing story.

IMPORTANT: If you or someone you know is at risk of self-harm or suicide, please seek help as soon as possible by contacting agencies specialising in crisis intervention and suicide prevention.

I sit in silence for a minute. I don't really know what to think about this. Didn't he say that he was going to do some stuff to help LGBT people? I guess he decided not to, in the end.

"Are you okay?" Caitlin asks.

"Yeah, I guess."

"How do you feel?"

"I'm not sure. I just feel... kind of numb to it? Like, why would he do that? I just feel confusion about it. Maybe it hasn't really hit me yet, I don't know. How about you?"

"Not good."

Caitlin slides up to me on the bench and gives me a hug, then starts weeping on my shoulder. It's unusual to have this situation reversed, usually I'm the one crying on her shoulder. I drop the phone on the bench and hug her back, I don't really know what else to do. After a minute she relaxes her embrace and stares into my eyes.

"He was really going to change things," Caitlin says.

I just stare back for a while, and then divert my gaze randomly to the ground. It's awkward to have such close eye contact, even with Caitlin.

"You're not that affected at all, are you?" she asks.

"I guess not. I mainly feel guilty. I feel like I should be having the reaction that *you're* having. I mean, that would make sense, right? Is something wrong with me, that I'm just not that bothered? I'm honestly mainly just thinking about what's going to happen to the song I recorded, will they still use it without Yohan advocating for me? But then I just feel guilty for that, I shouldn't be thinking of myself here, right? Does this mean I'm a bad person?"

"Everyone reacts differently to things like this. There's no judgement here. I just want to make sure that you're not repressing anything."

I think about this for a few seconds. Am I repressing?

"I don't feel like I am. I mean, I'm maybe a little upset, just because I feel like I'm a bad person, for *not* being upset... does that make sense?"

"You can only feel what you feel."

"I know I'm not repressing. I mean, I'm not the best person at hiding how I feel, even when I want to!"

Caitlin laughs a little through the tears.

"Yeah, that's so true actually! Hey, I got you these..."

Caitlin reaches into her bag and pulls out a small case. She hands me the case, it's my new glasses. I carefully take them out of the case and put them on.

"You look great in those!" Caitlin says.

I start looking around the yard, and remember what the optometrist told me. The top part of the lenses is long distance, so I can see far away, and the bottom part allows me to see things close up, and there's a smooth gradation between the two types of lenses, so it doesn't look like my mother's ugly bifocals where there's that stupid ugly horizontal line going right along the middle. That's good because I really didn't want my glasses to remind me of my mother. Looking around the yard, everything looks crisp and defined. I pick Caitlin's phone up from the bench and take a look at it, it's crystal clear.

"Caitlin, these are amazing. I will wear these constantly, thank you so much. I just have one question though."

"What is it?"

"Why didn't you show me the article after you gave me my glasses so I could actually read the fucking thing without straining my eyes?"

Caitlin starts laughing and gives me another embrace.

"I just forgot, I'm sorry. I was upset. I still am, but I love how you make me laugh Hana, you're adorable."

I sink into Caitlin's arms, thinking about nothing other than I'm glad I make her as happy as she makes me. At least I hope so.

138. MANDARIN

"We're going to go back to Mandarin lessons for this week. We will receive more work from Hancel soon, so it's important that we all have some understanding of the language. Even learning the rudiments will help us deal with the executives. Please open your exercise books and we will start."

Ijun opens up a pink laptop and starts typing quickly.

"Can we ask a few things first?" says Nari.

"Yes."

"Is the funeral date for Yohan announced yet? We'd all like to go."

"Not yet. But it is fine for you all to go. We will pick a time to attend that fits in with everybody's activities, and that way you all can attend together."

"Will they still use Hana's song?" asks Caitlin.

"There is no news on that. We will let you know."

"Are you okay?" asks Shu.

Ijun just stares blankly at nothing for a few seconds.

"Don't ask me personal questions. Let's do the lesson now. Shu, you're very fluent in Mandarin, yes?"

Shu nods. Ijun then says a sentence to Shu in Mandarin. Everyone looks at Ijun. I'm pretty sure that none of us knew she could speak Mandarin. Shu and Ijun then start talking to each other, having a full conversation between each other in Mandarin. The words roll of Ijun's tongue, it's obvious that she can speak it well, perhaps not as well as Shu but well enough to have a rapid conversation. As they talk more, I notice Shu smiling a lot, she's really enjoying this for some reason. After a couple of minutes, Ijun turns to face the rest of us.

"We are going to do some Mandarin phrase exercises now. Shu is going to say sentences to me in Mandarin, and I am going to type their meanings into my laptop in Korean, and show them to all of you. Phrases that you need help with, you can whisper to Shu in Korean, and she will say them to me in Mandarin. Please, everybody sit up very close to the desk here, so you can all easily read my computer screen when I turn it around to give you the answers, like this."

Ijun spins her laptop around so it is facing us. There is a message on the screen for us.

As you now know, you are all being recorded. I am also recorded at all times. Aside from (don't stare at it!) the camera in the vent that I showed you, there is a microphone (but not a camera) hidden in the top button of my outfit. The microphone is very sensitive and will pick up most sounds. My electronic devices are also monitored, they are always completely compromised, Mr Park checks my phone and computer five times per day and has access to all my online accounts. However, Mr Park doesn't know more than just the most basic Mandarin phrases, nor do his staff. He would become suspicious of Mandarin texts or emails, but we can talk freely in this room if we can make it look like a lesson. We can't do this often as Mr Park CEO is smart, he will catch on quickly if we make it a habit, but maybe once in a rare while.

Ijun turns her laptop screen back around so it faces her.

"Shu, please ask the first phrase. You can make it as long as necessary. Variety in phrases is good for learning."

Shu talks to Ijun for about a minute. Ijun then starts typing, she's a quick typist and it doesn't take long for her to type a lot of text. She then turns the screen to us.

Thank you for your concern about my welfare. I am struggling with life right now. Study is hard. Dealing with the demands of work is harder. It is very difficult. Also I am very lonely. I don't get to see my family, and I don't have people my age that I can talk to, at school they don't talk to me because they know about Mr Park so I am avoided. This is why I want to talk to you this way. Things are becoming more stressful and I want to talk to you face to face, but I have more restrictions now than ever before. Mr Park doesn't want me talking to you openly as a friend, he wants me to maintain the relationship as business only, but I disagree with this. It is one of the many things we argue about. Also language class is boring, so I think this activity will help the classes go quicker. If this works out well maybe we can do it more in future.

Ijun gives us all some time to read the message.

"Please take note of the message. Nod when you are done. Then Shu can either do another phrase of her own invention, or any of you can whisper a phrase to her and Shu will then repeat to me in Mandarin."

We all nod, Nari walks up and whispers in Shu's ear. Shu then asks Ijun something, a couple of sentences. Ijun spends a while typing before turning the screen to us.

When you all first arrived here, there were no cameras or microphones, but Mr Park has been gradually putting them in one by one ever since Ms Han your old dance coach left. The microphone in my outfit, that went in yesterday, so whenever you see me in uniform from now on, be careful what you say. The only place they are not is in the yard and the dorms. I will tell you if this changes, Youngsook keep checking the camera each time I give it to you so I can show you exactly where it is placed. I can promise you that none of you will earn any money while you are here. I would advise that you use whatever fame you now have to secure opportunities... but don't do any paid work that you don't have to while you are under contract to Mr Park! He will want a cut, and by 'cut' I mean 100%. Just plan for the future, and be careful.

We all read and nod. Iseul runs over to Shu and whispers something to her, it takes her a while to convey the question. Shu then speaks in Mandarin for a while. Ijun spends a few seconds thinking before responding and showing us the message.

I promise you that there is zero chance Mr Park will sexually assault any one of you. Physically, maybe if you irritate him enough, he might. Iseul and Hana, you two are the most likely to be hit, because you both irritate him, watch yourselves. But sexually, no, you are safe. He might send you to his disgusting "business locations" when you act up just to humiliate you, but he will never lay a hand on you himself in that way. Please don't ask me how I know this, I can't discuss it, not even like this. Just trust me that this is true. I swear it.

We read the message and nod. Shu then starts talking to Ijun in Mandarin again, I guess she has another question of her own. Ijun looks a bit shaken as she types a response into her laptop and shows us.

I auditioned for Halcyon, the same as some of you, but I was not selected. However Mr Park then contacted my parents about being staff instead so that's how I am here. Please do not ask me about the relationship, I won't discuss it, other than yes at this point we are still engaged. I don't know when the marriage is exactly. Mr Park is being evasive about it, I have a feeling that it might not happen. I can't reveal more than this.

We read the message and nod. Youngsook then walks up to Shu and whispers a question, it takes a while for her to convey it. Shu then says a long group of sentences to Ijun. Ijun's emotional state seems to get a little better, I can tell that she likes this subject more. Ijun types for a while before showing us the message.

Thanks for the compliment on my singing, Youngsook. Yes, I can sing well! It's frustrating to not be in your group sometimes, but then I see how you are treated and then I feel luckier that I was not selected. The diet here won't improve. I'm fully aware of what Nari is doing with the diet plan, as well as Iseul with the food smuggling. I am in full support of these activities! Mr Park has heard you talking about it (you were recorded in the kitchen when you planned it) but he wants to catch you in the act to be sure. I agree that the official health and meal regimen in this place is harmful. I have tried to advocate for better treatment for you girls but Mr Park won't listen. I will continue to help you here, as I can. I have limited power.

We all read the message and nod.

"It's my turn!" says Caitlin, as she goes up to Shu and says something to her, which doesn't take long. Shu starts laughing, and then starts talking in Mandarin, just a sentence. Ijun smiles and types something out quickly.

Caitlin, if you want to see his hydroponic setup just ask him about it plainly, he has a massive ego and will show it off gladly! He is oddly proud of his indoor garden.

We all read and nod. None of us can stop giggling.

"Please do not laugh at the exercises. It's important that we increase our Mandarin learning," says Ijun, doing her best to keep a straight face.

"I have more ques... um, phrases!" says Caitlin, who says a few more sentences to Shu. Shu initially looks concerned, but then starts giggling just before reciting it in Mandarin. Ijun's reaction is kind of awkward looking. She thinks for about half a minute before typing and showing us her response.

Hana and Caitlin, the "business locations", there are at least seven, most are worse than what you have seen, more disgusting. Mr Park likes to humiliate and belittle as punishment. This is why it is hard for him to retain staff, you might think it is the treatment you give them that makes them leave, but I think it is actually how he chooses to reprimand them when they are not able to control you. Privacy - I understand that not being able to be alone together is difficult. As you know we have ample private facilities in the basement, but how do I get you down there without getting us all into trouble, I do not know, I have not solved this problem. It's easy when Mr Park isn't around, but usually when he is gone, it's to accompany the group, so it's rare that he isn't here and you also are here. I will let you know if something comes up.

We all read the message. I see Nari rolling her eyes a little. Everyone else is smiling. I know exactly what I want to ask Ijun.

"It's my turn!" I say, as I move my chair over to Shu and whisper in her ear.

"Do you need any *help* with your situation? If you do, I would like an opportunity to *help*. I'm good at *helping*."

Shu starts talking to Ijun. Ijun spends a while thinking before typing her reply. She shows the screen to the room.

Hana, I am not sure what you mean, but if you want to help me: I had to change phone numbers when Mr Park smashed my piece of junk Hancel phone because I wanted to switch phone carriers away from them and they wouldn't let me keep my old number and transfer it across to the new company. Don't ever get a Hancel phone, shit company, shit phones, shit customer service even if you are a high-value customer with huge bills who always pays on time, I'm never using them again. So can you please get in touch with Jihu and give him my new number? I miss my gamer friend. Tell him my texts are monitored so he should text me with something that looks like a spam text (like "you have a package, click this link to track it"), and just put Jihu somewhere in a fake URL so I know it's him. I will then reach out to him later when I am able. Also tell him I am cheering for him in the quarter-finals.

I read the message and nod.

"I have another phrase."

I lean into Shu's ear.

"Thanks for making the videos, very useful. What was with that dance in the last video? I mean, the very end where you just kind of stopped? I think it's cool that you're learning our dances, by the way."

Shu speaks my question to Ijun in Mandarin. Ijun puts her head down and types something quickly.

I like the Halcyon dances. I just forgot the dance step. Sorry to concern you, I should have not left that in there. Just look after yourselves and don't worry. Let's not speak about it again.

I nod at Ijun. She looks upset. It's pretty obvious that something isn't right, but I don't know what. Maybe one of the other girls will figure it out.

139. GO-STOP

"A card game? Are you serious?"

Caitlin stares at Iseul as she shuffles the *hwatu* deck. "Sure."

"Yes, but we're at a funeral? Isn't this disrespectful?"

"Look around, does anybody care?"

Caitlin looks around and I can't help but do the same as I'm sitting next to her. We're seated with all the other girls in the group at a table in part of the funeral building. The room is a large dining hall area with traditional style square wooden architecture, full of benches and tables. It's really crowded here, there's about a dozen tables here and they're all full of men in black suits and women in black formal dresses, noisily talking. Although we're also dressed in black, we're probably the most casually dressed people here. I've chosen an ankle length black pleated skirt that fastens with a big decorative bow at the front and a fuzzy black jumper with a white shirt underneath, it's about as "funeral friendly" an outfit that I could arrange from what I currently have available. I can't help but stare at Caitlin even more than usual; she's wearing a knee-length pleated blazer dress with large buttons at the front, it's very stylish, one of her best outfits. Caitlin looks a bit flustered by Iseul's question, because Iseul is actually right; Caitlin doesn't understand the funeral culture at all. Not that I would expect that of her, but it's clear that Iseul does. I watch as Iseul rolls her eyes and acts like a snooty bitch, which she's very good at.

"Caitlin the *gyopo* telling me what's respectful in my own country, what would you know, idiot? Were you born here? Did you grow up here? Did I argue when you were giving me your dumb lectures about America?"

"Yes, you argued all the time actually."

Iseul ignores Caitlin's reply and looks at everyone else at the table.

"Okay, so does anyone here not know the rules of go-stop, besides Caitlin?"

"Me!" shouts Shu.

"Okay, I'll tell you how to play, I'll start by dealing out the cards. We'll do open hand for the first round just so I can explain how it works. Also we need something to gamble with, because this game is a lot more fun if there are some stakes at play."

"You're *gambling* at a funeral?" asks Caitlin.

"Oh wow, *gyopo* please screw off back to America."

"Don't be mean!" says Shu.

Nari suddenly stands up.

"Iseul can you please shut it or I'll smack it shut?"

315

Iseul glares at Nari but doesn't say anything. Iseul knows from watching me get hit by Nari enough times that Nari will come good on that threat if pushed.

Caitlin grabs my hand.

"Let's go for a walk, what do you think?"

"Fine with me, I don't care about a stupid card game."

We both stand up. Caitlin gives the group a little wave.

"Bye everyone, we're going for a walk now. Nari, how long have we got before Mr Park comes back to pick us up?"

"Two hours."

"Thanks! Bye now!"

I trail behind Caitlin, holding her hand as she walks into the aisle between the tables. She seems to be looking for somewhere we can sit together, but it's so crowded here, there's no seats free. Yohan was popular and it seems like the entire entertainment industry has been invited to his funeral. At least there's no fans and no press either, both of which have been mercifully banned from this event. Caitlin points to a hallway off to the side.

"Hey, what's down here?"

Before I can answer Caitlin starts wandering down the hallway, dragging me with her. The hallway we're in has several doorways off to the side, each with a sliding wooden door that is partway open. We walk into the first room together. It's a small room with a picture of Yohan displayed prominently on the far wall opposite the door, it looks like it was taken during one of his concerts and shows him mid-singing. On each side of the picture are some fabrics in various colours, arranged like a rainbow pattern. In the centre of the room is a small table with a box of tissues, a tea pot, and some teacups, and on the other two sides of the room are two lounge sofas. This looks like the perfect place to sit with Caitlin.

"Ladies, can I help you?"

We turn around, there's a woman dressed in a grey suit staring at us. She has the insignia of the funeral home on her suit jacket, she must be one of the staff.

"Hi! I'm Caitlin, I'm one of the guests! I'm just trying to find my way around! What is this room for?"

"This is one of the private mourning rooms. We have four of these, we have set these up for family members, relatives, and close associates who wish to grieve privately for Yohan."

"Have they been used much?"

"Yesterday there were many people wanting to use the rooms after the ceremonies. However as you can see they're empty now. I think most people who wished to use these facilities have already done so and are now in the main hall, but we are keeping them on standby."

Caitlin squeezes my hand slightly, not enough for the change to be visible to the funeral home lady, but enough for me to notice. I know exactly what she's thinking, I'm thinking it also.

"Hey... is it possible that we could borrow a room for a while? Myself and Hana here, we're... quite upset about Yohan but we don't want to cause a big display in front of the other guests. We'd be very grateful to have access to

317

somewhere quiet where we could... grieve in peace and won't be disturbed for a while."

"Yes, we don't want to cause any problems by being emotional or sullen in front of our seniors, they have high expectations of us to remain stoic and we're not sure that we could live up to them at this difficult time," I add.

"Yes, the rooms are not busy today so that is fine."

Caitlin smiles and does a little jump for joy.

"Thank you so much! Does the door lock?"

"No it does not. But I can place something in front of it to ensure that there is no access so that you are not disturbed."

"You're amazing, thank you! We promise not to be any bother to you!"

"It's fine. Just leave the door open when you are done so I know to make it available for access again."

"Thank you!"

Caitlin and I both bow at ninety degrees to the funeral home lady. She smiles and exits the room, gently sliding the door behind her closed.

"Just wait for it," Caitlin says.

We stand there and wait. We hear the lady walk down the hall, then her footsteps approaching again. The next sound is her sliding a couple of objects in front of the door on the other side, then her footsteps gradually trail off again.

"Think we're in the clear?" Caitlin asks.

"I think so."

"We still have to be a bit careful, just in case someone comes barging in. A lot of the people in the main hall were drinking, which is *bizarre* for a funeral, like, this whole shit is weird. But they are going to get more and more drunk as the day goes on, it's possible that they may not respect whatever that lady did to block the doorway. So let's not lose too many clothes, as we might need to put them back on and pretend that we're 'just grieving' really quickly."

Caitlin leads me over to one of the sofas and we sit next to each other. I should explain to her about how funerals here are different, so she understands.

"It's not so odd. People drink here at funerals all the time, it's really common in this country."

"Uh huh."

I suddenly gasp as Caitlin hikes the bottom of my jumper up to above my chest and starts caressing my torso through my shirt. I feel the warmth of her soft hands through the fabric. I want to feel her skin on mine, but I also want to explain to her about funeral culture because it's important, so I'm going to try to keep talking to her.

"It's... not like a funeral in the American movies, you know... where everyone is always miserable..."

Caitlin leans forward into me and starts kissing me on the neck, while working the buttons of my shirt lose. My breathing becomes heavier, it's becoming harder and harder to get the words out.

"It goes for... three days, you can't just... cry for three days straight..."

I hear a few quick pops in a row as Caitlin rips open the front of her blazer dress and the chunky buttons holding it together at the front give way.

"That's why there's the... games and the drinking... you know... you have to pass the time... ah..."

Caitlin reaches down to my waist and unties the bow that holds my skirt up against my body with one swift movement. She then grabs the pleats and pulls the top of my skirt down to my thighs.

"Don't you think you're... a hypocrite anyway... you're complaining about games and gambling and... drinking, but this... is way worse, totally not allowed, ah... oh my fucking god, fuck..."

Caitlin learns forward, pressing her body against mine and I instinctively press back, craving her touch more and more. With her left hand she moves gently between my thighs, applying soft pressure between my legs, and with her right hand she puts her index finger up to her lips.

"Shh. Just enjoy the ride. We both know this is exactly what Yohan would have wanted."

140. BAIT

"Hana, what time machine did you get this from?"

I'm sitting cross-legged on the bed with Astrid in her ridiculously pink bedroom. Astrid inspects the phone that I just gave her, some weird grey oval-shaped bubble thing with way too many buttons that I got from Jane.

"I'd tell you where this stuff comes from if I knew. I just get given it."

"It's so weird looking. What's this little black button here and why is it higher than the others? Oh wait, I think that's a stick, I can push it from the side. Wow, what a weird system. How do I even make a call on it?"

"The last time I used an ancient phone like this, I just pressed the numbers and then there was a button with a picture of a phone handset on it and I pressed that."

"Well there's nothing like that on this phone."

Astrid shows me the phone. All the buttons have either letters or numbers, or they're just horizontal lines. There's nothing that would be obviously used to dial someone.

"Oh. Then I don't know."

"I'll just try anything I guess."

Astrid reads off the business card which is next to her on the bed, punching the numbers into the phone. Each push gives an electronic beep.

"Ah okay, it says 'call' once I type in numbers. Hey the 'three' button doesn't even work on this thing?"

"Oh?"

"Oh never mind, I just have to press it really hard... okay, okay, I think I know what to do. I've worked this out, yep. Hopefully I can put him on speaker easily. Get ready."

Astrid looks at the ceiling and starts taking some deep breaths.

"What are you doing? Are you alright?"

"Just getting in character. I have to psyche myself into this a little... okay, I think I'm ready, let's do it. I apologise in advance for making you cringe. This is going to be so bad, seriously. Just... tell yourself it's for a good cause. Oh, and take this."

Astrid grabs one of the pink pillows from the head of the bed and tosses it into my lap.

"What's this for?"

"If you feel yourself wanting to scream, or laugh, or cry, just throw your face into the pillow to muffle the sound. Okay, here we go."

Astrid presses a button and puts the phone up to her ear nervously. We both wait for about ten seconds.

"*Yeoboseyo?*"

I can't hear if she's got Mr Jeong or not.

"*Yeoboseyo?*"

Astrid shrugs at me, before her eyes suddenly light up.

"Mister Jeong? Yes, I'm Astrid, from White Iris, do you remember me?"

I can't hear Mr Jeong's part of the conversation. Astrid takes her phone away from her ear quickly, I think she's looking for a way to put it on speaker. After a few seconds she shrugs and just continues. I think she's given up.

"Yes, you gave me your card ... Yeah, I just wanted to ring, because ... You know, ever since you gave me your card, I just can't stop thinking about you, you know ... like, I swear, I have no interest in my boyfriend any more, he wants to know what's up and I just can't tell him ... I guess I do, Mr Jeong! ... So I'm really keen to meet you!"

Astrid is right, this is horribly cringy, I feel so awkward listening to this. Astrid looks at me for a moment and puts her hand over her mouth. She's trying not to laugh. I turn my face away from her a little, I think me staring at her while she does this isn't helping.

"Yes ... I like a man who takes care of himself ... We could, but my schedule is really busy, plus you know what I want, and I think I know what you want, so why don't we skip dinner? ... I mean yes, we're busy people, sure ... It's good to meet someone so proactive ... Oh my!"

Astrid's voice becomes flirtier and breathier as the conversation progresses. I put my head face-first into the pillow to stop myself from screaming with laughter. Astrid is really hamming it up.

"You do that, Mr Jeong ... Is that right ... You know, I feel really comfortable talking to you, but I'd feel better about meeting in person ... Oh, you can meet tonight?"

Astrid looks at me, looking for confirmation. I give her a quick nod.

"Oh, the sooner the better, baby! ... I can't wait, just tell me where ... I'm a little restricted on that, agency rules, you know, but the time and place are fine! ... Oh, I wish ... Yes Mr Jeong *oppa,* I'll be there ... Oh, Mr Jeong I think I'm going to get in trouble if I don't hang up quickly, the staff are looking at me funny ... Goodbye Mr Jeong!"

Astrid takes the phone away from her ear and presses a button on it a few times.

"Okay that's hung up for sure! Oh my god!"

Astrid lies back on the bed and starts laughing.

"I tried to put him on speaker, but I'm now glad I didn't. You're actually so lucky that you couldn't hear what he was saying to me!"

"He was that bad?"

"He was... *very* keen. He's ready. I've got his address in my head, I'll look it up while I still remember it."

Astrid sits up, gives the ancient bubble phone back to me, and picks her own phone up from the bed. I should thank Astrid for her efforts, she did great.

"Thanks so much for doing that. I mean after my history with him, there's no way that I could make the call myself. He would never believe it coming from me."

"Let's just check out a map... oh wow, look at that, now that's impressive."

Astrid shows me her phone screen. Mr Jeong's place is like a small mansion, actually it's not that different to Astrid's own house.

"I think your place is better than his."

"He has a fountain! I *so* wish I had a fountain. I keep asking my mother about it but she thinks it's a waste of water, so I tell her that you recycle the water but then she says that you still have to power it, so then I say you can power it with solar panels but she says the panels need space, and there isn't anywhere to put them, and..."

"Why do you want a fountain?"

"Well, *feng shui* of course! A fountain is much better for *feng shui*, especially if you also happen to have a semi-circle driveway, because without something to catch it the *qi* energy will just flow into your front garden and then straight back out again."

"In Korea it's *pungsu*. You should check it with *pungsu* because the rules are slightly different here and your house might still be better. Only *pungsu* works here, *feng shui* only works if you're in China. We don't do cheap Chinese *qi* energy here."

"Well I guess I should worry more about how you're going to *pungsu* your way in and out of there."

"I have people for that. I'll be flowing some energy of my own straight into Mr Jeong soon, don't worry."

"I can't stress enough how ready for action he sounded on the phone. When you see him, don't hesitate. Just pull that fucking gun on him straight away, I swear to god."

141. EXECUTION

It's night and I've just arrived outside Mr Jeong's luxury mansion on the outskirts of Seoul. I'm wearing a black tracksuit and a black hooded jumper, a clothing choice suggested by Jane. I also have my gym bag with me, with the gun inside. Jane's dealer was able to get the gun that I wanted with the auto-fire switch, so I'm really looking forward to firing lots of bullets into Mr Jeong very quickly tonight. I've come up against a problem straight away though; there's a four-metre-high barred fence surrounding the house. I stare through the fence bars at the semi-circular driveway, it looks like I've approached the house from the side, so I'm at the side fence. The house looks exactly the same as the picture Astrid showed me, including the fountain that she liked so much, which seems to be switched off as there's no lights on it or water flowing. I guess having a fountain isn't that great after all. I wonder if a fountain that doesn't have water flowing still captures qi energy? I guess I can ask Astrid that next time I see her. Beyond the driveway, parked up against the house is a white sedan and a tiny red sports car. I recognise the sports car, I've seen it before in our CEO Mr Park's basement garage. Does that mean Mr Park is also here, visiting Mr Jeong? Perhaps now isn't the best time for me to do this, not that I really want to back out at this point. Then again, it could mean that it's Mr Jeong's car and he was the one visiting our premises when I saw his car in our garage? I shudder at the thought of Mr Jeong potentially having access to our dormitory. I guess that whichever way it is, if these two are visiting each other at their homes and that's something they do often, that might mean they're pretty close. Maybe they're best friends, which would explain why Mr Park never wants to criticise him for anything. I guess it doesn't matter as it won't be a problem soon.

I walk along the side fence and around the corner towards where the driveway meets the front fence, there has to be gates there to let cars and people in and out. I walk until I reach the driveway gate, it's closed. I search but I don't see anything obvious to open it with, I guess it must open electronically. I keep walking over to the second gate that services the other end of the semi-circular driveway, it's closed as well. There's a little black box with a button on it next to the gate, I guess that's the intercom for visitors. Should I use the intercom and bluff my way in by pretending to be Astrid, or should I just climb over the fence? The fence seems like it wouldn't be that hard to climb, the problem might be if I have to get out again quickly. I notice that the intercom box has a lens on it, that must be a camera that activates when someone uses the intercom. Even if I can fake Astrid's odd accent, as soon as Mr Jeong sees me through that camera he's going to know that I'm not her. Climbing the fence is definitely looking like the better option.

I walk a little bit away from the gate and start scaling the fence a few metres down, which is easy enough to do, but once I get about one metre high I start panicking. What if I fall? How will I get down again safely once I reach the top? What if I get stuck up there? I don't do well with heights and I'm not doing well with this, I can feel the fear kick in around my lower abdomen and the panic starts spreading through my body. I let myself slide slowly down the fence rails until I reach the ground again. So much for climbing, I guess I'm using the intercom.

I walk up to the intercom again. I should think about how to approach this, and what to say. Obviously he'll know I'm not Astrid because I can't hide the fact that I don't have long blonde hair and I'm not tall. However if I hide my face enough, maybe he'll at least not recognise me as Hana straight away. Mind you if he does know who I am, he might just come out here. After all he was going to 'get' me after Music Train, whatever that means, so he might just decide to do it now. Perhaps honesty is the best policy, after all it's what I'm good at. I'll just tell him that I'm Hana and I want to see him, fuck it.

I press the button on the intercom. A screen on the intercom box lights up, it's a camera feed from inside the house. Nobody is there. I wait a while, nothing happens. I press the button again. Still nothing. Could it be that nobody's home? That would seem weird with two cars in the driveway, I doubt this rich asshole would take public transport anywhere, if cars are there, he has to be home.

I'm interrupted by a sound of a car door opening and two men talking. I look over beyond the driveway. I recognise Mr Park's voice immediately, he's having a conversation with Mr Jeong. I can't really make out what they're saying to each other but they're laughing it up about something, I can't tell what it is but it makes me angry just watching them. They don't deserve to be this happy about anything. It looks like Mr Park was the one visiting and Mr Jeong is now seeing him off. I guess nobody answering the intercom was because Mr Jeong was busy seeing Mr Park to the door. That's good because it probably means nobody else is inside the house, so less chance for this to get messy. Mr Park closes the door of his car and starts the engine. I duck down behind the fence as the front gate automatically swings open and Mr Park's car drives through it. I watch his car vanish down the road and quickly run through the front gate into the darkness of the unlit front lawn before the gate closes back in on me. As it shuts, I realise... maybe I'm now trapped inside? I look at the front gate from the other side, there's a pole with a button on it a few metres back from the fence. I think that might be a manual gate release but it doesn't say anything on it, and I don't want to test it. I'll take a closer look after the deed is done, if I'm wrong I'll look for another way out.

I look back at the house, Mr Jeong has already gone inside. I guess he didn't notice me come in. I walk up to the front door, while putting my right hand inside my gym bag, feeling the grip of the gun. I need to think up the best strategy. Should I just knock, or would it be better to try and creep in somehow? I should maybe walk around the house and examine all the entrances, so I can make a plan. Before I can think of what to do next, the front door opens. Mr Jeong is standing in the doorway, staring at me.

"Oh hello, Astrid... you must have snuck in. Nice to see you."

This idiot thinks I'm Astrid? We couldn't look more different if we tried. What a moron. He'll be dead soon anyway so whatever. I pull the gun out of the bag, point it at him and pull the trigger. Nothing happens, just a click.

"Hana?"

He just stares at me, I think he's in shock. That's good it gives me a few seconds to act. Why didn't the gun fire? It's that stupid slider thing at the top, I know it. Why does every gun have a stupid thing at the top. Maybe I should consider a revolver next time. I pull back the stupid sliding thing and it makes a clicking noise, then I pull the trigger again. The gun erupts in a hail of bullets and smoke, firing so fast I can't even control it. After about a second I've fired every shot. Mr Jeong is still standing there. He's speechless for some reason. How is he still standing there? What the fuck?

"Did I seriously not even hit you once?"

"Hana..."

"No fucking way! How did none of my bullets hit you? That's such bullshit! You're not supposed to just be standing there!"

Mr Jeong bends forward slightly. Did I hit him after all, is that why he's bending over? No that's not it, he's just picking up a baseball bat which is by the door. I've got a second magazine but I don't really have time to reload that now. I start thinking that I should probably just run before he hits me with that bat. I start running but I suddenly realise that I can't. My feet are moving but why aren't I going anywhere? Oh, that's because I'm flat on my back. That's definitely a problem. How did I get like this? I don't remember falling over? Did he hit me with the bat or did something else happen? I should get up and run, otherwise who knows what will happen. I try to get up but there's a force stopping me, that's much more powerful.

"Hey! Just lie back down. Don't stress your body."

It's Jane's voice. Her hand pushes against my chest and forces me to lie back down. I suddenly realise that I'm lying down in the back of Jane's van.

"Where am I?"

"In my van."

I'm not sure why I asked that. I know where I am.

"Sorry, I meant... what happened? How did I get here?"

"We came and got you."

"Where is he? Are we in danger?"

Jane leans over so I can see her mask-clad face.

"Don't worry, you did good. You got him."

"I wasn't sure. I thought I missed all my shots."

"Well, you did miss most of them, but you can't really miss every single shot with a weapon like that, not at such close range. Not unless you're blind or drunk. You got him good, but it looks like he used his last few seconds of life to give you a bit of a bruising. Hold still, this might hurt a bit."

Jane turns my head to the side, I suddenly become aware of a stinging sensation above my ear, running down my neck to my left shoulder blade.

"Ah fuck, what are you doing?"

"Just checking you out. I think your shoulder took most of the impact. Your head doesn't look too bad. How does your body feel? Just run your hands over your body and try to move all your limbs."

I do as Jane instructs.

"I feel pretty sore all over my body. But I think I can move everyth... ow! Okay, I think my left thigh is pretty tender. The rest is okay, I think."

"Okay, that's probably another bat impact. You'll probably feel it more over the next couple days. Anyway just relax for now. It's over."

"What happens now?"

"Your clothes are a bloody mess, so we'll get you to take those off and we'll dispose of them and give you something else to wear. Then we'll drop you back at the agency."

"What about Mr Jeong?"

"We've got some people taking care of the mess you left, don't worry about it."

"Just so you know, Mr Park was with him, he left just before I arrived."

"Were you seen?"

"No, there's no way he saw."

"Good girl. You're getting better at this. Are you sure you're not looking for a permanent job?"

"I can't, I'm still under contract at the agency."

"For a criminal, you seem oddly concerned about legal matters."

"I'm not a criminal, fuck off!"

Jane laughs.

"Maybe not to my standard yet. Keep working at it."

142. SPECIAL VIDEO

"Damn Hana, that's quite a bruise. It looks evil. How did you get it?"

All the girls are in the dining room, we've finished our almost non-existent dinner and are killing time before we have to go back and do more practice. Youngsook is holding her camera and filming us all for the reality show. Nari is inspecting the bruise that Mr Jeong gave me on my shoulder and neck.

"I was in Caitlin's bunk and I fell out, and my neck hit the frame on the way down."

"You were in my bunk?" asks Caitlin.

I give Caitlin a slight poke in the thigh under the table with my finger. She stares at me and then suddenly realises.

"Oh yes, that's right, you were, how could I forget."

"That'll teach you two not to do lesbian shit in your bunk, I hope," scolds Nari.

I smile at Caitlin.

"Caitlin, it's official. Nari says you have to come down to *my* bunk to do lesbian shit."

"Okay, I can comply with that. No lesbian activity on the premises at more than one metre above ground level."

Caitlin gives Nari a salute and then starts laughing.

The door to the dining room opens. Ijun walks in, wearing her usual school uniform, and looking as flat and miserable as usual. We all bow in unison.

"*Annyeong!*"

"I just would like to inform you of some important updates. Firstly, from this Friday through to Sunday, Mr Park will not be on the premises. He will be attending the funeral of Mr Jeong, the PD of Music Train, for the entire duration."

"Thank you for letting us know," says Nari.

"Halcyon's appearance on Music Train will also not be going ahead, as Music Train itself is also on a week of hiatus for mourning. We will attempt to reschedule your appearance for later when the show resumes. This means that the next televised performance for Halcyon will be Platinum Hour."

"Understood," says Nari.

"Next, we are producing an official lightstick for Halcyon's fans. As we don't know how popular these will be, we are starting off with a limited run. We will provide you each a lightstick soon for you to promote on your social media."

"What does it look like?" asks Shu.

"It looks like a stick that lights up. Hana, I have some news for you. There is quite a lot of interest in the song 'The Love Complete' since the passing of Yohan, so we would like you to make a special video for it so we can promote the song and drive traffic to Halcyon's other activities. We want to move on this as quickly as possible as we don't know how long interest will last. Youngsook, you can record Hana doing this in the studio in a moment. Record her a few times, I'll edit it down later tonight when I get the camera back off you, and we will then put it up on our social media straight away."

"Sure, I can do that!" says Youngsook.

"Shu, news for you also. You will be hired again for a second appearance promoting Hancel phones."

"Yay! Is Hana coming too?" says Shu.

"Hana will not be required for the new advert, but the company did make special mention of her contribution to the virality of the previous film and paid accordingly. So Hana, I think you should not be discouraged, your activity for Hancel has had a positive outcome and was well rewarded."

Shu and I both nod.

"One last thing. Mr Park is very upset about Mr Jeong's passing, as they were in the process of becoming very close business partners when he passed. Please be mindful of this when dealing with Mr Park over the next week, until the funeral date. He is likely to be quicker to anger than usual, so please remain on your best behaviour at all times. Also please do not disturb him unless it is an absolutely critical situation."

"Oh, so he's not the delightful, even-tempered person that he usually is, then?" says Iseul.

I start giggling, I know I shouldn't but I can't help it. It's funny because it's true. Iseul can get away with statements like that without being reprimanded, but I can't, however I can still enjoy them.

"Just be careful what you say to him and how you act. If in doubt, come to me. Anyway, that is all," says Ijun, who then walks out of the room without another word.

"Careful," says Nari, while playing with her earlobe.

"I don't think I even give a shit," replies Iseul.

"Hey, does anyone here have Hana's song on their phone?" Youngsook asks.

"I do!" says Shu.

"Hana and Shu, follow me, let's do this recording!"

Who knows why the hell Shu has my song on her phone but whatever. I follow Youngsook and Shu as they get up and walk out of the dining room and down the hall. Youngsook unlocks the studio double doors and we enter.

"Here, stand behind the microphone. Shu is going to play the song on her phone. Hana, sing along in time to it, and just do the usual, you know, try to look convincing, like you're really singing it."

"Where's Mr Nam? We're not recording this?"

"He's not around, he gave me the studio key. No we're not recording sound, it's just visuals for the video. Ijun will sync it over the audio that already exists."

"Cool. So I can fuck it up then?"

"Yes, just go wild, it doesn't matter. As long as your lips are in sync with the words on the recording, and you look like you're really singing it, that's really all that matters for this. And hey we'll use a prettier microphone, it'll come out better on the video."

Youngsook takes away the big grey microphone that's on the stand, and replaces it with another only slightly different looking grey microphone on another stand.

"Okay Shu, start up the track."

Shu starts playing the song on her phone. I do my most convincing impersonation of a singer who actually knows how to sing.

Look at me and smile / I was so thankful for you / Coming into focus / The love complete

I hear laughter behind me. I turn around, Caitlin and Iseul have taken pillows from the dorm and are smacking each other in the head for some reason. I do my best to ignore them and continue on.

The place where we walked / New flowers bloom / Shapes in the distant sky / The love complete

I suddenly feel a pillow landing on the back of my head. I turn around and Iseul is laughing.

"Hey, I'm trying to look serious and stuff!"

"Yeah, stop it Iseul, you whore!" says Caitlin, smacking Iseul around the face. Iseul grabs her pillow from the floor and starts hitting Caitlin back. I try to keep miming.

Let us meet again / When we see tomorrow / Walk along a flower path / The love complete

"Shut up, you dirty bitch! Stop upsetting your lesbian lover!" Iseul screams.

"You're just jealous because you're still in the closet!"

"I'll never be jealous of you two clowns!"

"This isn't helping me get into the right mood," I say to Youngsook.

"Ijun is the editing master, she'll make it work."

Shu starts the recording again and I sigh. I'm not sure what's more stupid, singing or pretending to sing, but I could honestly live without both in my life.

143. PRIVATE BROWSING

Me: annyeong
   Gyeongja: Haaaaanaaaaaaaaaaaaaa our saviour
   Gyeongja: Hana Hana Hana Hana Hana
   Gyeongja: Hana Hana Hana
   Gyeongja: Hana Hana Hana
   Gyeongja: Hana Hana Hana
   Ora: if you keep doing this every time Hana joins the chat you're going to scare her off. She's very shy you know
   Gyeongja: Hana Hana Hana
   Gyeongja: Hana Hana Hana
   Iseul: Mr Jeong just found out how shy Hana is
   Gyeongja: MR JEONG IS IN THE POOL
   Astrid: we are so impressed, Hana
   Gyeongja: Hana Hana Hana

I'm sitting on the toilet bowl in the agency bathroom browsing on my phone because as usual I can't sleep, and I want some privacy. If I go out into the yard I just know I'll be interrupted by someone and I don't feel like talking to anybody at the moment. That includes the 'girls' group chat, which I now regret typing in. I decide that I won't type anything else in the chat tonight because it's too exhausting. There's wearing my brain out enough to get sleep, and then there's being assaulted by rapid-fire walls of text. I'm sure I can find something else to pass the time.

I go over to Halcyon's social networking front page where Ijun has posted the final version of the video for "The Love Complete". I press play on the video and watch it with the sound down, because I don't really want to hear our music any more than I have to and I already know what it sounds like. Youngsook was right, Ijun has seamlessly edited the footage of me miming to the track so it looks professional and all the recording studio silliness is out of frame. There are also a couple sections where Ijun cuts in some random stock footage of generic nature scenes like birds swimming in a pond, panoramas of mountains and so on. I guess perhaps there wasn't any good footage of me miming during those parts because Caitlin and Iseul ruined it by being stupid. I check the comments under the video from random fans.

They got this out quickly to farm the Yohan grief clicks didn't they

This is better than any song her group has

Hana doesn't suit this at all, she has an annoying voice, they should have used Youngsook or Shu for it

Who is this ugly bitch on my phone screen

Why does Hana get a solo and not Shu

Hana with glasses and the shoulder length hair is cute, I hope she never goes back to her old look

Halcyon's songs are trash and this is just trash as well but at half speed

Yohan's corpse is still twitching and this is already out

Some singer, she isn't even singing into the correct part of the microphone

Is it just me or is Hana fat, would still smash though

As usual our fans are all idiots. Since everyone knows about Mr Jeong's death, I should look at the news reports just to see what they say. Since he's a powerful industry person I expect there'll be something to read. It doesn't take much searching to find an article.

Producer/director of Music Train, Mr Jeong Kangdae has passed away at thirty-seven years old.

According to police reports, he was found deceased on Saturday morning at his home in Pyeongchang-dong, Seoul by a relative. There is no further information regarding the cause of death at this time, but police are treating the death as suspicious.

Jeong Kangdae first became known to the public fifteen years ago as a contestant on the first season of the popular hip-hop survival program "Street Arithmetic", where he finished in second place. Following his success on the program, he launched his own agency Ka-ching Records where he released his own music as well as collaborated with several prominent hip-hop artists, before crossing over into the world of television production by launching the long-running idol competition show "Music Train", now in its ninth year of production.

Jeong Kangdae was recently investigated by police for a violent nightclub assault, as well as assaulting and threatening his ex-wife three years ago. For the assault against his ex-wife, he was sentenced to a two-year suspended sentence and twenty-one hours of community service, with imprisonment if he committed more crimes during the two year term.

Following the death of EB-K's Lee Yohan, Jeong Kangdae represents the second recent death within the idol entertainment world.

Reading this article makes me angry. Why does this piece of human garbage get more words than Yohan? The media sucks in this country. Still, it's good to know that he really was a piece of shit and it was common knowledge, I had no idea about his history beyond him harassing all the other *maknaes* who would appear on Music Train. I suppose I should look at the comments under the article.

RIP Kangdae oppa
I liked him in his hip-hop days, he still had it
RIP
There's no way this isn't sus
Sad times for the music business
Kangdae my angel

Kangdae was involved in gangs and got into fights a lot, he had so many enemies, half of Seoul could have done this

I would let Kangdae step on my face, his ex-wife should have been grateful for the beatings

RIP my sweet angel

What the fuck is wrong with people. I don't want to think about this anymore, it's pissing me off so much. What can I search that will make me feel better? I should look for news on Jihu's e-sport group. I type "Virtuous Assault tournament" into my phone browser's search, and the details of all the contestants and coming matches around the country come up. I find out that Jihu's team of five is called "Critical Never Stop" and they've reached the national semi-finals, where they're playing off against a team called "Ice Clan Raiders". This reminds me that I need to tell Jihu to come to the dorms with his gaming gear on the weekend when Mr Park is at the funeral. Ijun will be happy to see him, I hope his schedule allows Jihu to come here.

144. COMPLIANCE

"Okay, let's do it again from the start! We all need to get this perfect! Come on, team!"

"Why the hell do you still care so much? We're not getting paid, you know."

"Youngsook, we still don't want to perform shamefully on Platinum Hour, regardless."

Nari is sitting on the desk in front of the TV screen in the gym, watching us do the "Love Carousel" dance. She's drilling us through the dance routine over and over again. The song starts up, and we all move through the tricky opening section. I hear a crunch and turn around; Youngsook has fallen on the floor again. Nari sighs.

"Come on, it's not that hard. How long have we been doing this dance for now? How many months?"

"I'm sorry, it's still hard for me!"

Nari flicks the remote control to stop the song and reset it back to the beginning.

"You should be a master at this by now. There's no excuse. Get on your feet."

"Can I just lie here for a while?"

"How about no?"

"Fine, fine..."

Youngsook gradually gets up. Nari is just about to start the song again when we're interrupted by some loud footsteps. We turn around. Police officers. I recognise the female police officer Yoon Nabi, who has interviewed me before. She recognises me straight away and smiles at me. I don't know if that smile is good or bad. The male officer clears his throat and speaks.

"Can any one of you ladies please point me in the direction of Mr Park Jeongmin?"

Nari points to the admin doorway in the gym.

"Just head through the door, and look for the only office in there that isn't open-plan, that's probably where our CEO is."

"Thank you."

The male officer walks up to the admin door. Just before he reaches the door, Mr Park opens it from the other side. I watch as Mr Park and the officer shake hands in the doorway before the male officer walks through, closing the door behind them both. I look back at Nabi, she hasn't moved, she's still staring at me and smiling.

"Hana, a word with you outside, please?"

"Sure."

Nabi walks out to the yard area and I follow her. We sit down on the metal bench together.

"Hana, I just wanted to ask you a few questions about Mr Jeong Kangdae. I understood that you had some meetings with him?"

"Yes. What's this about?"

"We're just following up leads. We're trying to get as accurate a picture as we possibly can about the types of interactions he was having with people in the lead-up to his death. How many times did you meet?"

"More than once."

"Twice, or...?"

"Three times... wait, no, twice."

Nabi produces a notepad and pen.

"You're not sure?"

"It was meant to be three times."

"Tell me about them. You don't mind if I take notes, do you?"

"No, that's fine."

I wonder what she would say if I had said that she couldn't take notes. She'd probably just laugh at me. I'm sure not going to try that though.

"Okay, so tell me about the first time."

"Well the first time was when Halcyon was on his show Music Train, this was the first time we went on. After the show we have to sit and wait for hours while the PD meets everyone. Because we were very unknown at that time, we were pretty much the last group so we had to wait the longest..."

"What was he like?"

"Disgusting honestly. He asked who the *maknae* of our group was and I said it was me, and then he started touching me, groping my body without my consent, in full view of all the other people in groups and the staff, everybody, he didn't care."

"Then what happened?"

"He met with Mr Park for a while privately, and I just tried to avoid him after that. Eventually our group were allowed to leave."

"Did you see him again that night?"

"No, I didn't."

"What about the second time you met?"

"Mr Park arranged a 'date' between me and Mr Jeong."

"A date?"

"Yes. Mr Jeong wanted to meet me, so Mr Park arranged that we meet in a restaurant."

"Why did he want to meet you? Was this a literal 'date', intended to be a potential prelude to sexual activity?"

"He didn't say that explicitly but it was pretty obvious that that's where he was going with it, that's what he wanted. I don't remember exactly what he said now, but he was all like 'I can give you so many opportunities, good things happen to people who play the game' and so on. He wasn't very subtle."

"I see. How did the date pan out? Did you end up going anywhere with him after the restaurant?"

"No. I was kind of rude to him, and he actually caused a scene in the restaurant and tried to beat me right there and then."

"Rude how?"

"I just wasn't using table manners and stuff. When he got upset about it I pretty much told him that he was disgusting to his face, and he got angry."

"He then assaulted you physically?"

"Yes. He hit me with his bare hands, he was very strong, it hurt a lot. The restaurant staff got him off me and threw him out. That was the last I saw of him that night."

"You said there was a third time, or not?"

"Well, no, but kind of. We went on Music Train a second time. Mr Jeong does this thing where... well, we wear these in-ear monitors, right? So we can hear sound from the stage engineers, like if they need to talk to us to give us instructions, like 'move to stage left now', that kind of thing. When I was on stage he spoke into my monitors and threatened to 'get' me after the performance, like he was seeking revenge from before. But I never ended up meeting him on that day because Iseul passed out backstage after the performance. I had to go straight to hospital with her because Iseul needed someone to be with her. It was actually Yohan who drove us there."

"Yohan?"

"From EB-K."

"Oh of course. But you didn't meet Mr Jeong again, or have any contact with him again after that day?"

Oh no. I have to lie here. I'm so bad at lying.

"No."

"You can tell me, you know. I understand if something happened that's traumatic and it's difficult to say. But it's important to be honest."

Shit, she's onto me.

"I didn't have a conversation with him again. We were going to go on Music Train again, but..."

"...he died before that happened."

"Yes."

Nabi just stares at me for a while and smiles, before then taking some more notes.

"You're shaking, Hana."

"I am?"

I look down at my legs. Nabi is right, my legs are wobbling back and forth. I put my hands on my knees to stop the shaking, but this only makes my hands shake as well. I try to steady myself but I can't do it. I suppose I'll just have to keep shaking.

"We know that there was a business relationship between your boss Mr Park, and Mr Jeong. Is it awkward for you that your boss and Mr Jeong were very close business associates?"

"Yes."

"Did you tell him about the incidents that you just told me?"

"Yes."

"What did he say?"

I'm starting to get upset thinking about this. I try to force the words out.

"He said that... I should not make a fuss, and... comply and just do everything that Mr Jeong says."

"Really?"

"He said he expected 'total compliance'... that's what he said, that's the words he used."

"Why do you think he said that?"

"He didn't want me to mess up whatever business thing they had going on, I think."

"Do you think he believed you when you told him what Mr Jeong was like?"

"I think he believes it, he just doesn't care!"

"Do you know if any money changed hands between Mr Park and Mr Jeong?"

"They do business? I'm sure that they exchange money all the time so Mr Park can get us on Mr Jeong's stupid show?"

"Sorry, I should clarify the question. I mean do you think money changed hands specifically to set up the date. I wonder if the 'date' was actually a situation where your time was being purchased."

"You mean..."

"Like an escort."

No way, how can this even be real?

"I was never told anything about that?"

"But do you think it's likely?"

How did the possibility of this not occur to me before? How could Mr Park sell me out like that? I already know he's a scumbag, but would he really try to pimp me out to Mr Jeong just for some extra money? I can't hold it in any longer, I burst into tears, sobbing into my lap. I quickly take my glasses off and put them on the bench because they're becoming so tear-stained that they're useless.

"You don't have to answer now..."

"Yes! Yes it's fucking likely as shit! I bet Mr Park sold me out just like that!"

Nabi looks at me sympathetically. She reaches out a hand and I hold it while sobbing.

"Oh my god I'm sorry for swearing, I shouldn't be rude in front of an officer of the law, it's not right."

"What makes you think he did it?"

"Because he's a fucking asshole, fuck!"

Nabi starts laughing.

"You're not doing too well at the 'not swearing' thing."

"I'm sorry! I'm so sorry!"

"It's okay. I've heard worse, don't worry."

Nabi squeezes my hand and I start crying harder.

"It's alright. Just one more question for you. Do you know where Mr Park was on the evening before Mr Jeong's body was found?"

I can't answer this right now. I just continue to cry. After a minute I finally dry up enough to answer.

"I'm sorry, I can't tell you."

Technically not a lie.

"It's okay. We already know. I just wanted to know if you knew."

"Where was he?"

"He was visiting Mr Jeong."

"We're always busy, and he goes in and out. We don't usually know where he is. I was very busy that night."

Not a lie.

"Oh. Doing what?"

"Just working on some important tasks."

Also not a lie.

"With the group?"

"No, individually. Our group has a lot of activities, some are group activities, and some are individual. For instance, I recently had to sing the song for 'The Love Complete' on my own, so I have to work on that a lot by myself, to get the parts right..."

"Yes, I know that song. That's a lovely song. I didn't know you did the vocals?"

"Yes, it's me."

"Your speaking voice sounds so different."

"Well, they change the voice a bit, with the machine..."

"Right. Anyway, that's enough questions for now. Thank you again Hana, you've been very helpful."

"I'm glad I could help. Will I be needed again?"

"I don't know if I'll need to ask you anything more at this stage or not. However we're going to be having a long conversation with Mr Park today."

"He's probably a bit upset about Mr Jeong."

"Yes, I'd imagine so. You can go back inside and join your group now. I'll stay out here for a little bit and finish off some notes. And Hana..."

"Yes?"

"You know that if there's anything you want to say, you can talk to me anytime, right?"

"There's a lot of things that I always want to say."

"You're having a hard time here, aren't you?"

"Yes sometimes, but I'm still happy to be here."

"Really? It doesn't seem like it."

"I don't like a lot of the way things are run here, but school was even worse."

"You had a harder time in school?"

"*Wangtta.*"

"What was that like?"

"Please don't make me talk about it."

Nabi squeezes my hand and I start sobbing again. I know that she understands. I wonder if that's why she's a police officer. I admit, it doesn't seem like a bad way to get revenge.

145. LIGHTSTICK

I wake up to the familiar sound of the dorm alarm clock going off. I gradually rub the sleep out of my eyes and sit up in my bed, when I notice something feels strange. There's a hard object on my bed poking into my ribs, it's a cardboard box. As my vision gradually unblurs I notice that the dorm door is open and Ijun is standing in the doorway. I also notice that for once she's not wearing her school uniform, but instead is in a plain black T-shirt and matching black skirt, which makes her look almost normal. The other thing that's unusual for her and which is making her look like a regular person is that she's smiling.

"*Annyeong,* Halcyon!"

"*Annyeong!*" we all reply, in varying states of sleep deprivation.

"On you beds are the new lightsticks that we ordered. Please open them up and take a look, then take some photos for social networking, and post them up. After you have done this, come to the dining room."

"Thank you, Ijun!" says Iseul.

Ijun leaves the room, and we all begin tearing open the cardboard boxes. I've just put on my glasses and worked out how to remove the sticky-tape around my box when Youngsook suddenly starts laughing.

"Oh my god! This is crazy!"

"What?" asks Caitlin.

"Just look at it!"

Caitlin starts giggling.

"Oh. Okay, yeah now I see it. Um... we really have to take photos of this?"

"The fans are going to freak."

"I guess if we have to, we have to."

Nari suddenly starts laughing as well.

"Caitlin and Hana, don't you go getting any ideas!"

Caitlin starts laughing even more.

"Come on Nari, how can we *not* get ideas? Just look at this thing! Hey, Hana..."

"What?"

"You know how when we went downtown to get your glasses fitted, I wanted to go to a certain shop, but we didn't end up going, because you were worried fans might see us in there, and you were a bit embarrassed about it?"

I know what shop Caitlin means but I'm not going to admit to it because I don't want to talk about this in front of the others.

"Sorry, what shop?"

"You know the one!"

"No I don't!"

"Don't pretend you don't know. I swear you are the crappiest liar in the world."

Fuck. Why does Caitlin have the ability to read me like a book, even when she's up in her bunk and can't even see my face? It's not fair at all.

"Okay, fine... but so what?"

"Well you'll be happy to know that we probably don't have to worry about going there anymore."

I finally get my cardboard box open. There's another box inside, which is made of clear plastic. It contains the official Halcyon lightstick, which is just a transparent cylinder, with a smooth rounded pink top and a handle in the official "nadeshiko pink" group colour, with the word "Halcyon" embossed into it. Next to the stick is a small clear plastic capsule with three batteries.

"It looks like a little hair curling wand?" I reply.

"It's totally just a dildo!" says Youngsook, playing with the buttons on her lightstick, switching it on and off.

"Ahhh! If you hold the button down it vibrates!" Shu says, giggling.

The entire room starts laughing, except me and Iseul. I watch Iseul as she studies her lightstick disapprovingly.

"I bet my dad designed this! I bet he did it just to be a creep and embarrass me some more!"

"You don't know that," says Nari.

"I know what my dad is like."

Youngsook starts laughing.

"I know what you're like, too! Like you're not going to be testing it later! If we hear a buzzing sound after the lights go out, I know who it'll be!"

"You're disgusting!"

"I'm just honest!"

Nari gets out of her bunk.

"Come on, cool it, you two. It is what it is. Let's all quickly take some photos of it and then we can go to the teaching room."

I decide to leave my lightstick in the box and just take a photo of it while it's still in the clear packaging. I then post it up on my social media profile. Immediately it starts getting likes and comments. The other girls are putting a bit more effort into their photos, actually bothering to pose with it, so I read the comments on my photo to pass the time.

That's a lightstick?

This company must think we're pretty dumb... or maybe just pretty horny

I've heard this has a vibrating function? Is it true? Because if it is then this is the best lightstick ever

It could be a bit larger

I can't wait to put it to the test

Shu is my angel I don't want to think about her being forced to dorm with the other dirty women in this group, she should come and live with me, I wrote her a letter she won't write back why why WHY

It doesn't look all that well made, what if it falls apart while I'm "using" it?

In the press release it says the vibrating function is for people with disabilities, stop being filthy you animals
It'll be busy in the dorms tonight

As usual our fans are idiots. The others seem like they're wrapping up their *selcas*, so I get out of bed and walk down the hall into the dining room, which is also the teaching room. I hear the others following behind me. When I get there my jaw drops. Ijun is sitting at the teacher's desk, and beside her, sitting on the desk, are half a dozen pizza boxes. Ijun truly is our guardian angel.

"Everyone sit down," says Ijun.

We all file into the room and find a seat at a random table as quickly as possible. We can all smell those pizzas and the sooner we get through whatever Ijun has to say, the sooner we can hopefully eat.

"Mr Park CEO left very early this morning to attend the funeral of Mr Jeong. He is helping with the funeral arrangements and he advised me that he will be there for the entire duration. Since it's my rules while he is gone, I have decided that you all have the next three days off."

This is amazing. Three days off is the longest break we've ever had since coming here. The entire room cheers with joy.

"The cameras and microphones are still recording, but I'll scrub the recordings later, so don't worry about it. Only Mr Park CEO checks the recordings. So you can speak freely."

"Completely freely?" I ask.

"I can't promise I'll answer, there are some things I won't talk about, you know what those are. But you can ask anything you want and we don't have to do the stupid typing game."

"I've got questions! Do you get bullied at school? Because I did and I would definitely help you."

"No, I don't get bullied, just ignored. I was bullied at first but Mr Park sorted it out. You know the guy with the blonde hair who you probably don't see that much, but he sometimes carries boxes and equipment for us? That's the bodyguard that Mr Park hired for me. He walks me to and from school sometimes, nobody says anything to me since he started that. It's good because I don't get picked on, but it's also bad because nobody wants to be my friend either. People went from bullying me to being too scared to say anything at all."

"Okay, that's good. Why is Mr Park such a fuckass?"

Ijun just stares at me like she doesn't know what to say. After a few seconds she puts her hand over her mouth. I realise that she's trying to restrain herself from giggling. After about ten seconds she puts her hand back down and looks directly at me with a straight face.

"Dropped on his head as a baby, that's what I think. Shall we eat pizza?"

146. PROMISE

We're all in the gym, sitting down, watching the television screen. We're not sitting on the floor this time; we've dragged the lounge chairs out of the recording studio and are sitting on those instead. I'm sitting with Caitlin on a chair off to the side of the television. In the most central lounge chair sits Ijun, and next to her is Jihu, my gamer friend who is quickly becoming Ijun's gamer friend also. They're busy playing with Jihu's gaming console, duelling each other in the Virtuous Assault desert arena, while we watch and cheer them on. I clap as Ijun scores a fatal headshot on Jihu, using a gun that looks similar to the large gun that the gun dealer told me would break my hand off if it fired full-auto and I was holding it.

"I just shot you. Some pro gamer you are, pathetic."

"Lucky shot, you're still losing by heaps."

"You think you're so good but you're not! No wonder you lost the semis with that weak aim of yours."

"Hey, I don't see you being invited to any tournaments, amateur."

"That's just because of sexism. They won't let girls in. If it wasn't such a stupid boys club I could train enough to kick your ass, and your whole team too."

"You've worked hard already, Ijun. Just lay to rest now. We will remember your mediocre skills fondly."

"Shut up and start the next round, idiot."

Jihu begins another round of the game. I watch as Ijun and Jihu dodge around the arena, hunting each other down. After about a minute of combat, Jihu scores a long range hit on Ijun with a sniper rifle.

"Hey, sniping isn't fair!"

"I thought you had skills?"

"I don't get to train as much as you do. You have an unfair advantage, you can play this whenever you want. Anyway I'm getting tired, I've been playing for a while. That's what it is, combat fatigue."

"More like lack of skills."

Ijun turns to us and waves the controller around.

"Who here wants to play against Jihu? I promise you he's super easy to beat."

"Me! I do!" says Shu, bouncing off of her couch.

Ijun passes her controller to Shu, and then curls up on the couch next to Jihu. Shu goes back to her own couch and sits down, bouncing up and down with the controller in her hand.

"I'm ready to shoot you, Jihu! Better watch out!"

"Okay, I'll be extra careful!"

Jihu starts a new game and Shu starts duelling with him. It's obvious to me that Jihu isn't playing to his full skill capacity. It's kind of lame to watch this, I would much prefer that Jihu destroy Shu completely and make her cry but he seems to want to be nice to her for some fucked up reason. I turn my attention to Caitlin, who is ignoring the game and playing with her phone.

"I'm bored of this," I tell Caitlin.

"Me too. I'm going to organise some adventures. I want to visit a few friends."

"Visit who?"

"I want to see Ora."

"Ora's fully recovered now, right?"

"Yeah, she's better, has been since the party."

"I'm not sure if I trust you with Ora though."

"You can come too, if you want. I'm sure she won't mind. You can make sure we don't get up to anything."

"I think I'm going to have to. I'm sorry."

"Don't be sorry. It'd be nice for us to all catch up together! Anyway I'm organising it now."

"Actually even with me there I'm still not sure if I trust you... or her."

"Well I'm going anyway. You can come, or not."

"She's going to visit us that soon?"

"No, we'll visit her. Away from the others. Hey, she just got back to me, it's on for tomorrow night! Pity it's not tonight though, I wouldn't mind going out right now. It's boring being in here. We should try and find some nightlife, what do you think?"

"The last time we walked the streets to find nightlife we got harassed a bit."

"Yeah, but we found a good club eventually."

"I don't know if it was worth it."

"Maybe we just need to know the good places to go. We need a tour guide or something. Back home I knew all the good spots but here I wouldn't have a clue."

"Well don't ask me about it."

I start thinking. Who would know about good places to go at night in Seoul for entertainment? I really don't have any idea. Caitlin suddenly taps me on the arm.

"Hey, I've got it. What about Sooae?"

"You think?"

"Yes! I bet she would know. She pretty much *is* Seoul nightlife, she would have some tips. Ask her about it."

"That's a great idea. I'll send her a message."

Me: hey, are you busy?

I wait for a reply. I don't see Sooae typing, I guess she's working. Suddenly my phone vibrates in my hand. She must be ringing me instead, awesome. I answer the call and put the phone up to my ear.

"*Yeoboseyo!*"

Silence.

"*Yeoboseyo?*"

"Nice to talk to you too, Hana."

Oh shit. It's my mother.

"Oh, hello. What's up?"

More silence. She's going to go off, I just know it.

"You rude child."

She sounds so scornful. I start shaking.

"I'm sorry Mother! I'm just busy!"

364

"So do you have time to talk?"

"No, I'm very busy! Training is really hard here!"

"Now that you're slightly successful you don't have time for me anymore, do you?"

"No, I don't mean that, it's just, I'll get in trouble..."

"You're already in trouble."

"I'll get in more trouble..."

My phone starts vibrating in my ear. This time, I check the screen to see who it is, which I should have done before. This time it really is Sooae.

"Mother, the CEO is calling me, I'll call you back..."

"Hana, I know *for a fact* that your CEO is..."

I press a button to put my mother on hold and answer Sooae's call. I instantly feel a little more relaxed.

"*Yeoboseyo!*"

"*Yeoboseyo!*"

"Hey Sooae, I have a question. Are you busy?"

"If you were busy do you think I would have rung you?"

"You're not busy?"

"I'm eating, but it's fine. Just ask it."

"Caitlin and I want to go out tonight, but we don't want to go somewhere lame. Can you help find us somewhere cool to go?"

"What, they actually finally let you out?"

"Some piece of shit that the CEO is friends with died, so we've got a few days of holiday while he goes and cries about it at the funeral like a bitch."

"That bad a person, huh?"

"Trust me, he deserved death. And I... I mean, yeah anyway he's dead and we have holidays and it's great."

"Then you're coming to see my band. We're playing tonight, in a couple hours. So get here quick."

"But your band sucks?"

"Come see us anyway. We're a good time, I promise. We'll get you backstage and everything."

"Why would I want to go back there? I see enough backstages."

"Is Caitlin with you?"

"Yeah, hang on."

I nudge Caitlin on the shoulder with my phone.

"Sooae wants to talk to you."

"Oh, cool! Thanks!"

Caitlin takes the phone and starts talking to Sooae.

"Hey ... oh fuck yes! ... Really? ... I'll definitely be there if *that's* true ... Yeah, I know, right? ... Okay, cool. We'll get there as soon as we can ... Sorry, the what? ... She will? Are you sure? ... I wouldn't be so sure. We don't get out much ... Okay great. See you soon!"

Caitlin hangs up the phone and gives it back to me.

"We're going straight away. Just let me get ready."

"Cool."

"Hey Sooae thought you might know where the venue 'The Lynx Bunker' is?"

"No, we don't even get out. Why would I know that?"

"That's what I told her. Anyway that's where they're playing, so you can look that up while I get ready."

Caitlin smiles at me. My heart sinks as I just realise something important.

"Shit! Caitlin, I just realised that you hung up on my mother!"

"I did?"

"She was on the other line."

"I had no idea? You should have told me!"

"Yeah, I just didn't think you were going to hang up."

"Hanging up is kind of what people do at the end of phone conversations."

"It was going to be a really bad conversation too. She's probably angry now."

"Maybe best you don't have that conversation, then?"

"But I have to!"

"Why?"

"She's my mother! Also she'll be mad!"

Caitlin shrugs.

"Let her be mad. What's she going to do if you don't ring back, send you home after that advert made all that money for Mr Park? I bet he won't even let you go back home if she begged."

"No, but she'll ring later and abuse me."

Caitlin looks me up and down.

"You're terrified of her, aren't you?"

"Yes! Yes I am!"

"Block her number!"

"I can't do that!"

"Why not?"

"She's my mother!"

"Well, what will you do if she rings back?"

"Answer it, and apologise and... I don't fucking know, be upset, I guess?"

"Why do that, though?"

"I don't know... don't I have to?"

"Hana, your mother didn't let you do literally anything at all except school for an entire decade, she kept you insulated to the point where you don't even know half of the most basic shit about life. That's like literal child abuse. Why are you constantly giving her a free pass?"

"But it's family... isn't it different, if it's family?"

"Hana, come here. Close to me."

I slide over so I'm right next to Caitlin. She wraps one arm around my waist, puts her other hand behind my head, and pushes my head gently up to her shoulder blade.

"I promise you, that if we ever leave this fucking shithole of an agency alive, that we're leaving together, and you're not moving back in with your mother. No matter what. I mean, unless you *want* to, but you don't want to, do you?"

"Fuck no. I hate her. But how are you going to manage that? I know you have some money, but there's no way you have enough to afford a house, or even rent one? How are we going to survive?"

"Honestly I don't exactly have a plan yet, I just decided this thirty seconds ago. Let's worry about the details when we have to. For now, just know that I mean it, it's a promise."

Caitlin smiles at me, she seems confident. I wrap my arms around Caitlin's waist and hold her tightly. I don't know if she will find a way to come good on her promise, but I know that she'll try.

147. KIMCHI SLAPPERS

I'm following Caitlin through the dense crowd of The Lynx Bunker, the maze-like club where Sooae's band are playing soon. We're trying to find either her, anyone who looks like they could be in her band, or the sound stage, and having no luck with all three so far. The challenge of locating anything in here is not helped by the fact that literally every single person in this venue seems to be wearing black clothes. The venue also has a weird military theme, with camouflage nets hanging from the ceiling, beaten-up metal panels lining the walls, and nothing but a few dim randomly placed coloured light bulbs lighting up various parts of the interior. To make the feeling of disorientation even worse, loud tuneless dance music plays in every room of the venue from speakers embedded into the walls, making it just as difficult to hear anything as it is to see anything.

"I'm so lost. Are we going around in circles?" I yell.

"I'm looking for a big room that could actually hold a stage, but I don't see one. All the rooms are tiny."

"I swear that this fucking place reeks of something. Did someone die in here or what?"

"Don't say that too loud in here, I don't want us to have problems with the regulars."

"It's so noisy in here, what makes you think anyone can even hear what we say?"

"Sorry, what?"

"I said... oh fuck it, never mind."

"Hey, look..."

Caitlin points at some stairs carefully hidden between two stacks of speakers. I follow her and we descend to a lower level of the venue filled with even more black-clad people. We're now in a slightly bigger room, but I still don't see anything that looks like a stage.

"Caitlin! Hana!"

I look over at where the voice is coming from. I see Sooae, moving towards us through the crowd of people talking and drinking. Like almost everyone else down here, she's wearing a black shirt and black jeans, but her red spiked hair makes her stand out easily. She gives Caitlin an enthusiastic hug.

"Caitlin, I haven't seen you in... ages!"

"I know, right?"

"Hana, come here! Give me a hug! Don't be shy, now!"

I reach out carefully to hug her but Sooae just grabs me and hugs me forcefully, patting me on the back at the same time. Her pats are so hard that they're more like slaps reverberating through my body, I probably would flinch but her grip is far too tight and strong for me to move much at all, voluntarily or otherwise. After a few seconds she lets go and I catch my breath.

"Hey, I'm on in a few minutes, the band are probably looking for me. I gotta go and make sure my shit works. We'll talk later, okay?"

"Sure, where's the stage?" I ask.

Sooae points to a corner of the room, where there isn't a stage, just a bunch more people. I notice that there's two speakers there that are on poles, and between them a small space which seems to be the only part of the room that nobody is standing in. In the space there's a drum kit, a couple of guitars leaning on amplifiers, and two cheap looking microphones on stands. Sooae's band doesn't even have a stage to play on.

"You're just going to play in the corner?"

"Yeah, and?"

"How are all the people here even going to see you when you start?"

"Stick around and find out! I gotta go now, talk later!"

Sooae waves and vanishes back into the crowd. A few seconds later she and two other people walk over to the "stage" area. Sooae picks up the smaller of the two guitars, it's busted-looking and covered in stickers. The drummer is a wiry-looking guy who is only wearing shorts and nothing else for some reason, he sits behind the drum kit and starts stretching, then hitting the drums randomly, seemingly testing them. A girl then comes up and picks up the bigger guitar, she's about my height with thick, messy black hair, and unlike everyone else here, is wearing a school uniform. She switches on her amplifier and plays a single low note, which makes the entire room shake. She looks at Sooae and smiles, they say something to each other but it's away from the microphones so I can't hear it. Suddenly, I recognise that school uniform, it's the one from *my* old school. My heart skips about three beats as I recognise who it is. It's Haneul, the girl I was forced to bully at school. The girl who forgave me, who was lonely and thought about self-harming, but told me she'd be okay. I can't believe that she's now in a group with Sooae, let alone one that makes the kind of cacophonous noise that I heard on the files Sooae sent me. Sooae walks up to the microphone and starts yelling.

"Hey shitheads, we're Kimchi Slappers! It's great to be back at The Lynx Bunker! How the fuck are all of you queers?"

Everyone around us starts cheering. Someone throws a *soju* bottle onstage for some reason. It lands on the drum kit with a crash. The drummer picks it up and hands it straight to Sooae who tips it upside down and shakes it, like she's trying to get fluid out of it. Nothing comes out of course, it's just an empty bottle.

"Hey whoever the fucking cuntfaced bitch was who threw this onstage, if you're going to throw bottles up here, make sure they have something *in* them!"

The crowd laughs and cheers. Sooae puts the bottle down and hits her guitar with her hand. A massive wave of distorted noise comes out of the speakers.

"This song is called 'Failure at Life'! Let's go! One two three four..."

Sooae starts playing some weird guitar riff that just sounds like noise. I instantly recognise it, it's the intro for the song that Sooae sent me on my phone a while back. Although the noise from her guitar sounds chaotic, it's exactly the same sound that was on that recording. Then the drummer starts up, with that same irregular rhythm. The crowd around me and Caitlin suddenly explodes with movement, people start dancing wildly, pushing and shoving each other around. Sooae then starts screaming into the microphone. This sounds different to the recording she sent me, she did mention to me that this band used to have another singer so I guess it was the other singer on the recording and not her. Not that I'd call it singing, I can't understand a fucking word of the song, it's just total screaming with no melody. Then the drumbeat changes a bit to a different type of beat, and Haneul starts playing as well, the low thudding pulses of her instrument vibrating right through my ribcage. The crowd goes even crazier, doing weird arm-flailing motions. Some guy flips himself up so he's floating on top of the crowd of other people, who carry him around for a few seconds before he drops to the floor. The movement of the crowd is becoming a bit unmanageable, I reach out for Caitlin but she's busy trying to stay upright. Before I can even reach her I suddenly fall to the floor as someone lands right on top of me. I feel hurt, I don't want to be pushed around, I want to punish the person who did this. A few seconds later, I feel several arms reaching down and around me; the same crowd who pushed me over are now pulling me back up onto my feet? I stand up and look for Caitlin but I can't see her anymore. I have to get out of the crowd, I feel claustrophobic and it's only a matter of time before I get seriously injured. I move away from the stage to the back where there's people just standing, but someone there pushes me right back into the crowd again. I lose balance once more and land on my knees, but again a few seconds later I'm picked up by a whole bunch of random people at once. I make another attempt to get out in the same direction and this time the crowd lets me straight through. I stagger along through the crowd of people standing around until I find the rear wall of the room and lean against it, catching my breath. I look back at the crowd, they're getting wilder and wilder, I'm glad that I got out when I did. Suddenly the song stops, way before it feels like it should. The crowd cheers. I can't see the band anymore from back here, but I can sure hear them.

"What a bunch of pansies you lot are! For this next one I want to see some fucking movement! Let's step it up, let's go fucking crazy! This song is called 'Circle of Kimchi Death'! Let's fucking go, assholes! One two three four..."

The next "song" starts, with everyone playing at once and Sooae and Hanuel both screaming their heads off. It's an unbelievable racket, so noisy and incoherent, and I still can't understand a word of what they're saying. However even though there's no melody to speak of, there's a real energy to it. Every time Sooae screams, and every time the guitars and drums do a change in their patterns, I feel like it's drawing me in, and affecting me inside a little, in a way I can't explain. I mean I still don't know if it's even "music" really, but whatever the hell it is, it's got a certain urgent, compelling quality to it that the shit songs Mr Nam writes for Halcyon definitely don't have. As much as I don't want to admit it, I'm not hating Sooae's band anywhere near as much as I thought I would. The song suddenly stops. Their songs are short, they only seem to go for a couple minutes, maybe even less.

"Hey this one's for Hana! I've heard she's here!"

That's Haneul's voice.

"Hana, please remember we love you! Stay strong!"

The crowd have no reaction to this. Haneul hasn't mentioned my group, only me by name, and this crowd don't look like they'd give a damn about idol pop anyway even if she did say where I was from. I crane my neck to try and get a look at the stage area. I can see that Sooae is back on the microphone but that's all I can see.

"This one's about school bullying! This song is called 'Victim Chant'! Let's tear this fucking building apart! One two three four..."

Another wall of sound erupts from the speakers. The screaming sounds different, I can't see the stage when the song is on because of the crowd going so crazy, but it must be Haneul singing this time. The song suddenly cuts to a quiet section, with Haneul saying "no" and "stop it" and "please" over and over again. *Just like she did when I used to bully her. I remember pushing her face into the toilet bowl at school with my shaking hands. Namgil, the iljin, and his two girlfriends, both right behind me, making sure that I did it right. "Make sure her face touches the water. If her face isn't wet when you bring it up, it's your head going in there next." "No, stop it, please," Haneul repeated, over and over. I didn't stop, not until Haneul's screams were obscured by the bubbling of the water hitting her mouth as she howled, then Namgil was satisfied.* Haneul's voice gets gradually louder and louder, and as she increases her volume, the guitars and drums also get louder again. I sink down to my knees against the wall and start bawling my eyes out as the song erupts back into distorted guitar and fast drumming. The room goes crazy once again, with the crowd pushing, shoving and kicking everywhere. I don't want to be like this in public, but I can't help it. *We love you. Stay strong.* I'm sorry, Haneul. I just can't stay strong, not like this. There's no way. I'll never be as strong as you, it's impossible.

148. ROOM 326

"Ora actually lives here?"

"That's what she said. Let's go up."

I'm standing with Caitlin in the foyer of Namsol Tower, a well-known and expensive high-rise apartment complex right on the bank of the Han River. The foyer has shiny grey metal walls and marble floors. Caitlin pushes the lift button and the middle lift out of three on the foyer wall opens immediately. We both walk into the small lift space. I notice straight away that I can see the street lights outside the building through the wall of the lift.

"This is glass? Oh, fuck no. Why?"

Caitlin laughs and pats me on the back.

"You can take the stairs if you want, I don't mind. Ora lives on the thirty-second floor though."

"I'll just close my eyes I guess."

Caitlin pushes the button for our destination and the doors close. I hold Caitlin's hand with one hand and grab onto the large lift handrail with the other. I then close my eyes and feel the inertia of the lift as it ascends.

"You're really missing out. The view is great."

"Sorry, I really don't give a fuck."

"Calm down. You're not going to fall, you can't, it's a lift. Wow, I can actually see our agency building from up here, this is cool!"

"Shut up, I so don't care! Anyway don't lifts break down sometimes? What if the thing that holds the lift up snaps and we fall down?"

"Hey you can relax now, we're here. Come on."

Caitlin's hand tugs at mine and I open my eyes. We step out into a corridor with white walls and beige carpet, We start walking along and Caitlin looks at each door as we pass it.

"Which door is it?"

"This one."

Caitlin stops before a white door adorned with a gold number "326". I take a deep breath, to calm my uneasiness about meeting Ora. Caitlin notices straight away.

"You're not going to fall now. What's wrong?"

"I'm just nervous, I guess."

Caitlin knocks on the door, and we wait. I start thinking about the last time I met Ora. It was fun, but so incredibly awkward. I'm hoping that this time around the meeting will be more relaxed and not so weird. I guess it should be, because Caitlin is here. I'm sure Ora won't dare do anything sexual with Caitlin around.

"The door is open, please push to enter."

A female electronic voice, it's not Ora's, it's just some kind of remote door unlocking system. Caitlin pushes the door and we enter the apartment. It's an open plan kind of space with a kitchen and lounge, no sign of Ora though. We close the door behind us and I bend down to take my shoes off.

"*Annyeong, naya!*"

That's Ora's voice. I look back up, she has suddenly appeared and is standing in front of us. I notice she's wearing the same black T-shirt and black pencil skirt that she wore last time we met.

"Hey Ora, it's a been a while!" says Caitlin.

"Sure has."

Ora walks up to Caitlin and grabs her around the waist. Caitlin pulls Ora into her and they start immediately kissing. The kiss starts off between them as a friendly peck on the lips, but then they start really going for it, kissing more and more deeply and passionately. This has gotten very weird all of a sudden. I don't know what to do about this. I guess I should get their attention and they might stop. I clear my throat. Caitlin starts talking to Ora between kisses.

"Hey, Ora... I think Hana... feels left out."

Ora stops kissing Caitlin immediately and looks at me.

"Oh, I'm sorry! Hi, cutie! It's good to see you again! Did you miss me?"

What do I even say to that? Before I can even think up a response, Ora walks up to me, puts her arms around my waist and starts kissing me. My lips melt into hers. She starts softly at first, but I know where this is going. I'm not ready for this, and I stagger backwards a little. Ora catches my fall with the back of her hand and pins me gently up against the door. I feel my heartbeat racing, I try to kiss Ora back but I feel so nervous that my lips don't match up quite right, I can't explain it but I'm messing it up somehow. I look over at Caitlin, she's watching us both and trying not to laugh.

"Hana, you look so uncomfortable!"

"That's because I am! This is so weird! You two are both freaking me out!"

Ora stops kissing me. Ora and Caitlin then both start laughing. Ora starts stroking my hair.

"I'm sorry Hana, I just haven't seen you both in so long, I just got a little excited. Why don't we all come into the lounge room and have a seat? I'll get some drinks for us. Come on."

Ora walks off in the direction of the kitchen, and Caitlin beckons me to come with her into the lounge. I walk over to the lounge sofa with Caitlin, sink into it and try to catch my breath.

"What are you drinking?" asks Ora from the kitchen.

"Whatever you've got is good!" replies Caitlin.

"Hana?" asks Ora.

"Um... do you have milk?"

"I do, but I've also got alcohol here, you know..."

"Milk is fine!"

"Okay, suit yourself..."

Caitlin grabs my hand and holds it. I move up right next to her so I can whisper to her.

"I didn't know it was going to be like this! I just thought we were catching up for a chat?"

"Well, we are! Ora just has a very, um... interactive way of chatting. Why not relax and go with the flow?"

"I'm not sure if I can! I'm freaking out!"

"Don't worry, you'll be fine. You're with me, I'll take good care of you, don't worry. Nothing's going to happen that you don't want to happen."

Ora walks into the lounge carrying three wine glasses, she gives one to Caitlin and one to me. Caitlin's glass has some kind of red liquid in it, whereas mine is obviously just milk but Ora has dusted some kind of chocolate coating over it. Ora then sits on the lounge chair at right-angles to our sofa, on Caitlin's side. I'm glad that she's not sitting on my side, because I need time to collect my thoughts. I sip the milk and think about what just happened, it tastes refreshing and the sugar from the chocolate makes me feel warm. My body is calming down a bit, but I'm also missing Ora's touch already too. The feeling of longing makes me feel pathetic and low. Am I really this easy? Or is Ora just that much of a good fit for me? Is it wrong to feel this way? I look at Caitlin, she doesn't seem bothered at all.

"So how's idol life?" Ora asks.

"Peachy, apart from the parts that are total bullshit, which is most of it!" replies Caitlin.

"Halcyon's been getting a lot of press lately. You've been having a lot of activities."

"No money though, no time off either, we're still being driven as hard as we were back when we were flopping. The only reason why we get to have holidays right now is because of the funeral for that PD."

"Ah yes. Speaking of which, a toast to Hana."

Ora and Caitlin both raise their glasses and touch them, I raise mine and do the same. Ora grins at me.

"Such incredibly good work, Hana!"

"Hana, you did well," adds Caitlin.

"She should be rewarded, I think."

"We can arrange it."

Ora gets out of her chair and sits next to me on the sofa. I'm now in the middle, squeezed between Ora and Caitlin on a sofa only built for two. The pressure of their bodies against mine makes me feel tense and excited, I feel the pace and depth of my breathing increase. Ora takes a sip of her red drink and then puts it on the coffee table. I continue drinking from my milk glass nervously.

"Hey, did you bring those lightsticks you were telling me about?"

"I sure did, take a look!"

Caitlin opens her gym bag and places it on my lap. Inside are two Halcyon lightsticks.

"Nice! The agency gave you two of them?"

"No. One's mine, and one's Hana's."

"You didn't tell me you were bringing my lightstick here?" I ask.

"I thought it'd be a nice surprise."

"Oh..."

Caitlin and Ora both start very slowly working loose my shirt buttons, Ora from the top and Caitlin from the bottom. My heart starts pounding. I can't believe this is even happening, but I don't want to stop it. I couldn't anyway even if I wanted to, because I still have one hand holding the glass of milk, which I suddenly don't know what to do with.

"Hey, you know it's a real shame we don't have three lightsticks," says Ora.

"Yeah I'm sorry about it. I did actually think of that. I asked the other girls about it, but none of them would let me borrow theirs!"

"They know you too well!"

Caitlin gently removes the milk glass from my grip and places it on the coffee table, then resumes slowly undoing my shirt buttons. I sigh with pleasure as I'm surrounded by Caitlin and Ora's touch.

149. PUNISHMENT

It's morning and we're standing in our usual line-up, in the gym. Mr Park is back from the funeral, and is standing in front of us. He's wearing a black suit which is unusual, I guess it's the one he wore to the funeral, perhaps he hasn't had time to change out of it. With him is Ijun, who is dressed in her usual school clothes and is playing with her phone. Mr Park stares at us menacingly. It's clear that he's not happy.

"So, who wants to be the one to tell me what happened here while I was gone?"

We all look at each other. Nobody speaks up.

"I'm already angry, but I'll perhaps be a bit less angry if one of you can come clean about your activities. I'm fed up with spending money just so you fat bitches can eat, talk shit and be lazy!"

"I told them all they could have the three days off," says Ijun, not looking up from her phone.

Mr Park turns to Ijun, who immediately puts her phone in her blazer inside pocket. She probably knows that Mr Park will try to destroy her phone again.

"So what did they do, during those three days?"

"It's their time off. How should I know?"

"You're the one running the show when I'm gone, you should know. It's your business to know!"

"That's right, I'm the one running the show, so I decided that it wasn't my business to know!"

"Like hell it isn't your business!"

"You said that it's my rules when you're gone. Is it really my rules or not? Why are you such a control freak?"

"It's my money invested in this operation! I'm the one who is taking on all the risk! Not to mention paying for everything in your life, as well as supporting this entire team financially! I've sunk billions of *won* into this! You've got quite a hide! Don't tell me that I shouldn't exert control over my own business!"

"The payment for Shu and Hana's Hancel appearance paid back all the debts though? We should be well in the black."

"That money has been reinvested into the business and we've already commissioned new videos."

"Why?"

"Have you seen the competition? We need to keep the team relevant."

"But surely the fanbase will..."

I gasp as Mr Park slaps Ijun across the side of the head. Ijun collapses on the floor, sobbing. Nari immediately runs up to Ijun and crouches on the floor next to her, inspecting the damage. Mr Park starts screaming at Ijun.

"Don't you DARE tell me how I should be running my own business! Nari, get up!"

"I'm just checking that she's okay."

"Get up, Nari!"

"Why don't you make me!"

Mr Park reaches down and pulls Nari up to her feet by her collar. It turns out Mr Park can make Nari get up quite easily. Nari twists Mr Park's grip off her with one of her wrist-bending moves and glares at him.

"Don't touch me, you creep!"

"Are you forgetting who runs this operation? Because I can surely tell you that it's not you, with your useless leadership skills!"

"My skills are equal to the amount you're paying me! Where's our money? Why don't we ever get time off? Why don't we ever get to eat properly and look after our health? How do you even expect us to perform like this? Why are there hidden cameras everywhere? Do you think we've not noticed those? Why do we always have to work with creeps who try to molest us? This whole enterprise is bullshit! It's a scam!"

"You're lucky that you have to be on Platinum Hour tomorrow, or you'd be getting hit as well!"

I hear the loud clearing of a throat. The entire group turns around. Four police officers are standing behind us. I wonder how long they've been there for. I immediately recognise one of them as Nabi. She smiles at me quickly before addressing Mr Park.

"Park Jeongmin, we'd like to have a word with you, down at the station, if you don't mind."

"Am I under arrest?"

"That depends. If you want to come quietly that's fine and we can work out the charges while you're down there, but if you'd like to be arrested right now we could arrange it. Oh, and we're searching the premises."

"You need a warrant for that."

Nabi pulls a piece of paper out of her pants pocket.

"Like this one?"

Two of the other police officers walk up to Mr Park and escort him out of the gym.

"Caitlin, come here," says Nabi.

"Yes?"

"I want to show you something."

Nabi pulls a phone out of her pocket and starts looking up something on it. She then shows the screen to Caitlin. I walk up to Caitlin and peer over her shoulder. It's the photograph that Caitlin took of her own lightstick when we first received them and Ijun asked us to post photos up. Nabi zooms up on the transparent lightstick pole. In the tiny reflection of the glass-like plastic, part of Caitlin's bong is clearly visible on her bed.

"Caitlin, that's an interesting item there. Do you know what it is?"

"Unfortunately, yes I do," Caitlin replies.

"We will have to confiscate it, along with any related items of course."

"Yes, of course."

Nabi smiles at Caitlin.

"Know that the department are keen to help people who are willing to comply with reasonable requests. If you tell me what I want to know, I promise you that you won't be joining Mr Park in the lockup tonight and you won't have to cancel any public appearances. Do we understand each other?"

"I believe that we do have an understanding, yes."

"So, tell me something that I'm interested in."

"Go through the door right in front of us. That's the administration area, mostly open plan offices. There's a door right at the back that might look a bit like it's part of a linen cupboard at first, because Mr Park changed it over recently, but it leads down some stairs. Once you're down there just look for the door with the glowing red light under the door crack, you can't miss it."

"I appreciate your cooperation."

"Happy to assist!"

"Hana?"

Uh oh.

"Yes?"

"There isn't anything that you'd like to tell me, by any chance?"

"No, not at all. I don't touch the stuff personally."

"Really?"

"I tried it, a long time ago. It gave me a headache and my brain went haywire. It doesn't agree with me. Never again!"

"Good girl. We won't see each other again about this, will we?"

"Definitely not."

Nabi walks away and starts talking to the other officer who is still around, they disappear through to the admin area. I look over at Nari who is talking to Ijun quietly. They both seem okay. Caitlin suddenly gets up.

"Where are you going?" I ask.

"To flush my stash down the fucking toilet before they come back!"

"Can I help?"

"No, stay here, or it'll look suspicious. Won't be long."

Caitlin walks briskly off to the dorms.

"Hey, Hana."

I turn around. It's Iseul.

"What?"

"What did Caitlin just tell that officer?"

"Where Mr Park's plantation is."

"She sold him out? The '420 erryday' girl?"

"They were going to find it anyway, it's not exactly well hidden. She might as well try to look helpful and get some points with the officers. Besides, fuck Mr Park. Nari's right. This entire thing is bullshit. We're just wasting our lives here."

"I don't agree with selling someone out like that. It's violating the code."

"Yeah well, you don't agree with a lot of things."

"I do agree that this is bullshit though. I've been really starting to regret this entire thing."

"I think we're all on the same page there. If even Nari has had enough to the point where she's willing to blast Mr Park to his face, I think the rest of us have, too."

"Tomorrow we have Platinum Hour. Why don't we do something major to fuck him up?"

"Won't he already be fucked with this drug charge?"

"Don't bet on it. Mr Park is powerful, this won't keep him down for long. I can't see him spending more than a single night in prison for anything."

"Okay, so like what? Fuck him up how?"

"Well, you know we're going to win the show, right?"

"Really?"

"Yeah, it's scripted."

"But don't the people vote on it?"

"They do, but the judges have a percentage of the vote too. That percentage is always enough for them to flip the votes to whichever group they want to win, so it doesn't matter how the people vote, as long as the judges vote as well, the result will always be whatever the show wants it to be. Anyway since we're winning, they'll have to give us a working microphone for a victory speech. So have a think about what you might want to say."

"Okay, I'll think of something."

150. PLATINUM HOUR

"It's time to announce the Platinum Hour winner for this week! Gyeongja, how was it for you, being the special guest MC for today?"

Our entire group is standing on the TV stage of Platinum Hour, looking out at the audience. Also on the other side of the stage is Boys909, who we "competed" with today for first place on the show by "singing" and dancing to "Love Carousel". We already know that we're going to win but we have to go along with the façade anyway. Between us is Gyeongja from Pearlfive, and Troy from Star-D, who are the MCs of the show for tonight. I watch as Gyeongja takes a deep breath. I wince and prepare myself, as I know that the entire room and TV audience are about to get hit with Gyeongja's unique conversational style.

"Thank you Troy! Thank you Troy! It's so great to be here! Thank you Troy! I enjoyed watching Halcyon! I also enjoyed watching Boys909! I also enjoyed watching Halcyon! Thank you Troy! I look forward to seeing the winner! I enjoyed watching Halcyon! I also enjoyed watching Boys909! I look forward to seeing the winner! Thank you Troy!"

Troy has been tolerating Gyeongja's verbal assault very professionally all evening, he grins and maintains his composure.

"Now let's announce the winner! Between Boys909 and Halcyon, who will win first place?"

"I enjoyed watching Halcyon! I also enjoyed watching Boys909! Thank you Troy! I look forward to seeing the winner, don't you?"

"Ah yes, thank you Gyeongja! Now..."

"Thank you, Troy!"

"Now let's go to the scores! The score is a combination of digital singles, airplay, fan voting, social media count, album sales and judges voting! Reveal the scores!"

"Thank you, Troy!"

A big screen behind us flashes up the scores which show that Halcyon trailed well behind Boys909 in every category, except the "social media count" and the all-important "judges voting". The final score shows us beating Boys909 by ten points. Cheers erupt from the audience and coloured confetti rains down from the ceiling.

"Congratulations to Halcyon! Tell us how you feel!"

Troy passes his microphone to Nari.

"It's been a long road getting here. There have been many struggles! We've been through many incompetent staff at our agency, also we don't get fed enough, that's why half of us are passing out onstage..."

Youngsook leans into Nari's microphone.

"It's true, we get nothing! We have to sneak food in."

Nari continues talking.

"People don't understand how hard it is, the long hours and the schedules with no rest, I'm a trained athlete and even I struggled with it, imagine how hard it is for your favourite performers... anyway we're grateful to receive this award, I hope it translates into a better quality of life for us, and maybe some money, but I have a feeling that it probably won't, because our agency keeps it all."

It looks like the other girls have had the same idea that Iseul had. Troy quickly snatches the microphone back off Nari before she or any of the rest of us can continue. I notice that Nari is crying.

"I guess it's time to now say goodbye! When you need an hour of music, make sure you listen to Platinum Hour! Goodbye!"

Gyeongja grabs the microphone out of Troy's hand and gives it to Youngsook. The backing track to "Love Carousel" starts playing, and Youngsook sings over the top of it, perfectly and effortlessly as usual, saving the rest of us the bother of having to sing any of it, which is great. I look at Youngsook, she looks really happy, just singing, just being allowed to sing, finally, with no dancing and no overdubbed backing track. The crowd get to hear her actual voice, finally, and they start cheering as she hits each note perfectly. I feel something grabbing my hand. I turn around. It's Caitlin. She waves at me with her other hand.

"Hey, Hana."

I notice there's a tear running from Caitlin's eye.

"Hi there. You okay?"

"It's not fucking worth it, is it?"

"No, it's really not."

Caitlin grabs my other hand with hers, and we face each other. I look into her eyes, and ignore everything else around me. The confetti, the noise, the fans, the people running everywhere on stage, none of it matters to me in this moment. Not that much of it ever did anyway.

"What do you think Yohan had in mind, to try and change things for struggling artists?"

"I don't know. I guess whatever it was, he knew it wasn't going to work and just gave up. Or maybe he was stopped. I guess if even he can't change things in this business, we're probably all fucked."

"I know a way we can change things, at least for us."

Caitlin tightens her grip on my hands.

"You do?"

"We can make it all come crashing down, right now, and we don't have to say a word to anyone. Do you want to come with me?"

"I guess it depends. Did you mean it, when you said that you'll always look after me?"

"I do."

"I've never had anyone say that to me before. It's hard to wrap my head around how someone could devote themselves to me like that. My parents sure didn't."

"Believe it. I'll always be here for you."

Caitlin takes her left hand and starts stroking my hair.

"You know, you're not freaking out about the hair thing anymore. That's really cool. I noticed that at Ora's place. I'm noticing it now, too."

"Yeah, I've somehow gotten used to it. Do you really think it looks better?"

"I don't care what hair you have, but I think it suits you a little more than the long hair."

"I guess I adjusted to it."

"You're more capable than you think. You've just got to believe that you can do the things you want. Anyway, do you really want to do this? Shall we burn it down?"

"Let's do it. Fuck this stupid corporate hell ride."

"There has to be a better life than this for us. I don't know what it is just yet, but we'll find it."

"I love you, Hana."

"I love you. Let's do this, for us, and for Yohan."

Caitlin looks into my eyes, I can see that she's crying. She holds me close and then starts kissing me, passionately, deeply. I kiss her back, matching the motions of her lips and tongue, and wrap my arms around her. Caitlin's warmth floods my body and I feel soft, protected. I hear the cheers in the audience gradually turn into gasps of shock and disapproval, but I don't care. I also know this will ruin our reputation as idols beyond repair. None of that matters anymore to me. Only Caitlin's love matters. I just want our love to never end.

GLOSSARY OF FOREIGN LANGUAGE TERMS
USED IN THIS BOOK

aegyo – acting cute, can also describe someone who acts cute or makes cute expressions.

anieyo – an informal version of "you're welcome".

annyeong – an informal greeting used among friends, etc.

annyeong haseyo – a standard greeting used in general polite company.

annyeong haseyo [name] imnida – "hello, my name is [name]" - a common form of greeting used by idols and idol pop groups for public appearances.

annyeong haseyo yeoreobun, je ireumeun Hana-imnida – "hello everyone, my name is Hana!"

annyeong hasimnikka – a very formal greeting which is rarely used, generally used only when meeting someone very important for the first time.

annyeonghi gaseyo – a formal goodbye, when you are staying and others are leaving.

annyeonghi gyeseyo – a formal goodbye, when you are leaving and others are staying.

annyeong naya – "hello, it's me", a greeting that can be used in a more flirtatious context.

bibimpap – a meal consisting of rice and vegetables, chilli paste, and beef or other meat served in a bowl, usually with the addition of a raw or fried egg on top.

bulgogi – grilled or barbequed beef strips, cooked in a marinade of soy sauce, brown sugar and spices.

daebak – literally "big win", a term to express excitement or admiration for something positive or "cool", similar to "awesome" in use and also similarly informal in tone.

feng shui – a Chinese system of geomancy.

gyopo – a term which technically refers to native Koreans who live overseas, but is often also used to refer to non-native Koreans brought up overseas who are living in Korea, especially Korean-Americans. Not necessarily a derogatory term depending on context.

hanbok – traditional Korean dress, that was popular in the nineteenth century and prior. Still worn today by Koreans for weddings, funerals, seasonal events, and other special occasions.

hwatu – the 48-card deck that is used to play "go-stop", a Korean fishing card game.

iljin – organised school bullies that operate like small criminal gangs, known for engaging in extreme violence, underage smoking/drinking and other criminal activity.

kamsa-hamnida – thank you.

maknae – literally "youngest", the youngest member of an idol group. Can also be used to refer to the youngest member of any other type of grouping of people.

molka – revealing/sexual video or photographs recorded in secret and without consent, usually with hidden cameras or when the subject is unaware/unconscious.

oppa – literally "older brother", but this term is also used for an older male friend, older boyfriend etc, often used affectionately but can also be used in other contexts. The term is exclusively used by women.

pungsu – literally "wind-water", a Korean system of geomancy similar to the Chinese *feng shui*. The main difference is that *pungsu* is primarily concerned with the harmony of outdoor locations and construction planning, rather than interior décor and increasing personal good fortune.

qi – (Chinese, *gi/ki* in Korean) a "life force energy", a concept in both *feng shui* and *pungsu*, where life force energy should be able to "flow", unimpeded by obstacles.

qipao – a Chinese formal style of dress, that was popular in the early twentieth century, also known as *cheongsam*. Still used today in China as a common style for uniforms, costumes, and formal dresses.

sasaeng – literally "private life", refers to an extremely devoted fan of pop idols. *Sasaeng* fans engage in stalking, harassment, and other intrusive activities in order to get closer to the idols who they follow, often while violating both their privacy and local laws. In very extreme cases, *sasaeng* fans have caused idols physical harm.

selca – a self-photograph or "selfie".

sillyehamnida – a formal request for attention, a very polite version of "excuse me".

soju – a popular Korean alcoholic white spirit, similar to vodka and gin but typically lower in alcohol percentage by volume. Much like vodka and gin, *soju* has a neutral flavour, is sold in both pure and pre-mixed flavoured varieties, and is often used as a mixer with soft drinks and other beverages. Many brands are sold cheaply, it is the preferred drink of juvenile delinquents and *iljins*.

wangtta – those socially ostracised in the Korean school system and marked as victims of organised bullying by

Korean *iljins*. *Wangtta* are often subject to a variety of bullying methods including but not limited to: taunts, threats, physical violence, sexual violence, extortion, blackmail, and being forced to perform subservient tasks for *iljins*, these tasks are known as 'shuttles'. Once the relationship between *iljin* and *wangtta* is established, coercion is often not needed as a climate of fear keeps the status quo in place. Those who associate with students marked as *wangtta* are also targeted, reinforcing the ostracism.

won – Korean currency. Exchange rates vary but ten thousand *won* is roughly equal to seven United States dollars.

yeoboseyo – a greeting which can be formal or informal, it is used exclusively for phone conversations.

yukpo – Korean style beef jerky, dried strips of beef often marinated in soy or chilli sauce during preparation.

The story of Shin Hana concludes in

THE LOVE COMPLETE

Coming in 2024

ABOUT THE AUTHOR

KPOPALYPSE is a musician and music industry veteran from Adelaide, Australia, and he has been writing about Korean pop music, music industry and fan culture since 2012 at kpopalypse.com. He was the first writer to publish completely unedited and raw tell-all interviews in English with people who had been through the gruelling and highly secretive Korean idol training system. He continues to advocate for artist rights and a progressive, pro-sexuality, pro-critical thinking view of Korean popular culture.

More information and relevant links at kpopalypse.com